Praise for *A Killer's Grace*

A Killer's Grace delves deep into the human psyche as journalist Kevin Pitcairn finds his understanding of right and wrong, retribution and forgiveness, and even choice shattered by a self-confessed serial killer. The book is a rich and deep story of self-understanding and redemption.
—Paula Renaye, Author, *Living the Life You Love*

Journalist Kevin Pitcairn is a man trying to do his best to bring to light stories and issues that matter while at the same time dealing with his own personal demons. No matter who we are or where we come from, *A Killer's Grace* shows the ability for redemption for us all.
—Cyrus Webb, Host, Conversations LIVE!

This book dives straight into the heart of one of humanity's oldest, most painful questions: How can we forgive the monsters among us? I admire Ron Chapman's honesty and courage in telling this story. He asks readers to see the mirror image of themselves in everyone—even those whose behavior causes us to recoil in horror. You'll enjoy the story for its own merits even if you don't read deep stuff very often.
—Jacob Nordby, Author, *The Divine Arsonist*

Chapman captures what it is like to accept that all people need to be heard. Reading *A Killer's Grace* allows you to open your eyes and think differently about your preconceived notions about humanity. A lot of swimming upstream must be done for us to get there. An important read.
—Patti Fox, The Fox Collaborative

I thoroughly enjoyed this book. It had me hooked from the first few pages, and I could barely put it down. It is well-written, but most of all, it is thought-provoking. The message behind the story is powerful.
—Amy Hood

From the West Mesa of Albuquerque comes a story of redemption and transformation. It unfolds with the taste of lightning on my lips and my heart touched by the main character's struggle to become more whole. Though the plot is fiction, the healing is real, both ours and the characters'. I loved the relationship between the two main characters, their love, their communication, and ultimately the redemption for both of them. What a treat to read!

—Mari Selby, *Lightning Strikes Twice*

I thoroughly enjoyed reading this book. The questions it raises are profoundly thought-provoking, causing the reader to rethink many commonly held assumptions. Chapman's protagonist, Kevin Pitcairn, deals with these questions in a very natural, very realistic manner which does not feel contrived. This is a book that I expect to read again.

—David N. Westfall

An intriguing, suspenseful story with a parallel exploration of the human psyche. Even as the story unfolds, the reader is often led to contemplate his or her own philosophy regarding some of humankind's most perplexing behaviors and actions. This book is both fiction and, in some ways, a college textbook—a fascinating read.

—Mervin B. Jersak

Through the journey of the main character, Kevin Pitcairn, a tale is told that explores mystery, beauty, love, relationships, redemption, forgiveness, and transformation. It challenges the limitations of our thinking and ability for compassion, and causes us to reflect on our own reluctance to let go of judgment and long-held belief systems. Ron Chapman's crystalline prose describing the desert landscape and its unique beauty—its particular light, sounds, and smells—is spot on. I thoroughly enjoyed this book, its plausible characters, and the message of healing oneself.

—Jeannie Sellmer

This book is well-written and has given me a new perspective on forgiving. It has helped me understand the power of forgiveness and why we forgive, which was not new to me. I feel a newer sense of freedom since reading this book. I highly recommend it to anyone who feels stuck or wounded. It has aided me in the gradual process of understanding the healing of inner wounds.

—Mariola M. Gorska

I really thought I would be reading a fictional novel. But not very far into it, I realized there were lessons: insights about forgiveness, self-acceptance, and compassion for everyone. If you want to see how you might "let yourself off the hook," I highly recommend this book. I will be reading it again.

—Lynda Gardner Pallette

Just finished *A Killer's Grace*. So didn't want it to end. When I realized I was getting to the end, my heart sank, didn't want it to be finished yet. Real characters and real life events to identify with, and thoughts I can carry with me. Can't wait for Book #2. You have a fan!

—Irene Fuson

A book for our times. It can make you stop and think that there is a better way to view the things in life that don't make sense, to look deeper into ourselves and others for a different perspective, to question our responses to others' behaviors as well as our own, and to give thought to opening our hearts to more compassion. I can feel myself changing even more as the book takes hold in my soul.

—Brenda A Elliott

A story of forgiveness and psychology. Chapman seems to be carving out his own literary niche which I'll call transcendental crime fiction. Think *Silence of the Lambs* meets the *Bhagavad Gita*. A heady read!

—Dan Gutierrez

A Killer's Grace is thought-provoking. The story is set in New Mexico, and the landscape provides the foundation and solace for the main character's search for understanding about redemption and forgiveness. A good read.

—Charm Lindblad

This book held my interest and opened my mind to a different way of thinking. The story line is well-developed. I do hope there will be more books to follow using the two main characters. Ron Chapman is my newest must-read author.

—Kathy Trimble

An excellent read! Author Ronald Chapman takes us through the story of Kevin Pitcairn, a journalist with a dark past, as he receives a letter from a serial killer on death row that propels him on a journey into the mind and motivations of an evil man—with an unexpected outcome. The revelations not only compel him to reevaluate how the world looks at a killer but lead him down a road of self-discovery and healing as well. It's a well-constructed story with deep, interesting characters that draw readers into Pitcairn's world and moral dilemma. As I followed his evolution throughout the book, I also found myself compelled to really think about my own perceptions of wrongs done both from a societal view and personal experience. That is the hallmark of powerful writing. I highly recommend this book!

—Kelly King

A Killer's Grace

Also by Ronald Chapman

My Name Is Wonder (2016)
Seeing True: Ninety Contemplations in Ninety Days (2008)
What a Wonderful World: Seeing Through New Eyes (2004)

Audio Sets
Seeing True: The Way of Spirit (2016)
Breathing, Releasing and Breaking Through (2015)

A Killer's Grace

Ronald Chapman

Terra Nova Books

SANTA FE, NEW MEXICO

Library of Congress Control Number 2016944136

Distributed by SCB Distributors, (800) 729-6423

Terra Nova Books

Published by Terra Nova Books, Santa Fe, New Mexico.
www.TerraNovaBooks.com

ISBN 978-1-938288-75-3

To those who fill my soul and inspire me.

There is no judgment upon you; there is no memory of the past; there is only the understanding of this moment.

—Joel Goldsmith

▶ 1 ◀

SPRAWLING ABOVE A BASALT ESCARPMENT THAT LINES THE VAL-
ley of the Rio Grande, the West Mesa was formed when
ancient volcanoes spewed a foundation of lava for silt to ac-
cumulate on over tens of millions of years. From that spare
soil grew a ragged carpet of bunch grasses and snakeweed,
spiked by gawky cholla cactus and stunted juniper trees.

Few people frequented that lonely place on the outskirts
of Albuquerque. Yet on this day, as on most, Kevin Pitcairn's
lanky figure was striding through the early morning light.
Beside him trotted a ghostly white dog while farther away,
a dun-colored one cavorted among pale mounds of Indian
rice grass.

The high desert was a perfect environment for Pitcairn—
countless trails for his agitated and seemingly inexhaustible energy, a perfect place to exercise his dogs. The open space was
like a second home. The emptiness of the mesa absorbed him.

He scanned the growing splash of color above the Sandia
Mountains to the east. "Lucy!" Pitcairn called, pivoting to
shout at the darker dog, trying to catch a glimpse of her.

There was no indication she had heard.

"Damn it, Lucy! Come on!" he roared. Lincoln, the pale
dog, gazed behind them into the fading night.

The purebred boxers were beloved companions. Lincoln
was five years old and perfect in stature. Despite his regal
bearing, a genetic quirk had robbed his body of its normal
pigment. And his pale, brown eyes didn't tear properly.
Hardened corneas left only peripheral vision. But he had
adapted well to the limitations of his defects.

On the other hand, three-year-old Lucy played the part of the clown. Her temperament would have better suited a cocker spaniel. In Pitcairn's eyes, the dogs were perfect.

Lucy remained oblivious to his calls. With a menacing gesture, he screamed, "Lucy, you idiot, listen to me!"

The boxer bolted toward them, and an instant later nearly leveled Pitcairn as she dove into him. Steadying himself, he lovingly scratched her outstretched neck. She stood with paws on his chest, a goofy, tongue-lolling look on her face.

Pitcairn released the dog and stared into the distance. Each night he woke long before sunup to a recurring nightmare or in dread anticipation of it. Since 1988, more than fifteen years had passed and he could count the number of uninterrupted nights on the fingers of two hands. But on this summer's morning, thoughts of the letter he received the previous day roused him from sleep before the nightmare had a chance. Bearing the marks and stamps of the prison vetting system, the careful script on yellow legal pages mailed in a plain manila envelope clawed at him. It was a lengthy and complicated read, a reflection of the exceedingly deliberate and disturbed mind of the writer. The first paragraphs seized his attention.

Dear Mr. Pitcairn:

My name is Daniel Davidson. I am a condemned man. When most people think of death row inmates, I'm the one they think of. To them, I'm the worst of the worst, a serial killer responsible for the rape and murder of eight women in three states. I have assaulted several others and stalked and frightened many more. I have never denied what I did and have fully confessed to my crimes. The only issue in my case was, and still is, my mental condition. For years I have been trying to prove that I am suffering from a mental illness that drove me to rape and kill, and that this mental illness made me physically unable to control my actions. As you can imagine, I have met with little success and less sympathy.

So here I sit in my cell in Santa Fe, soon to be returned to death row in Texas, waiting for the judicial system to complete the tedious process that will almost certainly result in my execution. Sometimes, when I close my eyes, I can envision the hundreds of people who are likely to gather outside the prison gates on that night. I can see them waving placards, drinking, and rejoicing, and I can hear their cheers as my death is finally announced.

Who is Daniel Davidson? And what could possibly motivate a clearly intelligent individual, a graduate of Villanova University, to commit such horrendous crimes? As you might expect, I have been examined by many psychiatric experts since my arrest. All of them, including the state's own expert psychiatric witness, diagnosed me as suffering from a paraphiliac mental disorder called "sexual sadism," which, in the experts' words, resulted in my compulsion "to perpetrate violent sexual activity in a repetitive way." These experts also agreed that my criminal conduct was the direct result of uncontrollable sexual impulses caused by my mental illness. The state's only hope of obtaining a conviction was to inflame the jury's emotions so that they would ignore any evidence of psychological impairment. In my particular case, that was quite easy to do in Texas, and the state succeeded in obtaining convictions and multiple death sentences. This diversion to New Mexico has only delayed the inevitable.

The urge to hurt women could come over me at any time, at any place. Powerful, sometimes irresistible desires would well up for no apparent reason and with no warning. Even after my arrest— while I was facing capital charges—these urges continued. I remember one day being transported back to the county jail from a court appearance just prior to my trial. I was in the back of a sheriff's van in full restraints—handcuffs, leg irons, belly chain—when we passed a young woman walking along the road. I cannot begin to describe the intensity of feeling that enveloped me that day. I wanted . . . no, were it not for the restraints, I would have had her. The situation was both ludicrous and terrifying. (And later, back in my cell, I masturbated to a fantasy of what would have happened.)

Even after I was sentenced to death, the urges persisted. One day, when someone in authority had a clear lapse in judgment, I was being escorted back to my cell by two female correctional officers. When we got to a secluded stairwell, I suddenly felt this overwhelming desire to hurt one of them. I knew that I had to get away from the danger, and despite my shackles, I quickly shuffled as far from them as I could just to feel some distance. I'll never forget them shouting at me; they had no clue how close I came to assaulting them.

You would think that being sentenced to death and living in a maximum-security prison would curb such urges, but this illness defies rationality. I eventually found some relief. Almost three years after I came to death row, I began weekly injections of an anti-androgen medication called Depo-Provera. Three years later, after some liver function trouble, I was switched to monthly Depo-Lupron injections which I still receive. What these drugs did was significantly reduce my body's natural production of the male sex hormone—testosterone. For some reason, testosterone affects my mind differently than it does the average male. A few months after I started the treatment, my blood serum testosterone dropped below prepubescent levels. (It's currently 20; the normal range is 260 to

1,250) As this happened, nothing less than a miracle occurred. My obsessive thoughts and fantasies began to diminish. If I had this treatment years ago, who knows how many lives it would have saved, including my own.

Having those thoughts is a lot like living with an obnoxious roommate. You can't get away because they're always there. What the Depo-Lupron does for me is to move that roommate down the hall to his own apartment. The problem is still there, but it's easier to deal with because it isn't always intruding into my everyday life. The medication has rendered the "monster within" impotent and banished him to the back of my mind. And while he can still mock me on occasion, he no longer controls me.

One thing is surely true: There are other "Daniel Davidsons" out there. It's easy to point a finger at me, to call me evil and condemn me to death. But if that is all that happens, it will be a terrible waste. Tragic murders such as those I committed can be avoided in the future, but only if society stops turning its back, stops condemning, and begins to acknowledge and treat the problem. Only then will something constructive come out of events that took the lives of eight women, left their families and friends bereaved, resulted in my incarceration and probable execution, and caused untold shame and anguish to my own family. I have read one of your columns and think you'll understand what I am saying. You have the ability to make the case for understanding disorders such as mine. With understanding, it becomes possible to change policy. The social values in New Mexico seem likely to support screening for youth offenders. That could make all the difference.

Sincerely,

Daniel Davidson

As a freelance journalist and regular columnist for the local afternoon newspaper, the *Albuquerque Chronicle*, Pitcairn often received unsolicited mail. He immediately recognized Davidson's name, and knew about the case. Davidson had been convicted for the murder of four of his six Texas victims after protracted delays for psychiatric evaluation. Oklahoma had opted not to prosecute him for the murder of a seventh victim. But New Mexico, where Marissa Sandoval's brutal death had brought a heavily politicized public outcry from the Hispanic community, had chosen to put him on trial for the murder of the seventeen-year-old Santa Fe high school girl.

That proceeding had become notorious for its conclusion two weeks earlier: no conviction. Unlike the Texans, these jurors had bought the psychological evidence and the mental defect defense. Perhaps not unexpectedly, considering the public rage over the crime and the jury's Anglo majority, a series of angry protests followed, fueled by heated accusations of racism. Police had to quell a near-riot. Now Davidson was to be returned to Texas to await execution.

His case was unusual. Despite the efforts of anti-death penalty agitators to appeal his case in Texas on psychiatric grounds, especially in light of the New Mexican decision, Davidson had asked that his sentence be carried out as soon as possible in order to break through what would otherwise be a lengthy process. It was reported that he understood he had broken society's covenants and actively sought his own death.

While Pitcairn could easily write a column or two based on Davidson's letter, he had no idea what to make of the murderer's request. He decided he would discuss it with his editor next week. The story would still be a big one. He could put it aside until then, he told himself, but for some reason, it was impossible to shake a pervasive uneasiness.

Davidson was to be transported back to Texas in a few days. Pitcairn had tossed and turned in bed last night, unable to keep the letter out of his mind. He couldn't escape the feeling that there was more than just a story there. Finally he got up, dressed, and slipped into the night. The early rising was nothing new, but the letter had provoked him in a way he couldn't explain.

Nearly at his Jeep again after several miles back and forth on the West Mesa's meandering trails, he paused and knelt beside a fresh gash in the earth. Heavy afternoon thunderstorms had pelted the area the previous day. The terrain he had just hiked was raked by nearly three inches of rain in less than an hour, bringing massive, rapid runoff that dramatically reshaped the steep ground.

To Pitcairn, the layering effect from the rushing waters seemed to have carved a miniature Grand Canyon. A billion grains of sand could be rearranged so quickly, he thought. Slowly, the wind would heal the scarred earth, one particle at a time. And then someday, another torrent would rip it apart again.

Walking the West Mesa always brought a measure of clarity for Pitcairn. Today was no different. He glanced toward the city, its lights twinkling as its residents slowly awoke. He had questions to ask before the day ended and the weekend began.

► 2 ◄

A HUMMINGBIRD HOVERED ABOVE THE THICK FOLIAGE AS PIT-cairn parked outside his house and went through the gated arch into the front yard. He watched the bird for a few moments as he breathed in the heavy fragrance of honeysuckle. The brief reverie passed. He opened the gate and stepped aside as Lincoln and Lucy rushed ahead.

He and Maria Elena had bought the house on Gold Street a few years earlier. The decision came after more than two years of dating, when they realized they would someday marry. It was their commitment to each other. The vine-covered adobe walls circling the house offered her a sense of security. It was not a particularly dangerous neighborhood, but the walls and dogs discouraged intrusion.

Pitcairn enjoyed the seclusion he felt in their home. Inspired by Spanish haciendas, the L-shaped house sat in a corner of the lot, with virtually no back or side yard. A single ancient, massive cottonwood shaded the house and most of the yard. He and Maria Elena had taken out the grass lawn sucking up so much precious water and laid out flagstone seating areas beneath the tree. Cinder walkways wandered amid the mulch surrounding the native plantings. They'd been told the honeysuckle vines that laced their way across the sunny front wall were planted years earlier by the original owner.

Stepping onto the covered porch fronting the house, he opened the door and let the dogs rush past him again. Maria Elena had already cranked up the swamp cooler for its daily battle against the heat. A waft of moving air carried the rich odor of carne adovada.

"Woman of the house," Pitcairn bellowed with a mock Irish brogue, "where's me breakfast?"

Maria Elena responded to his standard morning routine with a typical caustic response: "Up yours, Cito!"

The irony of the nickname was not lost on him. Kevincito, Cito for short—Little Kevin.

As he swung into the kitchen, Lincoln and Lucy were already wolfing down kibble and meat scraps in the corner. Pitcairn appreciated how Maria Elena always sought to feed every person and creature around her. It was a way of expressing her love, and, given his delight in New Mexican cooking, made for a near-perfect match.

He approached her tiny frame as she stood vigorously stirring the pork and fiery chile. Eggs sizzled in a huge cast iron skillet, and pinto beans simmered on the back burner. Towering over her, he carefully placed his hands on her shoulders, bent over, and gently kissed the top of her head. Tickling stray hairs the color of a raven caused him to recoil and furiously rub his nose.

Maria Elena turned and gazed up at him, her almost-black eyes shining brightly. Her face reminded Pitcairn of a native priestess: high cheekbones, tapered chin, full lips. She defended her heritage as blue-blooded Spanish, like so many native New Mexicans, but her looks were unequivocally Toltec. Maria Elena Maldonado had grown up near Old Town in Albuquerque, only a short distance from where she lived now. Her parents could trace back their heritage through many generations in New Mexico. But she was estranged now from the entire clan, as well as from the Catholic roots of her childhood.

"You were up even earlier than usual," she whispered. "The nightmare again?"

Pitcairn shook his head. "No, it was the letter. My instincts tell me to check it out. It could be a great story, but I don't really know where Davidson might go with it. And for reasons I don't understand, I'm reluctant."

Maria Elena's eyes blazed in response. "Why do you care about that bastard at all? He deserves what he's going to get!" She shook in a full-body spasm, mimicking the way she expected he would die. Her glare locked on Pitcairn's eyes before she spun on her heels to flip the eggs and stir the adovada.

Her infrequent bouts of steeliness always threw him off balance. He had learned to use the instant of quiet that followed to think before proceeding, and to swallow his tendency to react heatedly. It was simply a part of her capricious emotions.

"Look at it this way," he said. "If what Davidson writes is true, he's not an evil man. And that's a story that needs to be told."

The cords at the side of her neck knotted as he spoke. She whipped her head back over her shoulder. "Listen," she snarled, "any man who does what he did to the girl in Santa Fe deserves to be fried!"

Pitcairn draped his arms around her as she leaned away, whispering into her hair, "I may not always understand you, but you're gorgeous when you're pissed."

Her body sagged as a sigh escaped. "Pitcairn, if you defend Davidson, you're as much a bastard as he is. Now let go before I burn your eggs."

The tone in her voice told him the fight was over. Like a fast-forming summer storm, Maria Elena's emotions could rise swiftly only to pass without harm.

He slouched into a chair and grinned as she deftly placed three eggs on the blue-enameled tin plate and ladled beans beside them. Then she smothered the plate with steaming carne adovada before yanking open the oven and gingerly folding two tortillas along the edge of his plate.

"What are you grinning about, Cito?" she asked with an impish look as she saw his broad smile.

Pitcairn laughed merrily. "What more could a bastard want? A beautiful, tenacious woman. A platter of world-class New Mexican food. Doesn't get any better than that."

She leaned over and kissed his forehead before setting his breakfast on the table, then got her own meal from the stove.

The kitchen was quiet. The dogs studied him from the corner as they licked their muzzles in hopeful anticipation.

Maria Elena seated herself as Pitcairn lifted the first bite to his mouth. "Are you really going to do something with that letter?" she asked tentatively.

"I gotta check it out. Assuming his thinking holds up, it has huge implications, with all the debate about death penalties and stiffer sentences for felons." He pointed with his fork. "Controversial too."

Chewing thoughtfully as he paused, he shook his head. "Emmy, if it turns out to be bullshit, or Davidson is as rotten as you think, I'll drop it. Until then, I need to see it through."

Pitcairn watched as Maria Elena chewed, digesting both food and thoughts. He knew she would change the subject. The grin crept back to his lips as long moments passed.

"I'm meeting Darlene for dinner tonight," she said. "We're meeting two women at the Church Street Cafe."

A smirk came to Pitcairn's face. "Our Ladies of Perpetual Revenge do Old Town?"

Maria Elena rolled her eyes. "How can such a nice guy be such a jerk?"

Silence filled the space before she continued. "I know it's one of those jokes about women in recovery in Al-Anon: that we're out to punish alcoholics like you. But I really don't appreciate it. Especially because Darlene has been such a great sponsor. I could never have healed without her help. So I hardly think what she's doing qualifies as revenge somehow directed at you."

"You're right, Emmy," he said, with his playful variation on her initials. But you have to admit Our Ladies of Perpetual Revenge has a great ring to it."

She stared at him in mock disgust. "It's a good thing I have a job. If I were cooped up with you too long, I'd have to kill myself."

"Touché!" Then he quickly added, "I hope you remembered I'm speaking at the Saturday Night Live A.A. group tomorrow. I'd like you to be there, even though you've heard my drinking story ad nauseam."

"After the crap you put me through, Pitcairn, I should avoid you like an obnoxious teen-ager," she said. "But I'll be there. It's important to you. It's okay if Darlene comes with me, isn't it?"

"Absolutely. Just tell her to check her instruments of torture at the door," he said with a wink.

Maria Elena shook her head again, then glanced at the clock on the kitchen wall, and jumped up with a gasp. "You need to take care of the dishes. I've got a 7:30 meeting I can't miss."

"Done. I'll handle it. I'm a very competent guy."

She leaned down to kiss him. He grabbed her right breast. She laughed and dashed out the door.

* * *

With dishes done and dogs snoring on the futon in the corner of his home office, Pitcairn pulled out his file of names and contacts. He dialed Kate Delmonico, a talented brain researcher who had become a reliable confidante when he needed a sounding board for his ideas. She'd been the one who suggested when he stopped drinking that he experiment with using only his last name as his identity. Her research indicated that how people speak of themselves can reflect their perceived reality. If "Kevin" was a drunk, then "Pitcairn" could be sober. Though he couldn't call himself proof the hypothesis was right, somehow the name had taken hold with everyone who knew him.

"Kate, this is Pitcairn. How's your life?"

She giggled uncomfortably. He marveled that such a bright woman could be so socially awkward. But in a long ago interview about her first book on addictive brain chemistry, they had laughed together about what social inepts they were. The conversation had established a rapport that endured. Delmonico was brilliant and creative, especially when existing knowledge fell short.

"Pitcairn," she bubbled. "So nice to hear your voice."

"Ditto," he replied. "Have you got a few minutes?"

"For you? Always."

"Great. Now look, this is not really up your alley, but ..."

"But you figured you would give it a shot anyway."

"Kate, even on a slow day, you're sharper than all the shrinks in town."

Laughter punctuated by snorts burst over the phone line. "You are dangerously smooth."

"Maria Elena says I'm 'auténtico,' gen-u-ine. But that's a conversation for another day. I've got a hot project that involves brain chemistry. You in?"

"What's the story?"

Pitcairn described the letter, then read the paragraphs on the testosterone effect Daniel Davidson had described. "What's your take?" he asked.

"I suppose you want my professional opinion as opposed to commentary."

Pitcairn chuckled. "Come on, Kate. The whole truth and nothing but the truth."

"Well . . ." she began with uncharacteristic hesitation, "it's consistent with my findings, but the implications trouble me. As a scientist, I can defend that, but it's still disturbing."

He heard her take a deep breath.

"So it looks like it could hold up pretty well," he asked, "which would be a hell of a story, right?"

"Sure. Every year, there's more evidence that many behaviors are genetic and biological in nature. And every time one of these items hits the news, it provokes a backlash from people whose sensibilities are offended."

"Listen Kate, no way do I want to justify this guy's crimes. But the more I think about it, the more it seems that we're incarcerating and executing people who are sick simply because we don't want to admit they're not the convenient evil stereotype. That's newsworthy no matter how heinous the behavior."

After a long silence, she asked lightly, "How do you get involved in these strange stories anyway?"

"I'm karmically challenged," he laughed again. "Though of course, I don't believe in that nonsense."

"Well, it's a very interesting situation, which piques my interest. How can I help you?"

"I'll let you know." He paused a moment. "There's one thing I thought of. Do you have any suggestions on short-cuts to find out if a therapist has been assigned to treat Davidson in Santa Fe?"

"Pitcairn, I may be bright," she said with uncharacteristic charm, "but you're on your own in those waters. There are probably no shortcuts through the penal system."

"I knew you'd say that. But thanks anyway. I'll be in touch."

"See ya, Pitcairn."

His interest had been increased by Delmonico's support. He gazed out the window as he thought about what to do next, then opened his contact file again, searched method-ically through the bureaucracy, and started calling. A short while later, he'd made little progress. It was Friday. The best he could do was talk to clerks who offered little hope or di-rection, and then leave messages.

Lincoln and Lucy emerged from their slumbers with a great deal of yawning and stretching. Pitcairn took a break to limber his legs, walking around the yard as thoughts of Daniel Davidson filled his mind. With no clear direction until he talked to his editor at the *Chronicle*, he shrugged off further thoughts and drove away in his Jeep to run errands. The story would have to wait.

► 3 ◄

PITCAIRN SNAPPED AWAKE WITH A LOUD GRUNT, THE DAMP bedsheet clutched in his hand. Maria Elena threw her arm protectively across his chest and pulled herself tightly to him. The sound of panting announced the arrival of the dogs. Lucy nuzzled his forearm.

He took a deep breath and exhaled swiftly in several short bursts to force the terrible picture from his mind. It was part of the regimen he'd learned to help cope with post-traumatic stress disorder.

"Goddamnit," he muttered.

Her grip tightened.

The nightmare had begun in 1988. He was on assignment for the *Indianapolis Star* in the town of Mount Vernon a few miles down the Ohio River from Evansville, Indiana. A plastics manufacturing plant had accidentally released a mustard gas-like chemical that terrified local residents. After a day's reporting, he had visited Hawk's, a tiny bar and grill. When he mentioned how long since he'd had a good woman, the barman suggested he meander down the hill to the river-front titty bar, where he proceeded to get very drunk.

After fruitless efforts to get laid, he had somehow driven back to downtown Evansville. Rather than heading for his hotel, he had found another bar. After that, his memory was just fragments.

But the nightmare brought back the horror: the seedy hotel, the lurid wallpaper, the stench, his hands clenching an ugly little man by the throat and squeezing. Pitcairn's whitened knuckles stood out in vivid contrast to the man's face—its torrid complexion, the bulging blue eyes, the froth of little bubbles on his lips. In the periphery of Pitcairn's vision, the little man's arms and legs flailed. A terrible, focused fury pinned the man against the wall until his struggles ceased. The little man's eyes dimmed. He dropped with a dull, lifeless thud when Pitcairn eased his grip.

Pitcairn awoke at dawn, slouched sideways in the seat of his car. The dirt parking lot sat atop a wooded bluff above the river. At first, he had no recollection of the night, but when the image of the man he had strangled burst on him through the drug and alcohol-induced fog, he bolted for Indianapolis.

There was no way to know what had really happened. Pitcairn guessed that he'd left the bar to find drugs. There'd been a bad deal, or maybe the drugs just blew him into a rage—not uncommon for him in those days.

News reports said a man was found murdered at the Old River Inn. Police had no leads, but there'd be little effort to find a drug felon's killer. Pitcairn had escaped the law but not the guilt. And with it had come the nightmare. New Mexico had seemed like it might be a haven, but the powerful fear followed him. There was no freedom from the demons of his past. But over time, some change did come, an energy that propelled him toward a transformation of his life.

"Emmy," Pitcairn said as he leaned his head against hers, "the eyes in the dream were Daniel Davidson's."

He flashed back to the exact moment he had first told Maria Elena about the murder.

His memory replayed perfectly how her eyes had narrowed into a focused intensity as he dragged the words out of himself. Even the cottonwoods branching overhead in Albuquerque's Old Town had seemed to groan with his disclosure.

"Maria Elena . . . I'm . . . ." He looked away, shook his head, then took a breath and continued.

"No one knows the truth about me." He studied her eyes as she waited wordlessly. "Well, that's not exactly right since my A.A. sponsor has heard everything that matters." His voice trailed into a lengthy silence.

"Fuck . . . Emmy . . . I killed a man a while back . . ." he whispered with a downward gaze.

"And . . ." she prodded with a soft voice.

He looked at her and saw guarded curiosity. He closed his eyes, drew a sharp breath that pulled him slightly upright with resolve. "And I was never caught, but I've been paying for it almost every day with nightmares." He paused again. "And somehow I will make it right. I have to if I'm going to stay sober."

"And . . ." she offered again.

He laughed as the tears welled up. "And I have to tell you the fucking truth, 'cause I can't hide it from you."

She kept some emotional distance between them as they talked it through in the weeks that followed. Somehow she managed to reconcile the past with the present. More importantly, somehow it led to empathy rather than condemnation.

Back in the present, Maria Elena kissed his cheek and patiently caressed his forehead. He glanced toward the clock. It was 3:30 on Saturday morning. Discouragement threatened to overwhelm him. Sensing his despair, Maria Elena kissed him again.

"Want to be distracted?" she whispered.

Still thinking about the nightmare, Pitcairn took a moment to answer. "You're in charge."

Her forthrightness often surprised him. Given the childhood molestation she had battled to overcome, he'd once expected her to be timid or frigid. But he had learned. He had come to know she loved making love to him, that she experienced some healing catharsis when she initiated sex. She admitted part of her attraction to him was the hint of violence that lurked within him. Years of therapy had helped her see that her passion for Pitcairn was the response of a woman trying to transcend her childhood wounds, to confront and banish her history and fears.

Slowly, Maria Elena swirled her hand across Pitcairn's chest and stomach. One foot slid sensuously along his inner calf. She showered tiny kisses on his neck and chest.

Steadily, she raised herself and straddled him, then sat upright and pulled her camisole over her head. Her skin glowed in the pallid light as she leaned to press herself against him. He responded half-heartedly. She remained undeterred, slowly coaxing him.

Soon she had his attention. She rose upright again and began to grind her hips with deliberation. He felt the heat rising inside him and reached up to fondle her small breasts. A moan escaped her, and she reached down to make way for him to enter.

Pitcairn watched Maria Elena with fascination as her passion and movements increased. Her excitement was captivating. He closed his eyes as waves of sensation built in him.

A few seconds after her climax, he was swept into his own as she continued to draw him into herself. A protracted groan poured out of him, and she collapsed onto his chest.

As their breathing quieted, Maria Elena slipped beside him, then spoke softly with the side of her face pressed into his chest. "I love you, Cito. I wish I could take the nightmare away."

Pitcairn chuckled as his fingers played in her hair. "You just did. And I love you too."

They settled down, but his respite passed quickly. The tendrils of ugly images crept back into his mind. He waited until her breathing had sagged into the deep rhythm of sleep. Carefully, he extricated himself from her arms, leaned to kiss her on the cheek, then rose and padded from the room. Lincoln and Lucy knew the routine and followed him. As coffee brewed, he wrote of the nightmare in his journal, then added a few thoughts about his interactions with Maria Elena. He had long ago learned in A.A. that there was power in writing regularly about your struggles. At a minimum, it took away some of their power, and sometimes it could bring insights that changed a life.

* * *

Streaks of gray tinged by the first pink hints of sunrise painted the sky above the eastern mountains. Dawn's winds swirled around JA, the southernmost of the five volcanoes cresting the West Mesa. Air moved down from them to swirl in the valley below with currents from the mountains across the Rio Grande.

For time immemorial, men had come to these crumbling, lava-strewn relics to seek meaning beyond what they found in their lives. It was as if the presence of the volcanoes amid the vast openness signaled an answer to unclear questions. The mesa drew these men to its rocky bosom, and Pitcairn was among them.

* * *

Lucy joyfully led the way up the flank of the volcano. Lincoln trailed Pitcairn as he carefully dodged the worst of the broken ground. Thorns tore at his forearm as he slipped carefully through a narrow passage between two protruding knobs of reddish rock near the top.

He glanced up across the remaining twenty yards of slope to see Lucy whimpering as she gingerly lifted a paw.

"Lucy, how could any dog be more idiotic! You'd think sooner or later you'd figure out what cactus looks like."

He ruffled her ears, then hunkered down to pick out the spines. Once they were plucked from her flesh, she licked his hand exuberantly and bounded away.

Pitcairn shook his head and looked at Lincoln. "Unbelievable! You suppose we ought to be more like her, boy?"

Lincoln lifted his nose as if to nod in agreement. They resumed their ascent.

As Pitcairn stepped onto the level ground at the top, he turned to survey the coming dawn. He threw back his arms in a huge stretch, then eased himself to the ground, crossed his legs, and propped his back against a craggy outcropping.

Lincoln lay beside him with his head erect. Lucy snorted and snuffled around the perimeter.

Facing south, Pitcairn squinted to make out the terrain. Soon the light would shimmer on the waving grasses. Already meadowlarks were welcoming the day.

The walk from the road to JA had settled him some. He had counted his steps—2,654—a useful strategy, he'd found, for helping to manage the PTSD. Still, tears welled up as he closed his eyes. The voice of his mother taunted him.

Both his parents were dead. Scotty Pitcairn, the third generation of Welsh-Scottish immigrants, had worked himself to death in the steel mills of Gary, Indiana. His father was a huge man—made larger by memory—who'd given his son his first boilermaker at The Corner Tap at the age of twelve. Co-workers and barflies had gathered to watch the rite of passage, laughing when he choked and spat, cheering when he asked for another.

Hard-living men were drawn to his father. Partly, it was his reputation for never having been bested in a brawl, but more than that, it was the stories of the company men he'd beaten during violent union strikes. It was an image Scotty Pitcairn burnished often with well-told tales.

He had fathered four children. Mary died shortly after birth. Michael had been killed in an accident at the mills after Kevin, the second son, escaped to college at Indiana University. Elizabeth, the youngest by three years, still kept a blue-collar home a few miles from their birthplace.

Kevin's childhood had been filled with typical boyish adventures that sometimes became misadventures. He had a reputation for broken limbs and pranks, as well as tenacity. His high school football career had ended as a sophomore when he hammered a teammate into the ground during a tackling drill, resulting in a horrendous leg fracture. In a coach's comments, Pitcairn heard the murmurs for the first time: "That bastard is certainly his father's son. Mean as hell."

No one knew that the fuel for his doggedness came not from Scotty Pitcairn but from his mother, Anna. She had offered nothing but criticism of her son's accomplishments: honor society, class salutatorian, a full scholarship to college to study journalism. None of it mattered. For Pitcairn, each was simply one more failed attempt to please a power who could never be pleased.

He could not recall a single childhood sign of affection from her. Not one kiss. Not one hug. Not one touch. Instead, there was only the single terse phrase that he never understood in response to any success or adventure. He remembered her speaking the words after his first-place finish in a debate tournament: "Boy, you're just like Khrushchev."

He had hurried to the library to research Khrushchev. But nothing he found made sense. His only redemption was to excel at everything he could. He became a chronic overachiever, succeeding in every venture. But despite his determination, Pitcairn's inner wound would not be healed.

In time, the doomed disappointment of failing to please his mother in life led only to discouragement and worse. Nothing he could do felt adequate. His only response was to redouble his efforts, which also fell short. Only drugs and drink could grant fleeting relief from the stress of being in his life and body.

When Anna Pitcairn died in 1995, he shed no tears.

He understood clearly his need to escape into the drugs. It took sobriety for him to understand the merits of suicide. Without something to mask the feelings, torment became a regular companion. Yet he saw there were memories and emotions long suppressed that were only now emerging.

He couldn't kill himself. Not back then and not today. The value of living outweighed the alternative by the bare weight of a single breath as he sat on the windswept volcano. He wept for what he could not reconcile or understand— and most of all for the frustration of everything he could not make right. As tears fell, he hugged himself and rocked from side to side. Lincoln pressed firmly against his right leg. Lucy huddled at his left shoulder, leaning her nose on his collarbone and swaying with him.

When the waves of anguish had eased, he rested against the rock. He offered a silent prayer to the God in whom he did not believe. "It hurts. If you're there, help me. I don't want to drink or drug, and I don't want to die. Not today. Just show me what to do. I'm willing."

He remembered Maria Elena, and a tender smile slipped onto his face. He admired what she had overcome. Masters in economics, senior adviser to the city council, tough and resilient. Still, it was her capacity to care about him that he loved the most. She was one hell of a woman, and a very good reason not to drink or die.

Light shimmered in the green of the valley, then swept upward into the foothills of the Sandia Mountains. The darkness was vanquished.

Suddenly, Lucy sat erect and gazed toward an arroyo to the southeast. Pitcairn focused and watched two coyotes move furtively up the wash. He grinned as he grabbed the dogs' collars.

The adaptability of the coyotes enthralled him. A short piece he once wrote about them for *New Mexico Magazine* had opened his eyes. Pitcairn loved their wildness, and had tried to explain it to all the suburbanites who hated the wilderness beyond their walls. They had a simple view: Their cats and dogs could become snacks; the government should wipe out the coyotes.

The two brown forms disappeared into the brush. Pitcairn playfully tousled his dogs' heads. As a reward for their good behavior, he bonked his head into Lucy's. She backed off, stubby tail wagging, and began to growl.

"Dumbass," he said to her.

Lincoln watched placidly as Pitcairn rose and stalked Lucy around the rocks in a spontaneous game of slow-motion chase. Lucy yapped and cavorted. Pitcairn crouched wordlessly, feinting after her, occasionally darting toward her.

He played the game for several minutes until the boxer became distracted. After one last walk around the volcano's cone to see the mesa beneath the new day, he turned and herded the dogs down the broken slope.

► 4 ◄

PITCAIRN STUDIED THE ROILING CLOUDS OVERHEAD AS HE WAITED for his dinner on the patio at Villa di Capo. He knew he would have to beat a hasty retreat if the rain came, but testing limits was a pleasant pastime. Sitting there alone, it was perfect for thinking about the story he would tell at A.A. that night.

He and Maria Elena had been out most of the day. He had missed a call from Dr. Nathaniel Winter, the state-assigned psychiatrist for Daniel Davidson. Winter's message acknowledged that his call was unusual for a Saturday; he hoped Pitcairn would call him in Santa Fe on Monday. There was an obvious awkwardness in the doctor's tone.

Pitcairn was thinking about the call when the waiter arrived with his linguine carbonara and a pot of coffee to freshen his cup. It amused him to see the young man glance nervously toward the sky as he ground fresh pepper onto the pasta.

Though Maria Elena hated Capo's fare, it was comforting to Pitcairn. The retro decor and overstuffed, vinyl seats were reminiscent of his childhood. Perhaps it was the sense of ease they brought that made it an ideal place to think.

A stray drop of rain spattered on his wrist as squealing tires jolted him from his thoughts. A black, low-rider pickup with two serious-faced boys inside raced through the roundabout next to the restaurant. A free-floating fear he didn't understand swept down his neck in a shudder, compelling him suddenly to leave.

He polished off his dinner and glanced at his watch. Slipping a few bills under the plate, he swung out the gate onto

Central Avenue in full stride. For nearly an hour he walked at a steady pace, burning nervous energy as he looped the downtown area. Focused by the movement, he finished planning his words.

Just before eight, he arrived at St. James Church for the Saturday Night Live meeting. Nearly two hundred members of Alcoholics Anonymous milled about socializing. If you were a recovering alcoholic, this was the place to be. He spied his sponsor, Clint, standing in a corner and swung by to shake hands, offering a quick greeting before heading for the podium in the front of the meeting hall. He caught a glimpse of Maria Elena and Darlene sitting on the outskirts of the crowd, and waved as he gave an exaggerated wink.

The chairman rapped the gavel, and a few minutes later, he was introduced.

"Hey," he began, "My name is Pitcairn, and I'm an alcoholic."

"Hi, Pitcairn," boomed the response.

"My sobriety date is October 1, 1990. That's a long time, but my goal tonight is to be as honest as my dishonesty will allow me to be." He paused for the punch line, "Except for the things the statute of limitations hasn't yet run out on."

The group laughed as one, just as he knew they would. Some lines in A.A. guaranteed laughs.

With that, he launched into his story. It was a tale for those in the room, something he hoped could help further their recovery, and also for himself, to renew his sobriety and remind himself of how far he once had sunk.

After the straightforward and humorous parts had the group loosened up, he hit them with the uglier ones. Certain pieces of the past always made him squirm: viciously slapping a girlfriend despite his vow to never hit a woman; physically dominating a friend and fellow reporter to the point of driving him to leave the newspaper they worked at; waking up in beds soaked with his own urine. Each painted a degrading picture that brought forth healthy but uncomfortable shame. While he could never speak of the murder, it lurked like a shadow behind everything he said.

With that one exception, he held back little before his segue to the miracle.

"That's my truth. That's where alcohol takes me. And it's not a pretty place. No matter how I try to gussy it up, I'm not a nice man when I drink or drug. Years later, I still suffer from nightmares over some of it. But I guess that's a small price to pay for this gift of sobriety."

Pitcairn took a deep breath and rubbed his forehead with his fingers.

"Let me tell you how I got sober. It's pretty amazing. But let me begin by telling you I don't believe in God. Sure I pray and meditate like I'm told, because it seems to work. That doesn't necessarily mean there's a God. I know that's not a popular thing to say here. But if I can't tell the truth, I'm in deep, deep trouble. So I remain an agnostic. I have no knowledge of a God, but I do believe in the power of A.A.

"That said, let me tell you when I stopped believing in God. I was twelve years old, and my dog, Ruby, was run down by a speeding car. If ever there was a well-intended prayer, it came out of the heart of that little kid that day. I knew God could do miracles, and I knew he could bring Ruby back. I cried and cried. I prayed and prayed. But that son-of-a-bitch didn't bring my dog back."

Pitcairn made no effort to conceal his tears. "I stopped believing in God that day. And I didn't cry again until two years into sobriety. That's a long, long time, and a whole bunch of hurt."

He steadied himself as he leaned toward the group.

"I fled here from the Midwest in 1988. I got work with the *Albuquerque Chronicle*. In October 1990, I had this assignment to interview the Dalai Lama on his visit to New Mexico. It was a plum of a job." Pitcairn swallowed the lump in his throat.

"Just before going in to do the interview, I pulled a bottle of vodka out from under the seat. It was a warm, sunny day, and the booze was hot. I remember it burned my lips and made my eyes water. But by then, it had little effect on me.

I was beyond copping a buzz. I drank to stay away from the D.T.s and the demons."

"The interview went pretty well. For some strange reason, my work never suffered much from my drinking."

"Anyway, at the end of the interview, the Dalai Lama took my hand and just looked right into me. It was the most loving thing I have ever felt in my life. And then he smiled at me . . . the kindest smile in the world. He wished me well and thanked me."

Stunned by his own account of a generosity he could not understand, Pitcairn felt the urge to flee from the church. He gripped the lectern.

"That day, the desire to drink left me."

A deep silence filled the hall as he sensed his voice beginning to quaver.

"I don't know where it went. I don't know how it happened. All I know is it's gone, and it's been gone ever since."

He took a final deep breath and plunged onward to the conclusion.

"Now, just so you people don't think I'm a flake, I did some research and discovered that what happened to me has happened to others who encounter special people. There was a case with a drunk and the woman who founded Christian Science. It also happened with a woman who had an encounter with some Native American holy man.

"The desire just slipped away. But I had to go into a rehab for detox. The D.T.s were nasty . . . rats and spiders . . . retching and trembling. Then I followed the advice of the rehab pros and stumbled into A.A. I've been here ever since—because I probably have another drink in me but I'm not sure I could put it down again.

"I wouldn't trade this thing for anything. Sure, I'm still troubled. Just ask my girlfriend!" A gratifying laugh welled up from the group. "But I don't have to be able to explain it. I just have to know there is something like that for troubled people like me. I've got a place to go, and people who understand."

"Let me close by quoting your friend and mine, old Jim P. 'I'm the luckiest son-of-a-bitch alive.' Thanks for letting me tell my story."

Applause followed. A few shrill whistles. Pitcairn was aware of his hands shaking as he found a seat for the final business to be conducted. After the closing prayer, a flurry of people swept by him to say thanks. Clint came up and gave him a bear hug.

"That's the goddamnedest story, Pitcairn. For an old Baptist boy like me, no matter how often I hear it, I just can't figure out how you don't see no God in that." Clint shook his head for emphasis. "But what the hell do I know. It works, don't it? I guess God couldn't give a damn whether we believe in him or not. Must be above our opinions of him."

Pitcairn laughed. "Clint, I believe that you believe. Good enough?"

"Good enough, Pitcairn. Good enough."

At that moment, Maria Elena wedged herself alongside him and clasped Pitcairn's hand with both of hers. She hugged his arm as she greeted Clint.

Pitcairn looked down at her with a smile. "How'd I do, Emmy?"

"I guess I'll keep you. Just stay sober, okay? Otherwise, I might have to kill you."

"For you, anything . . . except I do need to chat with Clint. Okay if I meet you at the house?"

She nodded, then touched his cheek before leaving with Darlene.

"Clint," he said, "I've got some strange things shaking down. You got time for Luby's?"

"Sure. I've got a hankerin' for some pie."

When he arrived at the cafeteria, Clint's Plymouth was already parked in front. His sponsor was sitting patiently on a bench in the entryway.

Clint was a West Texan reared in Clovis, New Mexico. After a lot of small town trouble from his drinking, he'd served a stint in the Navy before moving to Albuquerque at the age of twenty-nine. He was promptly jailed for bar fights on three consecutive weekends. Soon afterward, he found A.A., and had been sober for forty-one years. He'd been a salesman at the old Paris Shoe Store on Central Avenue until he retired, dispensing wisdom to customers along with the pumps and flats. In actuality, Clint said the wisdom came in response to the needs of others, and God deserved full credit.

As they moved through the food line, Clint chatted with the staff. Most knew him by name.

"Xiomara, how're your parents back home?" he asked the cashier.

"Fine, Meester Pennington," she replied. "Thank you."

"And how's that boy of yours? No more trouble, I hope." He winked in a kindly way.

The Guatemalan woman rolled her eyes upward as she mumbled a few words in Spanish before switching to English. "Ay, that boy. He eez a good son. Just not too smart about who he runs with."

"You don't take no crap from him, okay? Not from them other punks either. Ya here me?"

She smiled. "Yes sir!"

"Good." Clint pointed toward Pitcairn. "You tell him this big ol' boy standin' here next to me will come kick his ass if he don't behave."

She handed Clint the receipt with a big smile and a respectful nod to Pitcairn.

The two men moved toward a table in a distant corner of the smoking section, Clint with a large slice of pecan pie, Pitcairn with a wedge of bread pudding.

They settled in. Clint chuckled and motioned toward the other diners. "I love this place. It's small townish. Everybody knows everyone, or at least acts like they do." He paused before glancing at Pitcairn, "What's on your mind, son?"

Pitcairn shook his head sheepishly. "Something has been stirring, Clint, but I didn't realize how it's affecting me. I feel foolish that I didn't mention it sooner."

Clint nodded sympathetically. "No small upsets, son. Better late than never."

Pitcairn described the situation with Davidson's letter, sparing none of the details. He ended by explaining that the killer had crept into the nightmare and painfully propelled him to the desert that morning.

Clint pointed at him with a piece of piecrust held between his thumb and forefinger. "Hell of an opportunity for you," he said gently.

"Opportunity?" Pitcairn replied, leaning back in exasperation. "You want to explain that to me?"

"I'm surprised you don't see it. You've wondered for a long damn time how you could make your peace with that man you killed. This guy Davidson appears to be givin' you that chance with his request. Goin' to bat for this guy might just be the way for you to right a wrong that's festered in you for quite a while."

Pitcairn sighed heavily and shook his head. "Damn, Clint. I just couldn't see it." He laughed at himself. "The amend I've not been able to make just got my attention, didn't it?"

"I think so," Clint agreed as he wiped his mouth and lit a Pall Mall. "Just remember, it don't matter how anyone receives the amends. You're the one that's got ugly on the inside. It's your forgiveness that matters. Screw everyone else."

"Why'd you say that?" Pitcairn quickly countered.

The waitress appeared and refilled their cups with a flourish.

"Thanks, Marnie," Clint said as he smiled at her. "How's your daddy gettin' along?"

"He's home from the hospital. Still sore from the surgery, though."

"Well, take good care of that crotchety old bastard. And tell him I said howdy."

The waitress nodded appreciatively.

Pitcairn stared at Clint and leaned closer. "You know her dad?"

"Nah," Clint whispered with raised eyebrows. "But she likes it when I ask after him."

They paused in their conversation while Pitcairn swept the last of the pudding into his mouth. "So tell me more about why I shouldn't worry about what anyone thinks."

Clint looked surprised. "Son, you know this. When you're clean, it don't matter what anyone else thinks. Believe me, with what Davidson's done, you'll get little support from anyone else. Most of them think the man's an evil bastard not worth one whit of your time."

Pitcairn laughed in one short burst. "Well, that pretty well sums up some of the reactions so far."

"'Course it does. This world can't forgive what Davidson did. So it doesn't want to understand him. If we understood everything, we'd forgive everything. But that would sure as hell screw the pooch, wouldn't it?" He shook his head thoughtfully. "Heavy work requires serious food, don't it?"

Pitcairn nodded through pursed lips. So I don't suppose you have any suggestions on what to do about Davidson, do you?"

"'Course I do," Clint answered with gusto. "Just keep doin' what you're doin'. You'll know it when you see it, and you'll know when you're done."

"That's helpful," Pitcairn replied with a cynical smirk.

"Son, everything ya need is inside ya. All you need an old fart like me for is to remind you."

"Clint," Pitcairn said in a serious tone, "I believe that you believe."

The old man snorted with pleasure. "Smartass. You youngsters got no respect for your elders."

They grinned at each other and lapsed into silence. A few moments later, they stood up and left, Clint chatting with nearly everyone along their path.

Pitcairn closed the Plymouth's door after Clint got in. He bent down to hear his friend through the open window.

Clint slipped a cigarette between his lips, but it stayed unlit. "Son, this is gonna be hard work for you. Hell, it's been hard on you for a long damned time already. But you can't kill a man without payin' a price. If you're willin' to do the work to make this right, you'll make your peace." Clint nodded in finality, then extended his hand.

"I'm in," Pitcairn replied as he took the hand. "This crap on my insides has got to stop."

"That's an honest reason, son. Keep me posted."

"Sure enough, Clint."

"Now I know you know it, but can't hurt to say it." The old man nodded in an assuring way. "Stick close to A.A., son. You're solid sober, but stir up enough of this shit and it's easy to get thirsty. It ain't the booze, it's that goddamn inner disturbance that'll cause you to forget. Don't be skippin' any meetin's."

Pitcairn laughed. "Good reminder. There's nothing that can't be made worse if I pick up a drink."

The Plymouth pulled away. Pitcairn climbed into his Jeep and slowly drove home.

► 5 ◄

THE REST OF THE WEEKEND SLIPPED BY SWIFTLY. THE LAST Monday in July dawned sluggishly. The rain-fed humidity plus the continuous heat of summer added up to torpor for Pitcairn. It was his most difficult season. He sweated profusely, swamp coolers almost useless against the thick, damp weight of the air.

After a long walk on the mesa and breakfast with Maria Elena, he began the week's work. Lucy and Lincoln collapsed into a near coma on the futon. He plugged in a small fan, then wrote down some of his thoughts about Davidson. Shortly after eight, he called Dr. Winter.

Surprisingly, the psychiatrist answered the phone himself on the third ring. He explained that his receptionist arrived later, and he enjoyed taking the occasional call himself. Pitcairn explained the reason for his call.

The psychiatrist spoke in a clipped, nasal tone. "I must tell you that while Daniel has asked me to speak with you if you contacted me, I walk a fine line concerning client confidentiality that precludes me from offering very much information."

Pitcairn spun a pencil in his fingers as he imagined a weasel-like face and a slight, stooped stature. "I understand completely, Doctor. Rest assured, I have no intention of asking you to breach confidentiality. I take a great deal of pride in maintaining my own journalistic code of ethics."

"Right-o," replied Winter in an obviously relieved voice. The pretense of the phrase from a man with no other British accent did little to improve his portrait in Pitcairn's mind.

"You knew about the letter Davidson sent me, didn't you?"

"Indeed."

Pitcairn scratched his nose with the eraser, not ready for so succinct a response.

"Hmmm . . . did he let you read it, or did he simply tell you about it?"

"Daniel asked me to review his presentation of the facts. He is very concerned about misrepresenting himself or his disorder."

Pitcairn leaned over his desk, thinking about the doctor's response. "Is this an honest letter, Doctor?"

The psychiatrist cleared his throat as he considered how to answer. Pitcairn closed his eyes to concentrate better.

"Mr. Pitcairn, let me assure you that Daniel's intentions are always quite earnest."

The doctor's careful responses were building a fair degree of respect in Pitcairn's mind despite his image of the man.

"Is his portrayal of the facts of his condition accurate?"

"Let me make it clear that I am not an expert on paraphiliac mental disorders. Daniel's circumstances required me to research the literature extensively. Much of what I know of his case came from the medical files prepared by his primary psychiatrist in Texas as well as the materials compiled for his defense by an expert in the field." Winter took a quick breath. "With that said, I believe Daniel stated the case very accurately."

"Is it possible to get the name of the Texas psychiatrist you talked to and how to contact him, and any articles you know of that could support what Davidson says?" Pitcairn asked.

"Indeed. I don't think it's something Daniel would mind my telling you."

Pitcairn realized he was curious now about Winter, who was not at all the stereotype lodged in his mind. "If you could send me the information, I would appreciate it."

"You'll have some of it as soon as my receptionist arrives. I'll send more later."

"Doctor . . ." Pitcairn knew he was pausing too long as he considered the question. He scratched his nose again, then asked: "Doctor, what kind of a man is Daniel Davidson?"

"In what regard, Mr. Pitcairn?"

Bemusement crept into Pitcairn's voice. "Well, if I met him on the street, what would I think?"

Winter allowed the silence, then said in an assured voice: "You would find him utterly normal as to appearance. His demeanor would seem a bit serious and strained. Daniel is not particularly social. When he spoke, he would be articulate, obviously quite intelligent and witty."

Pitcairn heard Winter clear his throat, perhaps reluctant to proceed.

"Mr. Pitcairn, Daniel Davidson is, in fact, a pleasant man. You would probably like him. Then when you heard his tale, you would be struck that he was quite unlike the monster portrayed by the media. If you are the thoughtful type, it would be a disarming experience."

Pitcairn's next question rushed out: "Do you like him?"

A soft, gentle laugh filled the phone line, "Yes, I do, Mr. Pitcairn. Yes, I do."

Pitcairn smiled to himself. "Thank you for your time."

"Will you be responding to Daniel's request?" Winter asked.

"If everything holds up, very likely. Funny you should ask. While his pitch is clear, I've never been in this kind of position before. I'm not really sure how to proceed."

Again the psychiatrist laughed. "Mr. Pitcairn, Daniel saw only one of your columns, which he liked very much. He describes you as erudite, but, more important, he finds you to be open-minded, which is quite unlike his experiences with the press."

"I'm not sure how to take that," Pitcairn replied.

"A compliment from a serial killer, you mean?"

"Yes, but it's more than that. It's uncommon to receive such praise from any quarter, and rather disconcerting to have it come from someone sentenced to die for their crimes."

"There is that, isn't there?" Winter replied. "But Daniel hopes you are as open-minded as you seem, and will perhaps put your thoughts into print."

Pitcairn replied thoughtfully. "Dr. Winter, I may or may not be any of those things, but I am afflicted with compulsive tenacity that doesn't allow much to pass me by."

"That would probably be a good thing. It likely serves you well if my senses do not deceive me."

"Indeed," replied Pitcairn. "Thank you, Doctor."

"You're most welcome."

"Dr. Winter, now that I've spoken to you and Davidson is going back to Texas soon, I think I'd like to figure out how to chat with him. Could that be arranged?"

Winter paused. "Obviously, that would be Daniel's decision to make, and we have some unusual limitations given his circumstances with the Corrections authorities, but I would be happy to see about initiating it."

"Thank you. I have a few more calls to make before I make my own decisions, but I'll be in touch. I appreciate your time."

"Not at all, Mr. Pitcairn. Cheerio!" Winter closed with an upbeat tone.

Pitcairn returned the receiver to its cradle and stood to gaze out the window. He shook his head in response to the unlikely conversation then fell into a lengthy reverie.

Shortly after his sobriety began, he had sought out a counselor. The experience with the Dalai Lama had been very confusing to him, and sobriety had revealed many challenges. One idea the counselor offered in response was the Old Testament story of Jacob's wrestling with the angel of the Lord. In the end, Jacob was smitten, but then the Lord blessed him, named him Israel, and made him founder of a great nation. The counselor summed up the story by telling Pitcairn that there was great value in struggle.

The counselor's Bible story reassured him as he sat at the computer scanning the outline for his column. A short while later, the initial information from Dr. Winter clattered from his fax machine.

He immediately called the Texas psychiatrist that Winter had referred him to. Dr. Norman Joseph was in Scandinavia, his receptionist reported, and would be unavailable for nearly the entire month. Pitcairn did not leave a message; he could call back later.

To better understand Davidson's disorder, he placed the second call to Dr. Arthur Burden, director of the National Institute for the Study, Treatment, and Prevention of Sexual Trauma, in Baltimore. He had testified as an expert witness for Davidson's defense. Burden's receptionist said the doctor would call back promptly.

Pitcairn read over his notes, made a few more, then emailed Sean Mortensen, his editor at the *Chronicle*, to let him know the column that would be coming might be controversial. With luck, he would talk to Burden later in the day and finish the column this week, to be run the next.

He leaned back in his chair and rubbed the heels of his hands on his closed eyes before sliding his hands behind his head and locking his fingers. A few minutes passed before the jangle of the phone startled him.

"Pitcairn here."

"Mr. Pitcairn, this is Dr. Arthur Burden. You called regarding Daniel Davidson."

The impression was different from what Pitcairn had had with Nathaniel Winter. Burden was relaxed but spoke with obvious authority.

"Dr. Burden, thank you so much for calling. Do you know anything about a letter Davidson sent me?"

"No, I'm afraid not."

Pitcairn extended his legs and relaxed deeply into his chair as he described the letter to the psychiatrist. He concluded: "Dr. Burden, I intend to write a column about Daniel Davidson. Right now, it looks like it will be a somewhat sympathetic piece that paints him in a way a lot of people won't like."

"I'm delighted to hear that."

"Why are you delighted?"

A measured silence followed, then a barely audible sigh. "When you've seen enough of these cases, you begin to realize that society needs to be shaken up a bit. While I can't say I know Daniel all that well, I like him. Frankly, he is a textbook case. After his medication began, he was utterly normal, or at least as normal as one could reasonably expect. I continue to be an advocate for proper diagnosis and treatment, and more than a little shocked that society refuses to consider the implications of its actions. It's really an unfortunate and unnecessary tragedy."

"Tragedy?" Pitcairn asked.

"Well . . . from how you describe the letter, Daniel said it beautifully. He brutalizes women. He dies. Nothing is learned. So more will die, because Daniel is not alone in this and similar conditions. For every death, there will be a ripple of loss and grief. That's a tragedy."

Pitcairn massaged his neck and shoulder. "So I take it you concur with what Davidson said about his illness."

Burden waited for a few seconds before responding. "Honestly, I would need to read his letter before confirming that. But on the face of it, it seems Daniel painted a realistic picture."

"If you would be willing to review the letter, I can fax you a copy."

"Happy to do so."

They concluded their conversation, and the doctor offered to provide any additional thoughts about the letter within the next day or so.

Pitcairn stood up, shook his legs, and kicked the futon. "Hey, you lazy asses! Let's go out in the yard."

Lincoln lifted his head and yawned. Lucy ignored him. He kicked the bed again, and Lincoln rose up and stretched. One more kick and Lucy crawled onto the floor, stopping to shake.

"Come on. I've gotta get to a meeting," he explained.

The three wandered lethargically into the heat.

► 6 ◄

MASSIVE THUNDERSTORMS POUNDED THE CITY EARLY IN THE evening and continued late into the night. Even by New Mexico's monsoon standards, it was an impressive display of power as well as a tremendous amount of water.

It was three o'clock Tuesday morning when Maria Elena woke him. "Cito," she whispered tentatively, "the roof's leaking."

"Damned flat roofs," he muttered, the standard New Mexico lament, as he shook sleep away. "Where is it?" he asked as he swung his legs out of bed.

"The sunroom." She reached out to stroke his back lightly.

"Well, at least I missed the nightmare," he said. "Off I go then." He stood up, then bent over and kissed her forehead. "Go back to sleep if you can."

She swept the blankets up in a flourish and rolled over with them, loudly whispering a favorite line from *The Wizard of Oz:* "Sleep . . . poppies will make them sleep . . . poppies . . . ."

Pitcairn snorted, pulled on pants and a shirt and started his day's work. The next several hours were spent on a temporary solution: placing, emptying, and re-placing buckets; tearing out soaked sheetrock; cleaning up the mess the water had made. As dawn broke and he watched the weather forecast on television, he decided he'd fix the roof that day, since the heavy rain had drained the skies for a couple of days now. It took almost until night to squeegee the water from the roof and repair the leaks.

By the time he settled into his desk on Wednesday morning, he was impatient to proceed with the Davidson column, even though its direction wasn't totally clear, as well as a couple of other writing projects. Burden had reviewed Davidson's letter and found it accurate, with some minor clarifications. Pitcairn was impressed; he wanted even more to talk with the killer now. It was unusual in his experience for a criminal to avoid embellishing a tale to make himself look better.

He'd received emails from Dr. Winter and Sean Mortensen at the *Chronicle*. The psychiatrist's note was a surprise: Davidson's return to Texas had been accelerated to the following day. "Shit!" Pitcairn muttered. It was unlikely now that he'd get to talk to his subject.

He rose with a scowl and thought about the situation as he walked to the kitchen for a cup of coffee. He knew his column would have been much stronger if he could talk with Davidson first. He might have to travel to the prison in Huntsville, Texas, for the interview. And he figured the Texas authorities would be much tougher to deal with. "Shit!" he said again.

He looked at the dogs piled on the futon. Lucy was snoring, but Lincoln's eyes moved blindly from side to side as if intuiting Pitcairn's dismay. "What do you think, boy?" he asked. "Sucks, doesn't it?" Lincoln's eyebrows rose in seeming comprehension.

He turned to Mortensen's message. "What the hell!" Pitcairn roared as the dogs shot to attention. "Mortensen, you bastard, what is this?"

The editor's email explained, in a strained and studious tone, that the column was not acceptable. Though Mortensen did not say why, Pitcairn knew his reasoning—either it was too controversial, "politics" had reared its ugly head, or both. With disbelief, he thought back to previous feedback from Mortensen. It was always constructive. Only a few times had Pitcairn been denied.

He grabbed the phone and dialed before he caught himself. Anger would not advance his cause. He hung up and took a deep breath, then whirled and snapped at the dogs, "Let's go for a walk!" They scrambled toward the door.

The trio raced around the neighborhood as Pitcairn burned off emotional energy. At moments like this, he appreciated the time-tested A.A. wisdom: "restraint of pen and tongue." By the time they all got back, he was calmer. He decided to check with Clint before challenging Mortensen.

"Good mornin'," Clint said cheerily when he answered.

"Hey, Sponsor, I'm encountering some challenges on this amend with Daniel Davidson, and I need your best thinking."

"Fire away, son."

Pitcairn briefly described the problem.

"Damn son, ya got a real interestin' situation here," Clint agreed before pausing for a moment. "Seems to me you got some resistance, which, as you know, is always a good thing. God's testin' your willin'ness to set things right."

"I know you're sure of that, Clint," Pitcairn responded, "but I have never liked resistance, and I sure don't think a God that I don't believe in would choose to offer me resistance."

The old man chuckled. "Hellfire, no one likes resistance till they understand it's the way of things—divinely required." He paused. "Yep, divinely required even for those who don't believe in the Divine." Clint's chuckle filled the line again before he added, "How would your life be without gravity, son?"

Pitcairn sighed in response to a conversation they had repeated countless times. "I know what you're getting ready to say, Clint. You've said it so many times I've got it memorized." He changed his voice to mimic the gravelly tone of Jim P: "Cuddle up to fear and pain . . . the resistance. Make it your friend. See what it has to teach you."

Clint laughed baldly. "Damn straight, Pitcairn. Damn straight. Ol' Jimmy would love it that you're quotin' him. But you still don't understand it, which is why you fight it. Nothin' in the world we know can be created without resistance. It's not just gravity. It's the metal form for injection molding of plastic or the hands of the potter that create a vase. Pain is the great gift that gits us into motion. Criminy, son, without resistance, nothin' happens."

A long pause followed before Pitcairn replied. "Clint, how in the hell do you stay so upbeat about everything?"

The reply was instantaneous: "Immaculate deception!" Clint laughed before adding, "Ya just got to keep choosin' your attitude, and if that means ya gotta fool yourself, then that's what ya do. Eventually, it ain't phony no more. Every day really is another day in paradise. It just never looks like what ya expect."

"Damn," Pitcairn replied. "You are so smooth it's frightening."

"Damn straight," Clint agreed. "Then there's that other Jimmy P. bit: 'Every day above ground is a great day.' " The roar of laughter made Pitcairn laugh along with him. "Keeps it real simple, don't it?" Clint added.

Pitcairn agreed, then steered the conversation back to Mortensen. "What do you suggest?"

Pitcairn heard the flick of a lighter and Clint's drag on his cigarette. He imagined the old man looking skyward for guidance. A few seconds passed.

"Well, son, seems to me that trying to bull your way through this is a bad idea. This here action you're takin' is supposed to be an amend, so ya need to relax and let God make the crooked places straight. Ya think you can give it a serious lettin' alone while that God ya don't believe in lines it up for ya?"

Pitcairn took a deep breath. "Yeah, I don't like it, but I'll trust you on it. It's probably a good idea, Clint. I can do that. The last thing I need to do is add mischief and mayhem to an already-prickly problem."

Clint laughed lightly. "Ya know, them spiritual gurus call this a matter of timin'. Ya can trust a solution is already barrelin' at ya . . . but no way will it look like what ya expect."

"Okay, Clint. Is there anything else I ought to be doing?"

"Take a long walk. Have dinner with the little woman. Go to a meetin' and shake hands with a wet drunk. You'll know what to do next."

Silence settled over Pitcairn before he continued, "I just remembered an old Peanuts cartoon where Snoopy is in some kind of mess. He turns, walks away, and says, 'There is no problem too great to be run from.' "

"Smart dog, that Snoopy." Clint paused. "And get some rest, Pitcairn. This deal is gonna wear you out."

"Got it. Thanks, Clint."

"Love ya."

"I love you too, Clint. Talk with you later."

With the day's heat building, Pitcairn decided to head for the bosque, the cottonwood forest that lined the Rio Grande. He called Maria Elena to let her know the latest news and to make a dinner date. Then he packed a sandwich, some water, and a few biscuits for the dogs. The better part of the day was spent wading in the river as it roiled brown from runoff made heavy by the rains.

► 7 ◄

A WET MUZZLE WOKE PITCAIRN. MOMENTARILY DISORIENTED, he pushed Lucy away as he rubbed his eyes. Pleasant memories of dinner and lovemaking swept through his mind, then he realized: There had been no nightmare! He opened his eyes and was surprised to see early morning light seeping into the bedroom.

He credited good sex for the curious abatement of the horrors he'd faced almost nightly, and leaned over to kiss Maria Elena as she stirred lightly. She opened her eyes as he gazed at her, then looked toward the window. "What are you still doing in bed?" she asked.

"No nightmare," he replied simply, shaking his head.

The morning walk was later than usual, a relative stroll around and through La Boca Negra, the canyon on the West Mesa escarpment named for its massive black basalt boulders left by long-ago volcanic eruptions. Afterward, he took the dogs for a leisurely breakfast at the Flying Star cafe in the North Valley, a mecca for dog owners because of its expansive, canine-friendly patio, as well as serving the best breakfast in town. With Clint's instructions to ease up his focus on Davidson, ninety minutes passed uneventfully. While the dogs made new and old acquaintances, Pitcairn thought about an article for *Vision Santa Fe* magazine that he would spend most of the day finishing.

The time passed languidly, and his writing went smoothly. Around three o'clock, he knocked off to run a few errands. Thunderheads had moved in from the Southwest, more moisture pouring in off the Pacific. South Albuquerque was shrouded in black. Dark curtains of rain swept down, obscuring part of the city as exhilarating streaks of lightning forked from clouds to ground. For a time, Pitcairn simply sat in his Jeep on a rise above the Rio Grande mesmerized by the show of light. In characteristic desert fashion, the storm inundated some areas while completely missing others.

Returning home, he grappled with the always-exuberant Lucy and petted Lincoln before noticing the light on the answering machine blinking rapidly: four calls in the ninety minutes or so he'd been away. Punching the replay button, he settled into an easy chair.

The first message was a short, terse demand from Mortensen, "Call me about Davidson." Pitcairn's eyebrows rose in curiosity as he remembered Clint's remarks about timing.

Maria Elena's voice was next, but in a strange conspiratorial tone. "Cito," she almost whispered, "did you hear about Daniel Davidson?" There was a short pause before she continued more loudly: "We've got to get you a cell phone! Call me as soon as you get this!"

Pitcairn was moving toward the phone as a recorded message from a pollster started. He skipped to the next message: Clint's slow drawl talking about Davidson's death. "I think the timin' is right now, so give me a call."

Confusion welled up inside him. *Davidson's death*, he wondered as he punched the speed dial for Maria Elena's cell and went over to the television. The local evening news would begin in a few minutes.

Maria Elena answered on the first ring, "Cito," she said breathlessly, "somebody stabbed Davidson at the airport. Did you hear?"

"No, Emmy, I got messages from you, Mortensen, and Clint. And I just turned on the local news. What the hell happened?"

Pitcairn heard her inhale. "Sorry, I'm out of breath from running up the stairs at the parking garage. Gotta keep my legs like you like them!"

He didn't respond, so she went on. "I don't know the details, but I guess he was killed at the airport. Darlene said he was stabbed by another prisoner. What are you going to do?"

"Damn," he replied. "Well . . . I want to catch the news, then I'll run over to the airport and see what I can find out. I'll call you later, okay?"

"Sure . . . but be careful!" she responded with concern in her voice.

"I'll be fine. I've gotta go. Love you!"

He hung up as a woman on the air ratcheted into an overly dramatic account of the events. Despite her excitement and gestures, Pitcairn noted, her hair didn't move at all.

Against a backdrop of the tarmac pooled with rainwater and swarming with law enforcement officers, she reported that the killer was being transported to Texas with another prisoner who had stabbed him with a homemade knife while corrections officers were distracted—or perhaps had knowingly looking away, she intimated with flair. The shank had entered his abdomen just beneath the breastbone, the upward thrust severing the aorta. He died in less than a minute on the asphalt outside the airport's private terminal, Cutter Executive Airport.

Turning the television off, Pitcairn made a quick call and left a voice message for Don Nichols, the airport's security chief. He was sure Nichols would make every effort to accommodate him. The city's small-town dynamics played themselves out over and over again. Pitcairn and Nichols had crossed paths a number of times on stories, in ways that built mutual respect between the two men.

A call to Mortensen likewise ended in voice mail. Pitcairn considered trying to track him down but dismissed the idea with a vague sense of resentment at the editor's response to his proposal. Mortensen could wait. He said simply, "Pitcairn here. I'm on my way to the airport. I'll call you tomorrow."

He raced over to what the city grandiosely called Albuquerque International Sunport. Mariachi music swept over him entering the Great Hall of the central concourse. The gaily clad troupe of Hispanic minstrels stood tucked in a corner churning out the bright sounds beside Pitcairn's favorite Sunport painting, an expansive desert landscape by Wilson Hurley,

He had written three columns over several years about the Sunport. Its neo-New Mexican architecture marked it as an unusually beautiful airport. Massive, hand-carved wooden beams loomed above multicolored brick floors laid in a herringbone pattern. Turquoise accents complemented an earthy color scheme, and museum-quality art filled walls and niches. He marveled that a community so opposed to taxation could have supported building this artistic gem.

Nichols stood out from a crowd of reporters gathered near the escalators. He was taller than Pitcairn and a member of the relatively small African-American community in Albuquerque. Both traits qualified as distinguishing characteristics.

Pitcairn dodged a handful of children playfully dancing to the music in the center of the Great Hall. With his attention focused on Nichols, he almost collided with Angie Montaño, the airport's arts coordinator and a friend of Maria Elena's whom he'd written one of the columns about. She had seen him approach and moved to greet him enthusiastically. They hugged.

"Pitcairn! Isn't the music wonderful?" she asked with a smile.

He nodded with matching enthusiasm as he glanced toward the mariachis. "Another brilliant performance in the city's most idyllic venue. Angie, you don't get enough credit," he offered with a wink.

"You're so full of it!" She laughed, then added with sincerity, "But, thank you. I've got the best job in the world."

"Angie, I've got to see Chief Nichols about the killing. I'll catch you on my way out." He touched her arm reassuringly but noted a disturbed look creeping onto her face. Perhaps reality had put a dent in her careful stagecraft.

Pitcairn stepped to the fringe of the crowd. Nichols nodded

slightly toward him in acknowledgement, then continued to answer questions. Pitcairn noted the reportorial feeding frenzy, a phenomenon he sought to minimize in his own work.

The questioning continued for a few more minutes until Nichols said there would be more information later and turned to walk away. Other officers moved in to restrain the push of the crowd, Nichols caught Pitcairn's eye and with a twitch of his head pointed toward a side hallway. Pitcairn slipped away, knowing the other reporters would be angered to know the privileged access he enjoyed.

A quiet corner in the unused hallway beckoned, and Pitcairn leaned against the wall. A few more minutes passed before Nichols strode into sight and extended his slender hand.

"Howdy," he said with a slight but sweet Southern inflection and a curt nod. "Davidson?" he asked before Pitcairn could utter a word.

"Yes, sir," he replied in a friendly tone.

"Pitcairn, that boy sure did stir up a hornet's nest. What the hell you want with that?"

"Just some routine follow-up, Chief. Never know where a story lurks. Could I take a look at the crime scene."

"Well, I can't go with you, but I'll send you with one of my men, Clive Barker. He was dispatched as soon as the radio call came. He can fill you in."

"You're the man, Chief. I appreciate your help."

"Just do me one favor, Pitcairn. Don't slander us with whatever you write. We had no role in it. This baby belonged to Corrections. If there's someone needs to take a hit, it's not us." His eyes squinted slightly as he nodded with a quick downward look that made clear to Pitcairn what he meant.

"You got it, Chief. Not one discouraging word about you or your people."

They steered into a nearby stairwell and descended swiftly. Nichols flagged Barker down, introduced him to Pitcairn, then waved them away.

It was a short trip punctuated by small talk as they drove around the perimeter of the tarmac to Cutter Executive Airport. Barker seemed tense, which was fine with Pitcairn. Maybe his nervousness would make him less careful with his words.

The strategy worked. As soon as they hopped from the security truck, the officer started blurting out the events as they'd been described to him. As Davidson and the other prisoner, Steve Cordova, were getting out of the Corrections Department car, an ominous curtain of rain rolled in from the west, causing the corrections officers to rush the men toward the plane.

A moment after a burst of lightning split the sky and struck the ground with a monstrous crack, Cordova spun, and in an instant, Davidson was down, his chest gushing blood around the sharpened metal blade. Cordova was quickly restrained as medical personnel and the airport police were called. The rain cascaded down as Daniel Davidson bled to death on the tarmac.

Pitcairn slowly absorbed the scene before him, imagining the chaotic event. Barker asked if he had any questions, but he knew the security officer had only secondhand information and little more to offer. Pitcairn thanked him as his thoughts churned.

The drive back was quiet. Pitcairn thanked Barker again, then paused briefly. "Officer, what do you think happened exactly?"

A hardened grin creased his youthful face. "Off the record?" he asked.

Pitcairn nodded.

"Bastard got exactly what he deserved." Barker's tone was ugly.

Pitcairn nodded again, but with a different meaning. He saw how it was. With a slight wave of his hand, he turned and climbed briskly up the stairs, then walked thoughtfully through the concourse. He hardly noticed the mariachis as they continued to play for a delighted crowd.

► 8 ◄

A MILD VERSION OF THE NIGHTMARE WOKE PITCAIRN AROUND three the next morning. His early hike was what he called "the topper," traversing the crowns of all five volcanoes with his boxers, then making his way back on a trail that crossed the undulating slope.

He swung by a newsstand to pick up the morning paper. The headline wrenched at him: Serial Killer Dies at Sunport. He sat in the Jeep in the early light reading the accounts. There was nothing new.

Maria Elena had left for the day before he wandered in. After his morning routine was complete, he touched base with Clint before calling Mortensen. His sponsor simply listened as Pitcairn explained the latest developments—including the guilt he felt for failing to make contact with Davidson.

"Son," Clint began, "that guilt ya feel ain't about Daniel Davidson. It's the old shit that's surfacin', which means it's time to get it done."

"But I had no idea it would take this direction, Clint."

"Hell, it may take some more strange twists before it's done with ya," he added. "It's bone deep."

"Any words of wisdom before I call Mortensen?" Pitcairn asked.

"You'll know what ta do. Just make sure you're listenin' for inner guidance, son. The path will be shown if you're payin' attention."

Goodbyes said, Pitcairn called his editor, who answered promptly. Mortensen listened to the details without saying a word.

"Look, Pitcairn, the politics in this make it real hard for me to run this piece. I don't see this as a time for a sympathetic piece, because I don't think there's any sympathy for Davidson. I want an evil begets evil angle, or maybe something about a bitter harvest. There's a point to be made, but it's not one that condones violence . . . either Davidson's or Cordova's."

Pitcairn chewed on his lower lip, fighting off an urge to launch into Mortensen.

"Are you there, Pitcairn?" the editor asked.

"Yeah, I'm here, but I'm holding my tongue," he said curtly. "I think you're wrong on this account, Sean. What you're saying is true enough, but there's even more important commentary to be made about our misunderstanding of seeming evil. And what a punchline with Davidson's murder!"

Mortensen sighed with exasperation. "That's a piece for some other place. It will not appear on my editorial page. Is that clear?"

Pitcairn took a deep, measured breath to settle himself before replying, reminding himself not to push back. "Okay," he said in a simple monotone before hanging up.

The next call went to Don Nichols at the airport.

"You must be calling about Davidson," the security chief began.

"Yessiree, Chief. What's the latest? Is there anything else I should know about what happened?"

"Nothing."

"Nothing?" Pitcairn frowned.

"Yep."

"Don, isn't that just a tad unusual considering the circumstances of the murder. How could he be killed with so many officers around him?" A flush came to his cheeks as the frustration grew. He turned in his chair to let the stream of air from the fan hit him full in the face.

Tension filled the line. Nichols replied tersely. "Pitcairn, the police will make an official announcement next week. I can't say anything else. Have a good weekend."

The sound of a dial tone followed. Perplexed, Pitcairn scratched the back of his neck. Then he closed his eyes. His reporter's intuition told him he was in the middle of a vortex, and that the messiness would only increase. With a sigh, he acknowledged to himself that seeing this through was going to be a real hard push. He nodded to himself, affirming the commitment.

Impulsively, he called Maria Elena. "Hey, do you want to take the day off, drive down Highway 14?"

"Perfect timing. The mayor is all whacked out by Davidson's murder and acting like a big baby. Sometimes my heart just isn't in this work.

"Then again," she said as she lapsed into a moment of self-reflection, "the truth is I really do love it. That matters … a lot."

Pitcairn imagined her refocusing her thoughts. If anything, Maria Elena was deeply principled, and he admired her for it.

Then with a burst of energy, she announced, "I'll be home in a few minutes."

A short time later, Pitcairn was navigating the Jeep east through the city, then up into the rocky terrain via Interstate 40 through Tijeras Canyon. Exiting on Highway 14 South, they steadily gained elevation. The drive would take them down the eastern flank of the Manzano Mountains through Chilili and other ancient Spanish land grants. It was their favorite drive, with cooler temperatures, few cars, and several great stops—the idyllic family drive neither of their families had ever taken them on.

At the top of the climb, Pitcairn pulled onto the dirt road of Sierra Farms, a producing dairy whose exquisite soft cheeses Maria Elena loved to put in her enchiladas. Goats bleated softly from the corrals as they got out of the Jeep. They clasped hands and leaned on the top rail of the fence. A few animals nearby gazed at them with twitching noses held aloft, probably wondering if the visitors would offer food.

Pitcairn laughed with Maria Elena at the antics of some of the kids, then threw his arm over her shoulders to pull her into the store. Ceiling fans hummed over the room as an elderly Hispanic man, stepped through a door and called to them, "Buenos días!"

"Buenos días," Maria Elena replied.

Pitcairn leaned against a wall as the two struck up a pleasant, rapid-fire conversation in Spanish. As she gaily engaged the somber old man with talk about various cheeses, Maria Elena would point, they'd exchange a burst of words, then he would hand over another cheese for her stash in the little cooler she always brought for Sierra Farms' sumptuous selections.

When the cooler was full, Maria Elena turned to Pitcairn, "I guess I'm done. My favorite compulsion—spending your money so I can feed you." She beamed at him.

He extracted his credit card with a woeful expression, noticing the slightly conspiratorial look on the old man's face.

"Oh! Cito, grab two of those cherry ciders from the cooler. We'll drink them and snack on some cheese while we drive."

Back on the highway, sipping cider, they settled into a comfortable silence as high country piñons swept by. Minutes passed.

When Maria Elena spoke, her voice was barely audible. "The old man reminds me of my grandfather. He's so patient and kind." She paused to sip cider, then said wistfully, "Especially his gentleness." She was silent for another moment before adding, "And his calloused hands."

Pitcairn steered as he cast careful glances toward her. "I'm glad you enjoy him, Emmy. He has a nice place ... and great cheese." He sensed her growing melancholy.

"Sometimes I wonder why Daddy couldn't have been more like Grampy. There are stories that Grampy had some problems when he was younger, but he was so wise and gentle when I knew him. He always paid attention to me. He was the father my dad couldn't be." She looked out the side window.

An awkward quiet followed. Pitcairn placed his hand gently on her leg and squeezed lightly. She edged her hand atop his and reached up to brush away tears. He knew encounters like these often brought back her old injuries. After much therapy and even more spiritual recovery work, her healing was now often experiential. He could never tell when some aspect of an old trauma might arise—a memory, a fear, or even anger—nor what would follow. The best strategy was simply to allow her the space she needed to process whatever came.

"I just don't understand it. Momma knew. As far back as I can remember, she warned me away from men, even Grampy and Daddy. It was always not right to sit on Grampy's knee or have Daddy tuck me in. She knew."

The only sound was the rushing air and the tenor roar of the Jeep's engine.

Maria Elena took a deep breath. "Why couldn't Momma admit it when I finally told the truth about Daddy molesting me? She and the priests just tried to brush it aside."

He felt her hand spasm and clench.

"Bastards!" she muttered.

Just then, the pine forests gave way to high plains. Pitcairn turned to scan the eastern horizon.

Maria Elena cried out. "Oh look! Pronghorn! Stop so we can watch them!"

With a smile, he pulled to the side of the road. They climbed out and leaned against the front fender to watch the graceful creatures a couple of hundred yards away. Pitcairn counted nine of them. The buck studied the two humans from a promontory, obviously aware but feeling safety in the distance. Had they been much closer, the herd would have fled.

A gentle summer breeze made the grasses and wildflowers flutter. In the distance beyond the pronghorn stood an old shepherd's camp. A rustic cabin slouched beneath several cottonwood trees, signs of water in an arid terrain. The only sound was the wind and the hot engine's little clinking.

Pitcairn stood behind Maria Elena, his feet outside hers, his arms wrapped protectively. She placed her hands on top of his.

The pronghorn wandered away as a pickup slid toward them down the rolling road. The rancher waved with a single finger above the steering wheel.

Maria Elena turned and asked, "Why don't we drive down to the Owl for green chile cheeseburgers?"

"A perfect suggestion." As a native of the Midwest, Pitcairn had been surprised by how far people would drive in the Southwest. The Owl Cafe was in San Antonio, more than an hour away but renowned for its signature chile and superb local beef. It was a common destination for New Mexicans wanting a great burger.

He helped her into the Jeep, and they roared off toward Mountainair, then turned west back to the valley of the Rio Grande. Before starting the descent, they detoured at the last minute to the pueblo ruins near the highway at Abó. It was a favorite place for Pitcairn: subdued, solemn, and sacred. The site was generally devoid of tourists, who sought more-prominent ruins but at the expense of missing an extraordinarily stark and beautiful place set beneath the quintessentially New Mexican high desert light.

Towering thunderheads loomed over the western desert. Brilliant cloud tops billowed in sharp contrast to their flat, greenish-black undersides. Pitcairn and Mari Elena held hands and walked in the late afternoon heat as it eased before stray breezes arriving in advance of the storms. The sun vanished behind the line of clouds.

Abó was deserted as expected. They meandered along footpaths that led beside broken rock walls. Pitcairn paused to trace the tidy, intricate pattern of the rocks with his finger. He had researched the history of the many pueblo ruins around central New Mexico. Theirs was an unusually rich culture that endured in a myriad of forms. He admired the natives' persistence; they adapted as necessary, and thrived regardless of their circumstances.

Maria Elena suddenly pressed herself against his arm.

"If those storms weren't so close, we could sneak behind that thicket and I could take advantage of you," she said teasingly.

He felt an instantaneous response in his groin and looked down at her with narrowed eyes. Pitcairn glanced to the west to gauge their chances. It did not look promising, a ragged curtain of rain coming steadily closer.

He leered back at her. "You naughty woman. You might get wet."

"I already am," she growled in a husky voice.

Pitcairn spun her quickly, then led her in a dash through the thicket. Beneath the massive boughs of an old cottonwood tree, she pressed him down into the thick grasses. She knelt beside him and quickly loosened his belt and opened his fly. Giggling at her efforts to release him from his boxers, Maria Elena hitched up her denim skirt. There was nothing on underneath it.

"A well-laid plot, Emmy?" he asked with a lewd look.

She responded with a suggestive raising of one eyebrow as she eased herself down onto him.

Highly aroused, they took only a few minutes, moaning together as the tree limbs strained in the wind, emitting eerie, creaking noises.

Maria Elena leaned down and kissed him quickly. "My plot well laid," she said with another giggle, then leaped up and dashed over to the trunk of the cottonwood. She hoisted her skirt rakishly and squatted to lean against the heavily ribbed bark and relieve herself. Her tooled Western boots gave the entire portrait a strange and curious twist.

Pitcairn stood up to reassemble himself. "Do you realize how ridiculous you look?"

"Too bad you don't have a camera. We could call it 'Western Madonna' and put it in a museum. That would stir up the local art police."

"Well, you'd never have to worry about returning to the Catholic Church, would you?"

Maria Elena snorted in disgust. "No loss there!"

The conversation waned as windy gusts propelled a smell of ozone. They sprinted toward the Jeep. Sporadic, pelting raindrops gave way to a deluge just as he unlocked the doors.

Laughing joyfully as they returned to the road, they gradually turned west and descended through the down-pour toward the valley. The initial onslaught of rain was easing thirty minutes later as they cruised through the verdant bottomland around Bernardo. A quick trip south on Interstate 25 delivered them to the Owl Cafe.

They both ordered burgers, fries, and shakes, then chatted about nothing in particular. The flow of customers provided an unending stream of subjects to comment on. Two tall, lean cowboys looked fresh off the range. A gang of young punks with outrageous hair colors, black clothes, and extreme body piercings had obviously driven down from Albuquerque. There were extended Hispanic families and a Navajo man and woman eating wordlessly. A young Indian girl wandered through hawking jewelry.

The food arrived as Pitcairn was commenting on the remarkable diversity, even here in a rural setting.

Maria Elena took a surprisingly large bite of her burger, then asked, "What's Clint thinking about Davidson?"

Pitcairn shrugged. "Clint thinks this is a great opportunity for me to finally make peace—that if I can see this through with Davidson, it will be my amends work."

"I don't understand how defending a serial killer is an amend for another dead man, Cito."

"I know. Clint doesn't see the making of amends like most people do. He's mostly concerned about me finding peace, which he insists is the real point. Since I can't directly make it right for the guy I killed, the next option is to do the right thing for someone else. I can't duck it, Emmy."

Maria Elena looked down. "I know. You don't have to tell me the importance of making things right. Clint may be sure, but I don't have to like anything about Davidson."

He pursed his lips and began, "Look . . ."

"I know!" she cut him off with annoyance. "Don't sell me. I can see you have to do it, and I'm sure you will. But I don't like it. Something stinks, and that scares me."

A look of acceptance spread across his face. "Got that," he said as he reassuringly touched his fingertips to the back of her hand. "How about we just enjoy our dinner."

She nodded in agreement but could not squelch a troubled look. "Damn it! In my family, you learned to pay attention to how things felt. And something's coming, Cito." She stared at him, then with an almost-imperceptible lifting of her chin repeated with conviction: "Something's coming."

The drive home was pleasantly cool. The rain had briefly washed away the summer.

► 9 ◄

EARLY SUNDAY MORNING, PITCAIRN TOOK LINCOLN AND LUCY to the mesa. He parked the Jeep in a sandy basin, and they made their way into a narrow defile that opened into an otherwise-hidden canyon running a mile or more.

This trek was one he would make only early in the morning or in winter. The crevices around the many basalt boulders were thick with rattlesnakes, but now, the morning chill kept them in their dens.

It was an uneventful hike, and two hours later, he was home. Much to his surprise, he saw lights in the kitchen. It was still before seven, much earlier than Maria Elena usually woke up. When he opened the door, he promptly tripped over Lucy scrambling to be first in line for breakfast. The kitchen smelled of chorizo frying and biscuits baking.

"What are you doing up?" he asked as he swung into the kitchen.

Maria Elena wiped her nose with the back of her hand as she turned with a spatula held firmly in the other. Her eyes were red from crying. "I was scared, so I decided to cook."

"What frightened you, Emmy?" he said as he wrapped her firmly in his arms.

She stifled a few sobs and shuddered. "When you left for the mesa, I was sort of awake—you know, that not-asleep-but-not-really-awake state. It didn't feel like a dream, more like a premonition."

He felt her tremble again and began to stroke her back.

"I imagined you were dead," she said haltingly, "that Davidson killed you too." She began to sob.

Pitcairn pivoted their bodies a little to reach the stove and turned off the burner. He held her as she cried, his face pressed into the top of her head.

"Son of a bitch!" she spat out loudly, tearing loose from his embrace. "The biscuits!" She yanked the oven door open, grabbed a towel, and quickly pulled them out. Then she laughed. "God, what a mess I am."

Pitcairn lifted her chin gently with one hand and kissed her. "But you're my mess, and I love you."

Maria Elena shook her head sheepishly. "It seems so foolish, but the feelings are so real."

"I know," he replied. "It's okay."

She smiled weakly, then turned to the stove. The skillet was filled with sliced potatoes, wedges of red and green bell peppers, chopped scallions, and the savory Mexican sausage. "Let me grate some goat cheese on here, and breakfast will be ready."

Pitcairn grabbed a basket and tossed in the biscuits—except for one he broke open to cool. "Maria Elena, I'm sorry this shit is so hard on you."

She thought first, then said, "It'll pass, Cito. I'll be okay." A gentle look filled her face as she piled food from the skillet onto his plate, then looked up at him.

Pitcairn could see her resolve returning. He simply nodded in acknowledgment. "Are you going to eat?"

"No. No appetite. I think I'll go sit in the tub for a while. Some lavender oil will be nice."

He took the cooled biscuits halves and tossed them across the room to the dogs. They had finished their breakfast, but Lucy caught hers deftly while Lincoln's caromed off his head. He scooted after it quickly as Lucy nosed around for crumbs.

"Pitcairn, you are such a pig," Maria Elena said. "I'm going for my bath. You can clean up."

He saluted sloppily. "Yes ma'am."

She exited and Pitcairn tended to his breakfast. He read the Sunday *Times* as he ate, an indulgence he and Maria Elena both enjoyed.

She emerged from her bath with spirit renewed, which brought him relief. They shared the *Times* as well as the *Albuquerque Journal*. The morning passed leisurely.

Shortly after noon, Maria Elena reminded him it was time to get ready for a party. Natalie and Bee, the two daughters of her friend Angie Montaño, the airport's arts coordinator, were celebrating together with a quinceañera, the traditional coming of age celebration, since they'd turned fifteen only ten months apart. She scurried off to steam tamales, while Pitcairn showered.

It was just before two when they arrived at the party and wove their way through the many guests to greet Angie. They found her arranging dishes of food. Maria Elena hugged her fondly. Their relationship had endured for nearly two decades, and Bee was Maria Elena's goddaughter.

Pitcairn's innate introversion emerged as Angie took Maria Elena in search of the girls. He steered through the gaily decorated home looking for a place to hunker down. In a secluded corner of the den, he found Maurice Gomez, a Taos Pueblo native who worked in maintenance at the airport. Pitcairn knew him from A.A. meetings and quickly settled into the next chair.

Gomez looked as uncomfortable as Pitcairn felt, and freely admitted it. They fell into a conversation about their challenges in social settings like these.

The afternoon passed, though Pitcairn spent much of it sticking close to Gomez while they ate and chatted. Toward the end of the party, the subject of the murder at the airport came up. Gomez told him his wife worked for the state in Santa Fe, and the scuttlebutt there was that Steve Cordova had made a deal. In return for killing Davidson, a close-knit network of friends and relatives of the slain Santa Fe girl would provide for his wife and children. Gomez also said the talk was that police weren't putting much effort into investigating the case.

Pitcairn was always interested in rumors. Sometimes they were useful, even the ones not totally true. "What else is your wife hearing?" he asked.

"Nothing surprising. Most everyone figures it's okay to kill a killer."

Pitcairn made note of the remark. It had a ring to it

► 10 ◄

WITH THE BEGINNING OF THE NEW WEEK, PITCAIRN BEGAN TO review the case he wanted to make about Daniel Davidson. He pored over what the psychiatrists had told him and reread his research. He checked and rechecked facts with Dr. Winter and Dr. Burden, then tested his thoughts and logic with Kate Delmonico, who again proved to be an astute thinker. Her many questions pressed him inexorably toward certainty about how he would proceed. Intrigued by what he was becoming immersed in—the conclusion that Davidson's claims were legitimate, even if they seemed impossible to accept—Pitcairn also spent the next couple of days reading abstracts of studies the psychiatrists had recommended on sexual violence, mental disorders, and related subjects.

To give his story balance, he planned to interview victims of sexual violence, members of advocacy groups, and others—including, if he could, relatives of Davidson's victims.

On Wednesday afternoon, a joint press release came from the state Department of Corrections and Albuquerque Police Department. Worded simply, it stated that Steve Cordova had acted alone in killing Daniel Davidson. The weather had played a part by distracting the guards, but no culpability was assigned to them. The corrections commissioner commended them for their effective response in ensuring there was no further violence.

As Pitcairn read the statement, instinctive doubt rose in his mind. "You can't bullshit a bullshitter," Clint always said. Pitcairn smelled bullshit. The explanation was too simple, to say nothing of absolving everyone involved other than Cordova. He made a note to call Don Nichols in the morning. There were always interesting avenues that deserved a look and a little curiosity.

Some time later, as he and Maria Elena lay in bed reading, he rolled over and shared the latest information. She listened impassively, then nodded curtly.

"So Emmy, I know you don't have a dog in this fight," he said, borrowing his favorite of Clint's West Texas phrases, "but whaddaya think?"

She cocked her head and smiled. "I think you're going to lose all your good English-language skills if you keep emulating your sponsor." She grinned jokingly. "Then you'll be unemployable in your field and completely dependent on me."

Pitcairn snaked a hand onto her belly and pressed an ominous look onto his face. "Tell me or I'll tickle you till you cry," he said in a deep voice.

She parroted a bad Russian dialect: "Nutink you can do veel make me tawk."

"I warned you," Pitcairn said sternly as he yanked her toward him. His massive hands played lightly up her waist and along her rib cage as she began to squirm.

"Ees dat da best you got?" she sputtered as she laughed.

Pitcairn launched into her. Her gales of laughter set Lucy barking excitedly as the linens rapidly fell into disarray and she tried to escape.

A few seconds later, she gasped, "Uncle! Uncle! I give!"

Lucy stood with her front paws on the bed, stubby tail wagging, snout up, howling as the lovers collapsed together like spoons.

"Come on up, dumbass," Pitcairn said with a wave.

Lucy piled onto the bed.

Maria Elena poked Pitcairn with an elbow. "Lincoln too."

He turned his head and whistled toward the pale dog lying quietly in the corner. Lincoln yawned, then leaped up to curl around Maria Elena's legs. She gently caressed the dog's head.

Pitcairn tried again. "Really, Emmy, tell me what you think about the Davidson case."

She pressed her head back into his chest. A long, nasal inhalation ended in a chuckle.

"Damn, you're persistent."

"It's one of my best traits," he replied quickly.

"Okay," she said firmly as she reached back to place a hand on his thigh. "Look, I'm deeply conflicted about Davidson. Really couldn't care less about his circumstances or his death. But . . . I care that you care . . . and I hate what that bastard did. So I don't know what to think."

She paused and cocked her head as she thought. "This whole thing just feels like bad news, Cito. I don't know why, but my intuition tells me to tell you to get the hell out of it."

He interjected. "So you think something's fishy too."

"I honestly don't know about that. But I do trust your instincts, just like I trust mine. Somehow, something about it seems a threat to you. And that worries me."

He tucked his chin between her neck and shoulder and held her more closely. "I'm fine, Emmy. Thanks for telling me the truth."

The conversation ended. Soon Maria Elena was asleep. Pitcairn shooed the dogs from the bed and tidied the covers as best he could without waking her, then slipped into a fitful sleep.

* * *

The nightmare came a little later than usual and was relatively calm. Pitcairn lay in bed until shortly after five, then opted to walk the dogs around the neighborhood rather than the mesa.

When Maria Elena had left for work, he tidied the kitchen and headed to the study. He called Nichols. After a long wait on hold, he heard the security chief's rich baritone fill the line.

"This is Chief Nichols."

"Chief. Kevin Pitcairn. I saw the press release. What's up?"

"Look, Pitcairn. Since Davidson was a Department of Corrections case, I have no official position and no official information. Got that?"

"Sure, Chief."

"There wasn't an investigation. There won't be an investigation. Davidson's got no friends. More than a few people think he got what he deserved."

It was quiet. "Is that it, Chief?"

"That's it."

Pitcairn stared intently at the phone. "So what's it boil down to, Chief?" He imagined Nichols carefully focusing his thoughts. "That it's okay to kill a killer?"

Nichols cleared his throat. "It means you should run from this one."

An awkward pause followed. Pitcairn closed the conversation, "Got it, Chief, but I won't do that."

The security chief's laughter filled the line. "Never doubted it for a moment, Pitcairn."

The call ended. He gazed out the window.

Shortly after he'd been struck sober with the Dalai Lama, Pitcairn had happened to wander into San Felipe de Neri Catholic Church on the Old Town Plaza. A kindly old priest had sat with him beneath a soaring stained glass window and chatted in the stillness of the chapel.

The priest had some experience with recovering alcoholics, and offered a significant observation that had come to him from that work. He said, "The ones who find peace are the ones who keep seeking, keep asking, and keep knocking. But I do not think they have a choice. They must do what they must do."

That wisdom had guided Pitcairn countless times, as it did now. He called several contacts in the Corrections Department, made plans to follow up with some of them, and was luckily able to get invited for a group intervention session that evening with youth offenders at the Santa Fe Center for the Prevention of Sexual Violence.

He let Maria Elena know he wouldn't be back from Santa Fe until late evening, then drove over to the Dog House for a couple of green chile cheese dogs for the road.

Two hours later, he sat down to a difficult interview with a rape crisis counselor and the center's director of public information. Sexual violence was about exerting power, they insisted—unable to consider even the remotest possibility that someone like Davidson was suffering from a mental illness. In itself, their stance was not surprising, since a more flexible view would undermine the validity of their approach. But it was troubling that they seemed so close-minded.

The evening intervention session with the six teen-agers was even more disturbing. Each had been deemed capable of rehabilitation, and sentenced to the program as an alternative to incarceration. But he could see how bewildered the young men were as the staff members kept following their power model to get the youths to admit they'd knowingly and willingly exerted their power over the women they harassed or assaulted. Over and over, the questioning led toward the same conclusion. Though the words changed, the point was the same: "You knew it was wrong, and you did it deliberately."

The confusion was clear in the boys' eyes, but Pitcairn could also see their desire to please those running the program. Who knew why they said what they did? But their desire to stay out of detention surely played a part. In the end, all six professed guilt exactly as desired.

During the drive home, impressions of the night swirled in his thoughts. Something about Davidson's perspective had the ring of truth to it, and was wholly at odds with what he'd just seen. Moreover, it seemed that what the serial killer had to say about new policies for youth offenders really did make sense in light of what he'd just seen.

► 11 ◄

PITCAIRN SCREAMED IN TERROR, THEN WOKE TO FIND HIMSELF
standing naked beside the bed. The dogs barked in confusion as Maria Elena flicked on the bedside light and
turned to him with a look of worry.

"Are you all right?" she asked fearfully.

Bewildered, Pitcairn looked around, still caught in the
nightmare. He blinked several times, then shook the hazi-
ness from his head.

"You scared the hell out of me. Are you okay?" she asked
again as her fear gave way to agitation.

"Jesus!" he swore angrily as he pressed his hands firmly
against his temples. He toppled onto the edge of the bed,
then slumped over in a sitting position, elbows on knees,
hands rubbing desperately through his hair.

Lucy poked her head between his legs. "Goddamnit,
Lucy!" he exploded as he shoved her forcefully toward the
corner where Lincoln sat. "Stay there!" He gestured with a
trembling finger.

Pitcairn could see Maria Elena out of the corner of his
eye. She kept her distance. He rubbed his eyes, then glanced
toward her as she flipped on the nightstand light.

"Sorry, Emmy," he said as a forlorn look came to his face.
"The nightmare again." Pitcairn paused as he felt the terror
course through him. Maria Elena moved closer and pressed
herself against his arm.

"The man stopped struggling and didn't die. He tried to
talk to me, but I couldn't take my hands from his neck. His
eyes darted up over my left shoulder, but before I could look,

someone spun me around and knocked the shit out of me. Next thing I knew, I was pinned to the ground being choked."

He began to weep. "I couldn't breathe." Sobs burst out as he cradled his head in his hands. Maria Elena held him gently. "I couldn't see who it was, and I couldn't get loose. Somehow I managed to scream, and then I woke up."

"Cito, you're okay now," she whispered.

He turned fully toward her and looked into her eyes.

She gasped, "Mother of God!"

"What is it?"

She looked stunned.

"Maria Elena, what is it?" he repeated as he leaned toward her.

"Cito, come with me to the mirror! You won't believe it!"

She turned on the overhead light and led him to the mirror on the dresser.

Standing in the now-bright light, Pitcairn turned his head. His breathing grew shallow. There on his cheek was a stark, pale handprint rimmed with flushed skin, as if he had just been slapped.

He tilted his head up. The marks at the base of his neck—a circular bloodless spot tinged by red—was precisely where thumbs would have been pressed on his windpipe.

"Maria Elena," he said in a hushed, quavering voice, "what the fuck is happening to me?"

She was silent, but he could see her dark eyes wandering over his image in the mirror.

He touched the marks. "Have you ever heard of anything like this, Emmy?"

She shook her head slowly. "It's like the stigmata of the Christ."

Pitcairn snorted. "The Christ!" His voice dripped with sarcasm that failed to mask his fear of something he couldn't understand.

"Well, I don't know what else to tell you."

"I know. But . . . the Christ?" He looked back in the mirror. The imprints had faded slightly.

"What time is it anyway?" he said as he turned to look at the bedside clock. "Four." He studied himself in the mirror. "Clint's probably up. Think I'll call him. Why don't you go back to bed."

She looked at him through narrowed eyes.

"Are you okay, Cito?"

A puzzled look came over him. "I don't know what I am. And I sure as hell don't know what's going on. But maybe Clint will."

He momentarily regained his emotional balance in response to the comforting thought of Clint. He spoke softly. "Climb on into bed, Emmy," he said, trying to restore a shade of normalcy. "I'll come back after I've talked to Clint."

She turned with reluctance and straightened the covers as he walked out of the room. The dogs followed, Lucy slinking. He slumped into the office chair and dialed quickly.

"Sorry to call so early, Clint. It's Pitcairn. The nightmare was pretty bad. Can we talk?"

"Mornin', son. And it's okay. I didn't know when I'd hear, but I was expecting you'd be calling."

Pitcairn quickly described what had happened. "Damn!" Clint said when he described the imprints on his face and neck. "Haven't heard of that in a while. Them's deep memories, boy. Do you suppose it's about the killing? That doesn't feel right, but if it's not that, what the hell else could it be?"

"But memories of what, Clint?"

"Don't know, son. Do you remember gettin' beat as a kid?"

Pitcairn sat up, tucked the phone between his shoulder and ear, and extended his arms over his head as he thought.

"Nothing like that. My Dad whipped us with a belt if we got way out of line, but that's about it."

"Hmmm," Clint replied. "Well, it'll come to ya. You're just gonna have to stay the course. Ain't easy, but it does seem to be necessary."

"So you've heard of this sort of thing with the handprints?" Pitcairn asked with a quaking voice.

"Abso-damn-lutely son. It's been a while, though. You can bet your ass that it's important. And the secret is gonna be revealed by you diggin' inta this thing like your life depended on it.

"Son," Clint said after a long pause, "your life does depend on doin' this deal. I can feel it all the way down to my bones. So pull out your journal and get busy writin'. See if you cough somethin' up."

"Okay," Pitcairn answered with a sigh. Then he heard a chuckle. "What's so funny?"

"Well, tell Maria Elena that she ain't livin' with Christ. Not hardly."

"I'm sure she'll be surprised by that." Pitcairn joined in the humor, feeling a slight easing of his concern. "Thanks, Clint. I really owe you one."

"Couldn't do it without you, son. Glad ya called. Don't hesitate to call as often as ya need to. Now I'm gonna go read the paper and have some coffee. Tell that beautiful chiquita of yours I said 'howdy.' "

He was gone. But Pitcairn felt the edge still sharpening his emotions; he could feel it in the pit of his stomach. Rather than going back to bed or to the mesa, he made coffee. While it brewed, he searched out the partly filled journal in which he scribbled down thoughts. Coffee in hand, he sat down and began to write at length.

► 12 ◄

PITCAIRN DID EXACTLY AS CLINT ADVISED. HE WROTE AS IF HIS life depended on it, page after page of his life story pouring forth, most of it simple regurgitation of matters known. But every now and again, something new would emerge. He could feel vague insight building: a hint of sexual overtones and deeply shadowed stains of memories.

He wrote through the weekend, taking occasional breaks. Each time he saw Maria Elena, worry showed on her face. A couple of times, Pitcairn was heartbroken to see a glint of uncertainty in her eyes. Her unease disturbed him. He did what he could to reassure her, which may have been as much to reassure himself.

On one extended break as he ate an egg salad sandwich, he slammed out a column along the lines of what Mortensen wanted, more of a news account mixed with observations. He felt himself shaking his head as he read it again. It was not the story Pitcairn wanted to tell, which was still forming within him, but it met the immediate need to give Mortensen something. He had surrendered to the flow of things. It would run in the *Chronicle* on Tuesday.

The hardest part was the dissonance he felt with Maria Elena. The thought pulled at him all the while. Fortunately, she knew how he worked things through, and had seen it before. She left him to his writing and sought solace elsewhere.

Beyond the dissonance, his thoughts were growing murkier. Even as bits of clarity seemed to form, his emotions and psyche swirled in an inner torrent. It was exhausting him.

On Monday morning, after a weekend of neglect, Lucy and Lincoln were pleased to head for the desert long before dawn.

* * *

Monsoon clouds hung low over the open expanse of mesa, desert flushed green from record-breaking rains. Moisture blended clouds to ground and muffled sound. The mesa held a depth and substance almost foreign to its arid nature; torpor hung heavy, poised to embrace those with willing hearts. At times, this sacred land was a crucible, a place of transformation. Always, the mesa delivered, though rarely as expected.

* * *

Slogging along through muck, Pitcairn felt the sweat pour down his body. The cloud cover insulated the ground, preventing heat from releasing into the atmosphere. And the closeness of the moisture in the air was like a low-grade perspiration pump.

He labored as Lincoln moved beside him steadily. Lucy frolicked from puddle to puddle. They would need to be hosed down back at the house.

The westerly track turned nearly ninety degrees and downward to cross an arroyo. On a whim, he whistled Lucy back from ahead of him and turned up the sandy wash. The sky was just beginning to lighten with the coming of day, and the shades of gray around him were soothingly consistent with his mood.

They followed the arroyo for some time until it began to get shallow and then slowly disappear. A knob of earth reared up slightly to the north, and he quickly climbed it. Atop the rise, he stopped to scan the still-darkened horizon.

A thought seized him, and he knelt to build a cairn from volcanic rocks that were strewn widely across the ground. As it neared four feet or so in height, a sense of anticipation grew within him.

He had just begun to tuck sprigs of sage into the top of what seemed to have become an altar when a spasm of pain suddenly wrenched his gut. He toppled forward with a gasp, feeling it rip through the pit of his stomach as the cairn collapsed under his weight. The boxers bounded to him as the pain wrenched his body into a fetal position, contorting him as he struggled desperately to breathe.

Just as a whimpering Lucy began to lick his face, the spasm relented, and he drew a ragged breath. He rolled like a ball onto his knees and was swept into a fit of coughing that quickly gave way to gut-twisting vomit. Vile tasting liquid spewed forth, emptying him, though the retching would not cease.

Finally, after an indeterminable length of time, he was able to raise himself up and take a few deep, tension-releasing breaths. Seemingly from nowhere, a memory from childhood raced through him.

He was five years old, Little Kevvie they called him, and playing in his room with Carrie, the little girl from next door who was his best friend. They had closed the door and were innocently playing doctor.

His mother barged in and flew into a rage. Disembodied, he saw himself turn and watched in slow motion as she swung her hand viciously, striking him full on the face. Then she leaped at him with a fury, knocking him to the floor, and pummeling him as she hovered over him. She screamed unintelligibly as her fists windmilled wildly. After many blows, her energy waned, but with one final burst, she cast herself upon her son and began to strangle him with a cold passion.

Studying the scene from a point of view outside his body, Little Kevvie felt a strange detachment before his own white hot rage surged. Suddenly he was back in his body with the urgency of survival. With clear-eyed focus, he drew all his strength and head-butted his mother.

She screamed in pain as blood spurted from her broken nose. She tumbled from him as he slipped from consciousness.

Pitcairn felt a strange quiet as the memory faded. He was spread-eagled on his back with Lincoln hovering protectively over his head and Lucy tucked between his legs.

Some time later, wasted by the grief and tears that had poured from him, he rolled up into a sitting position. The boxers braced him from both sides, each curling around his hips with heads patiently on either of his thighs.

He surveyed himself. Soil-stained clothes and hands marked him outwardly. A profound but comforting sadness filled his entire being, an inward sign of truth seen. With a deep breath, he realized the experience had broken him open, and that the melancholy he now felt might never leave. But it was certainly tolerable, much more so than the ragged edge of unconscious rage he now knew he had long borne. It was that unbridled rage unleashed by drugs that had caused him to murder.

Strangely, he felt no anger toward his mother. If anything, understanding dominated. And in that comprehension, he saw himself in a new light.

He stood painfully, realizing that his time on the ground had been much more physical than he could recall. His fists ached from clenching as did his gut, while his head and neck throbbed, a few spots tender with bruises. He leaned down to scratch each of the dogs' ears, then began the walk home with steady steps. A short time later, he stopped and knelt beside the dogs. Placing his head between theirs, he whispered a thank you for the love and protection they offered without condition. Tears welled then as he also felt a deep sense of gratitude for Maria Elena.

He began to walk as the column he wanted to write started taking shape. The childhood memories were drawing him closer to the heinous events that had shaped the life of Daniel Davidson—a life not evil but understandable. The recollections, though awful, now galvanized him, somehow seeming more concrete. He felt certain that writing would bring it into focus.

First, he needed to call Clint. Then he would contact Aunt Jeanne, his mother's sister. It had been some time since they last spoke, but Pitcairn recalled her fondly. Perhaps she could shed some light on his memories. Then there were calls to be made to the families of Davidson's victims.

When he settled into the driver's seat of the Jeep, it occurred to him that what had just transpired fit well the descriptions he'd read of so-called demonic possession. The depths of the psyche and its protective mechanisms were unfathomable. "Possessed indeed," he admitted.

► 13 ◄

H IS COLUMN FOR THE *CHRONICLE* WAS DONE AND GONE. BUT Pitcairn knew that Daniel Davidson's story was not finished with him yet. Ideas to be worked out, reporting to be done, conclusions to be fought for—all distracting him as he washed Lucy and Lincoln. Leaning over to towel them dry, he was so preoccupied with his thoughts he didn't hear the screen door behind him.

The boxers bolted as Maria Elena's voice cut through his self-absorption. "Cito?" she asked in a trembling voice.

Pitcairn heard the concern in her tone, but there was also a guardedness that did not fit. He turned and cocked his head. "Hey," he said gently. His eyes caught something terribly amiss in her tear-stained face. She was still in her robe, and her arms were wrapped protectively across her chest. Without moving but with great care, he asked, "What's wrong, Emmy?"

Her lower lip quivered as she raised a hand to wipe away tears. "Clint's sponsor, Jeff Hopkins, just called." She shook her head as if to ward off her thoughts. "He died a few hours ago, Cito. They think it was a heart attack. He's gone." She burst into tears and blubbered, "I'm so sorry, baby . . . on top of everything else . . . ."

He felt himself slump as his eyes closed and a sharp stab of pain lanced through his chest. Almost disembodied again, his mind disjointedly leaped to a recent interview with a local pain physician who'd told him that heartache—the feeling Pitcairn was filled with—had become the greatest untreated malady in modern medicine. A dissonant chuckle popped from his thoughts: *Heartache . . . what an understatement that is!*

Opening his eyes, he and Maria Elena moved toward each other as if in a dream. As they held each other, it was unclear who was comforting and who being comforted. For Pitcairn, the well of sadness that had come to him on the West Mesa seemed to expand to encompass this new blow. It was as if the expansiveness of that open space had somehow found its way inside him, that his emotional capacity was larger than ever before.

Still, there was a bittersweet ache that clung to him. It was not unpleasant.

The next two days were a blur with little time for grief. Friends and acquaintances from A.A. called to offer condolences. And Clint had previously asked Pitcairn to lead a memorial service. So amid the social swirl it was necessary to think deeply about what needed to be said on Thursday night.

On the morning of the memorial, Clint's sister Ellie came by to drop off a few items Clint had designated for him. Ellie never approved of Clint or A.A., so the meeting was brief.

It was very quiet in the house as he sat to open the parcel Ellie had delivered. Outside a light drizzle muted and softened the world after still more overnight thunderstorms.

Drawing a deep breath to center himself, he pulled the cover from the box. On top was an envelope with Clint's small script: "Kevin Pitcairn—Do not open until October 1st." It would be the birthday of his sobriety, and he found himself suddenly amused by his sponsor's quirkiness as he set it aside. He trusted Clint's intuition and wisdom.

Next was a worn, large-print copy of A.A.'s Big Book. Pitcairn leafed through and was deeply moved to see it was heavily annotated by Clint. Margins were filled with comments, and multiple colors highlighted a great deal of the text. This was the compilation of Clint's life in recovery, a treasure trove of insights and commentary. Wistfulness crept over him as he realized this was probably Clint's most prized possession. It was a great gift.

Last was an item wrapped in brown butcher paper. Peeling away the cover, Pitcairn laughed out loud as he saw Clint's mantra in needlepoint mounted in a simple wooden frame. He'd stolen the phrase from somewhere but could never recall where:

"We are the otters of the universe."

Tears crept into his eyes as he replayed countless episodes when Clint had cited those words. No matter how bleak or challenging things might have seemed, he would remind Pitcairn about the otters: "Remember son, we're just playin'. It might be drama, or it might be comedy, but it's all play. Goddamn, don't forget to have fun!"

Lincoln and Lucy leaped up and ran out, intuiting Maria Elena's entry. He heard the door followed by her shout, "Cito?"

"In here!" he hollered in response, assuming she had come home for lunch.

She swept into the room an instant later and eased sideways across his lap, her arms cast around his shoulders, her face tilted toward his. Looking him in the eyes and scanning slowly, she announced, "First, tell me you love me."

His heart welled as he said it. "I love you, Maria Elena."

"Now, tell me you missed me."

He dutifully repeated the words. Somehow she had overcome the fear his strangeness provoked. Her resilience was always inspiring. Over and over again, she rose to respond to difficult circumstances, always after what looked to him like some kind of deep, emotional breath she took before plunging forward. It was a trait he had come to rely on. She was an extraordinary woman.

"Okay," she said with a smile, "now tell me what you've been doing."

Given an opening, he began with the items from Clint, then recounted his day thus far. He included an interesting experience he'd had with Martin, a mutual friend from A.A. who at one time was Clint's sponsor, when the two had met at a morning meeting.

Martin said Clint had confided in him about Pitcairn's situation. It was a surprising revelation. While Clint was Texas through and through, Martin was entirely Seattle, right down to his REI garb and an ever-present designer travel mug. It was a stark contrast but not the first curious connection Pitcairn had observed in A.A. Recovery made for strange bedfellows.

"I won't presume to give advice," he had said, "but if you need someone to talk it through, just let me know. I'd be honored. I really admired Clint."

"Thanks, Martin," he replied. "I'll take you up on that offer if it seems right. For the moment, it looks like an inside job."

With a nod, Martin assented. Then a curious look passed over his face. "Pitcairn," he began, " I think I know a few things about you based on what Clint told me. I have a feeling you ought to spend a few days at my place on the Rio Puerco. It's an old rancho a ways north of Interstate 40, but as the crow flies, it's just a few miles northwest of the West Mesa. I've refurbished it a bit. It's rustic but comfortable—no telephone or television, so it makes for a nice retreat. There's some acreage around it I lease out to a rancher for grazing, but other than the cows, you'll find it quite secluded."

Pitcairn accepted the offer. He knew Clint's former sponsor was someone he could trust. It touched him that a man he knew only slightly would offer such a kindness.

Back in the present, he stroked Maria Elena's arm. "If it's okay with you, I'm going to head over tomorrow morning and stay through Sunday. I need a few days to collect myself."

She smiled warmly. "Cito, you can't fool me. You're going to cry like a baby up there." She poked him on the shoulder before snuggling closer to him. "And I can't blame you. Clint was good for you." She sighed heavily. "I'll miss him too."

Pitcairn nodded in agreement. "I gotta tell you, I've never felt so disoriented. I don't know what to expect anymore, but now's a good time to tell you what happened to me Monday morning before you told me about Clint."

The story poured out, including the obvious link between the markings on his face and neck, and the incident with his mother. While he talked, the feelings washed over him anew. Maria Elena comforted him as he talked. He was left again with a pervading, but not uncomfortable, sense of sadness.

"I guess the truth is I probably have some grieving to do, for Clint and maybe for my mom. And I need to sort out how I'm going to proceed. So far, every plan I've made since Davidson's letter has gone awry. There are obviously things at work that are beyond me. Christ, who could have known memories could be lodged so deep they could express themselves physically?"

Quiet swept up around them as they sat together wordlessly.

Finally she spoke. "I know how memories can feel sometimes, Cito," She looked at him through eyes now deep and clear. "I'm sorry."

He returned her gaze. She understood.

► 14 ◄

I F THE MEASURE OF A PERSON'S LIFE CAN BE TOLD BY THE NUM-
ber of people who are affected by your death, then Clint's
life could only be viewed as an immense success, Pitcairn
thought. He was also pleased to see a slightly bewildered
look on the face of Clint's sister. Nothing could invalidate
her disapproval of her brother more than the several hundred people who had shown up. It was a testament to the
power of Clint's spirit.

While a great deal of grief showed, the recovering crowd
was notable by its laughter and gaiety. They would miss Clint
terribly, but the memorial was a celebration, and they knew
how to celebrate. Their own battles with darkness and loss
had bred in them an incredible joy for living that could overcome great difficulty. Many friends were in attendance, plus
Clint's wide circle of acquaintances. His body had been cre-
mated, but those gathered at the Taylor Ranch Community
Center had been asked to bring inspirational stories to share.

When the crowd had mostly settled, Pitcairn moved to
the front of the auditorium. Other than a stage filled with
flowers, it was a simple setting.

"Hello everyone. We're gathered to honor and celebrate
Clint Pennington just like he asked us to. We're not here
to lament his death but to share the many gifts he gave us.
In fact, his instructions were specific in having his good
friend Charlie Rice kick things off; he knew Charlie would
set the right tone. After Charlie has shared, you're all free
to take the microphone and pass on whatever you think
Clint would like to be said. But remember his guidance;

we're here to celebrate and to be inspired. So Charlie, come on over here and get us started."

A worn and weathered man sauntered up to the front. There was a mischievous look in Charlie's eyes as he glanced at Pitcairn and took the microphone.

"Some ya'll know that Clint and I go way back to Clovis where we grew up. I knew him for a long, long time." Charlie glanced around with a squint that resulted from years spent in the outdoors. "What ya'll don't know is that he and I made one of them blood brother pacts when we were fifteen. We was close all along.

"I promised Clint I wouldn't cuss, so those who are waiting for the F-bomb can just relax." He laughed as a titter ran through the crowd, though a few looks were nothing short of mortified.

"But he did want this shindig to be as real as it could be, so I'm going to tell you one of the funniest stories I know about Clint. It was during his stint in the Navy, and he was all drunked up and got in a fight in port in the Philippines. His buddies had dragged his ass back to the ship, but the guys they'd been fightin', a bunch of jarheads, followed 'em as far as the fence. It was all they could do to get Clint up the gangplank, cause he was cussin' and spittin' like a wildcat. But they managed."

Charlie chuckled to himself as he shook his head. "Well, Clint ran up and stood on a few steel drums, whipped down his pants, and peed straight at those guys while wavin' his arms and hollerin' at 'em. He told 'em, 'I piss on your mommas and daddies for bringin' up such worthless bastards.' God, that set 'em off, and they started howlin' right back."

Pitcairn saw the recovering alcoholics in the crowd laughing with delight, while Clint's other close friends bore amused looks on their face. Ellie was aghast, and looked almost ready to leap up and flee.

"Before long, a bunch of MPs had to come and clear those guys out and haul Clint off to the brig. Even then he was fightin' everyone and everything."

Tears came to Charlie's eyes. "One of those guys had insulted one of Clint's buddies. Clint was fightin' for someone else. And that's what I loved about Clint. No matter the price, that's what Clint did . . . stick up for others."

The audience was now silent as Charlie blew his nose into a huge, red handkerchief and headed toward his seat. The tone had been set, and what followed was heartfelt and profound, filled with both laughter and tears.

Pitcairn simply facilitated the storytelling, occasionally punctuating it with whatever seemed appropriate. As always, the candor and humanity of the drunks who spoke was refreshing. Mostly, he felt the pervading sense of sadness. After more than an hour, he moved to wrap up the service.

"I want to acknowledge that Clint's sponsor in A.A., Jeff Hopkins, sends his regrets. He's ailing but knew you'd provide a great sendoff regardless. And no doubt Clint would have loved hearing all your recollections. I'm sure he would have laughed and wept right along with us. He was that kind of guy. And his life and behavior was just as outrageous and had just as much impact as you've heard. For every one of your stories about how he affected others, there are countless others untold.

"Now I'd like to close the memorial with a story of my own. Like all of you, I could go on and on about how Clint touched me over many years. But one day I watched Clint at a Westside youth detention facility. He was there to talk to them about alcohol and drugs, but shifted gears to families. He got up and walked around that room as he talked, touching boys on their shoulders and heads as he seemed to think was right for each. One kid just started bawlin'. Clint sat down next to him, put his arm around his shoulders, and told the boy he loved him. Those kids in that room all started crying about their families, and they were probably never the same again."

Pitcairn, feeling a lump in his throat, needed some time to collect himself. "That's my story too, just like a lot of you here today. We've been greatly changed from knowing Clint, and we'll never be the same again."

A number of heads nodded as he closed. "Thanks for honoring Clint with your presence tonight. He'd ask only one thing of us all, 'Freely have you received, therefore freely give.' Travel safely."

A number of people stayed talking until they were encouraged to leave by the community center's staff. Pitcairn stayed with Maria Elena until everyone had left. Then they drove home.

A few hours later, Pitcairn startled awake in a heavy, cold sweat with a feeling of dread clutching at his diaphragm. There had been no nightmare he could recall, but the anxiety he felt was nearly overwhelming. He glanced over to see that it was a bit after three o'clock. Maria Elena was snoring lightly.

He blinked several times in the dark before closing his eyes again. He felt only emptiness, an unfathomable depth to the sadness that had been dogging him. Panic flitted around the edge of his awareness, but he settled into deep, steady breathing as he tried not to think.

Still, thoughts crept in. *What the hell is this now . . . at least before, I had the nightmare to blame . . . this is terror . . . relax, it's only a feeling, not a fact . . . it seems far more than a feeling . . . just breathe.* Eventually, the breathing quieted the voices in his head, though the feeling of dread remained palpable.

He rose quietly so as not to wake Maria Elena, and moved to the kitchen. The boxers followed and settled into a corner. Pitcairn brewed some coffee, then settled down with his journal to write.

Some time later, he arose to prepare oatmeal for Maria Elena. The feeling of doom had not yielded, so he opted to busy himself in a hope of distraction.

A short time later, Maria Elena moved dreamily into the kitchen. The pungent smell of the Irish oatmeal had woken her. Heavy with half-and-half, it was one of her favorite breakfast foods. She slipped beside him and sleepily laid her head against his chest.

"Oatmeal . . . you are so sweet," she said drowsily.

"The finest for the finest," he replied distractedly, then turned to kiss the top of her head.

Ever sensitive to the slightest nuance, Maria Elena pulled her head back and cocked it to look at him. "What's up?"

He exhaled. "It's a good thing you're the only woman I chase; I couldn't get away with anything. You always know when something's going on."

She snarled at him in jest. "You wouldn't even get away with your cojones if you cheated on me, baby." She gestured with a cutting motion. "Snip, snip!"

He hugged her to him as a feeling of adoration welled up in his chest. He kissed her head again, then told her to sit down.

After serving the oatmeal, Pitcairn described the dread he felt. "Emmy, if it's possible, this feeling is worse than the nightmare. It's beyond sadness, and I'm not sure I even have words for it." He paused to think. "I always thought getting rid of those desperate, dead eyes would be a blessing. Never dreamed anything could be worse than that."

He sighed as she reached out to caress his arm. "I'm so sorry, Cito." He noticed a somber look that spread across her face.

Leaning back and pressing his hands over his head to stretch, he returned them to press firmly on his eyes, rubbing them rigorously. "Nothing to do but go forward. Maria Elena. I sure as hell can't go back."

He changed the subject then, a tactic Clint had taught him to stay out of self-pity. "After you go to work, I'm headed to Martin's place. He calls it Rancho Sereno, but he laughs every time he says it. So I really don't know what to expect. There's no phone, but I'll drive down to the truck stop to call you. And I'll be home Sunday afternoon."

She nodded without a word. Her eyes pored over his face for what felt like a very long time. Then she leaned forward and kissed him. "I love you."

A wry look crossed Pitcairn's face. "Thank you. I need that."

She nodded again. With a gentle touch to his cheek, she swept herself up to get ready for the day.

Pitcairn cleaned the kitchen, then packed a few things before she left. As usual, she was running late. A quick peck on the cheek, and she was gone. A few minutes later, and he'd loaded the dogs into the Jeep for the drive to Rancho Sereno.

► 15 ◄

HE TRACK RUNNING NORTH FROM THE INTERSTATE ALTERNATED
between heavy, muddy ruts and bone-jarring washboard
on sections of higher ground. More than once, Pitcairn uttered his gratitude for four-wheel drive. The way snaked
along the eastern edge of the Rio Puerco, a typically muddy
trickle with alkali-stained banks that had become a torrent
with all the rain.

He crossed several cattle guards, then passed through a
particularly muddy wash that almost swallowed the Jeep.
Swearing under his breath, he rattled up out of the swale to
see Rancho Sereno tucked between the river and the cusp
of the mesa. Surrounded by a few scrubby native trees, it
was an ugly site.

Immediately, Pitcairn thought about changing his mind
and returning to the city. Were it not for Clint's voice in his
head urging him to be open minded, a byproduct of many
years of coaching, he would have turned around. A few
bounces and mud puddles later, he came to a stop in front
of the place.

Scanning the "rancho," he was amused to realize he had
no idea what to call it. It could never pass as a house. After
a short contemplation and a snap decision to call it an im-
proved shack, his gaze was drawn to the sweep of green
rising up to the mesa. Lucy's whimpering to escape added
to a compulsion to walk this new yet familiar terrain. He
opened the door and was nearly bowled over by the excited boxer scrambling past him to romp. Lincoln sat patiently in the back of the Jeep until Pitcairn opened the

back, then leaped down gracefully and began to slowly sniff his surroundings.

It was late enough in the morning and the sun high enough that snakes were probably holed up for the day. So he grabbed two bottles of water and strode past the still-unexamined rancho. Within a few yards, they picked up a game trail that meandered efficiently toward the escarpment as it intertwined with the more-notable trails of cattle crisscrossing the terrain.

Pitcairn stopped to survey the landscape. It was markedly green from the rain, though Martin had told him a large part of the lushness came from having a rancher who knew good grazing practices. Indeed, the grasses were more luxuriant than anyplace he could recall in central New Mexico. He noted a pile of largish, round turds, a sign of mule deer, then turned to scratch Lincoln's ears. While he could not see Lucy, he could hear her romping through the thick brush.

He fell into a steady walk. Sometimes just walking was the only choice to soothe a deeply troubled mind. So he brought his attention to his steps, his breath, and the terrain. For a time, thoughts left him.

Just as they approached the crest of the upheaving slope, he began to cry. It was an oddly gentle weeping compared with the usual inner torment that ripped from him. The tears flowed steadily as he continued to walk, stopping occasionally to blow his nose and wipe his eyes. There were brief ebbs to the tears, but then feelings would well up again, and he would cry some more.

He and the dogs tromped along the edge of the mesa where the eastern vista swept across grasslands while the western view covered the Rio Puerco drainage. Finally, he stopped and sat on a smooth outcropping of basalt atop a knoll. He could see the top of one of the West Mesa volcanoes, his usual area now a few miles to the east, as well as Mount Taylor far to the west on the edges of the land of the Navajo. Farther north, cattle dotted the terrain.

Strangely, the tears had stopped. Pitcairn imagined the walking to be like a pump for his sorrows, and laughed at the thought. He tried to place the sadness but was unsuccessful. He spoke to Lincoln, who had settled comfortably beside him. "It feels like it's all linked, boy. Loss is loss is loss. Clint. Mom. The guy I killed. Every pet that ever died." He screwed up his forehead. "Hell, even me and alcoholism and Maria Elena and her abuse. One continuous strand of loss and grief."

Lucy bolted out of the brush then and collapsed beside them, tongue lolling as she panted. Pitcairn cupped a hand and squirted water into it as the boxer lapped at it noisily, droplets spraying.

He stared at Lincoln as the dog looked back through opaque eyes. "Even your eyes, buddy. Just one more thing to be grieved." He patted the boxer's head. "Loss is loss is loss."

Turning his eyes to the western horizon, he remembered the words of a friend as the feeling of sadness welled up: "So many losses never tended, piling up waiting for expression." He shook his head with new appreciation for all he had failed to feel. "Feel, deal, and heal," he muttered, one of A.A.'s mottos.

As soon as he began to move again, the tears resumed, unattached and ultimately unnoted. Pitcairn and his dogs angled across the slope toward the river and a return to Rancho Sereno.

A short while later, he opened the door to Martin's retreat. With a backpack in one hand and a sleeping bag in the other, his immediate reaction was one of comfort. Though dim and slightly musty, it was not at all unpleasant. A single large room included everything: a counter with a basin and an old broken hand pump, another counter with a propane camp stove, a wood stove centered between two old couches, and a mixed lot of tables and empty book shelves. Candles and partially used books of matches were everywhere.

He opened drapes to let in light and noted that the shack was otherwise very tidy. Walking to the corner and into the bathroom, Pitcairn was surprised to see a very modern composting toilet beside another counter with a basin. He laughed out loud at the sight, so in keeping with Martin's environmentally avant garde, REI identity. After settling in and writing for a while, he lay down on a couch with his long legs sprawled over the end and was soon fast asleep.

When he finally woke to the sound of thunder, stupid from the heat that had gathered inside, it was dusk, and a light breeze passed through the door. He was covered in sweat. He lifted himself groggily and stopped to let feeling creep back into his numb legs. Then he shuffled around to the windows to open them so the wind from the storm could pass through.

The nap had been long and deep, and it took a few minutes for the fogginess to clear, leaving in its wake feelings of dread. Pitcairn tugged a chair over to sit in front of the door and watch the rising storm. Sipping at a water bottle, he let the feelings just be as sheets of rain began to sweep across the land accompanied by rolling thunder and occasional bright forks of lightning that branched downward to the earth.

Later, after a period of what felt like thoughtlessness, he fed Lincoln and Lucy, then ate a sandwich in the darkened doorway. The rain had stopped, and it was now cool. Lighting candles on the table next to the door, he pulled out his notebook and began to write to the sound of coyotes wailing.

First he tried a spontaneous version of the new column he intended to write about Davidson. It proved to be pointless, so he began noting what was going on inside him—something learned from Clint. The act produced a steady ebb and flow of tears. Soon he was writing about all the losses in his life. It seemed important to acknowledge them.

Late in the evening, exhausted, he unrolled his sleeping bag near the doorway, latched the screen door to keep the dogs from wandering, and called it a day.

* * *

The sense of doom woke him just before dawn. It was chilly, and his body was very stiff from the floor and the cold.

He disentangled himself from the sleeping bag and stepped outside to pee. Lincoln and Lucy moved slowly around the site snuffling.

After a breakfast of beef jerky and fruit, he carefully drove down to the freeway truck stop to call Maria Elena. Beyond checking in, there was little he felt like discussing, though he did admit that her prediction of tears had been right on the money. He told her again he'd be home Sunday afternoon.

Back at Rancho Sereno, the day unfolded slowly. Pitcairn and the boxers took several long walks. And he wept intermittently, never clear on a specific cause. That evening, the clouds rolled in again, though it only spat rain. Beneath flickering candlelight, he continued to write until he slept.

Very early in the morning, Lincoln began to growl menacingly. An instant later, Lucy hurled herself at the screen door snarling, almost smashing it off its hinges. Pitcairn wrestled her away and held her firmly as he fumbled for a flashlight. When he finally beamed light into the brush, it glinted on several sets of shining yellowish eyes. Coyotes had crept in close. Pitcairn was glad he'd latched the screen door.

On a hike when Lucy was just a gangly puppy, she had romped away. Pitcairn saw her a hundred yards or so in the distance on the side of a slope, her stubbed tail waggling at the pack of coyotes that were slowly encircling her. He called, and fortunately, she bolted back to him through the closing gap of the predators before what would have been an ugly outcome. Now matured, she had no love of the creatures.

He closed the door to prevent any problems, then stretched as he became aware of what was becoming a routine on awakening—a sense of dread. Breathing deeply to try to get some release of the feeling, a single word popped into his mind . . . *innocent.*

Pitcairn rolled the thought around in his mind. *Lucy's actions with the coyotes as a puppy were perfectly innocent. So was her defensive response a moment ago. She only did what was appropriate to time, place, and circumstance. So too with the coyotes.* He took a long, slow breath as the implications of the epiphany rushed into him. *So too with Daniel Davidson. And me. And Mom.* Unexpected, a memory of the TV image of the second plane crashing into the World Trade Center rushed into his consciousness. *Even the terrorists were acting out of what they believed to be their highest good . . . honoring their God through the deaths of infidels.*

"Crap," he muttered to himself as he flashed to a line Clint had used on more than a few occasions. "You're innocent, son. And so are all the rest of those bastards."

Quickly he lit a candle and grabbed his notebook. Resisting the urge to pee for fear he would lose the strand, he wrote fervently as the words raced forth and spewed onto the page. Simultaneously, voices clamored in his head. *This is bullshit . . . No one will want to hear this . . . You're perverting the very meaning of innocence.*

Steadily, he shook off the voices and captured the words and ideas on the page. When they were done, he knew precisely how he had to proceed.

► 16 ◄

MARIA ELENA WAS INCREDULOUS. "WHAT DO YOU MEAN YOU'VE seen Davidson's innocence? That has got to be the most absurd thing I've ever heard! I suppose that's what you're going to tell the victim's families now that you've decided you need to track them all down and meet with them. Hi, I'm Kevin Pitcairn, and I'm here to interview you about the purity of the man who killed your daughter. Are you nuts?" She paused to take a breath, rolled her eyes back into her head, then gestured with an exasperated flailing of her arms.

Pitcairn appreciated her points, but her attitude angered him even though it did not surprise him. He'd driven home from Rancho Sereno early in the afternoon after another hike with the dogs and found a note from Maria Elena that she was shopping with Darlene. He had bathed the dogs, stowed his gear, and proceeded to type up the column for publication. He titled it "Kill the Killer," then sent a copy to Amy Miscione, a friend who managed the progressive weekly newspaper, *Albuquerque Contours*.

After a shower, he called Martin to thank him for the use of Rancho Sereno. They had a brief chat, though Pitcairn didn't share the details of his experience. But he did acknowledge it was a productive time.

Martin was fairly quiet and offered again to help him if the need should arise. Pitcairn acknowledged the offer with appreciation and added that with everything he had happening, he might have to take him up on the offer.

Maria Elena came home after he had read a few sections of the newspaper. With a rush she cast herself snuggly beside him on the sofa. She listened quietly to his plans and the description of his writing but exploded when he mentioned Davidson in the same sentence with innocence.

"Listen," she resumed after her outburst. "You know this whole situation is frightening me. I'm absolutely clear something is just not right, and then you come home with some strange ideas that simply don't make sense. Ideas no one else will find reasonable either." She glared at him as if to drive her points home.

He nodded an encouragement for her to proceed.

"Worst of all," she continued as a film of tears glazed her eyes, "*you* scare me." She pursed her lips. "I always knew you had a violent history, but it never seemed real. When you snapped at Lucy a few days ago, which you've never done like that before, it was like you were changed. And it really, really scared me."

He started to speak, but she stopped him with an extended hand that rose like a football player's stiff-arm tactic.

"You don't need to defend yourself. I love you. But you need to know how this is affecting me."

She stood quickly. "Now I need some space."

After she left, he remained on the couch contemplating what he should do. A sense of anxiety caught at his diaphragm, seeming to be the perfect but unpleasant companion to the background of dread he bore. He decided there was little he could do about Maria Elena, who would likely follow her usual roller coaster ride of emotions until she found some balance. As he returned to the paper, he could hear her muffled but animated voice as she spoke on the telephone. Darlene was probably getting an earful. Fortunately, she could be counted on to give good guidance.

At precisely five-thirty, Maria Elena appeared at the entrance to the living room, her face an unreadable mask. "I'm going out. Be back later." Before he could respond, she spun and walked out of the house.

"Goddamn," he announced to himself. Clasping his hands behind his head, he sprawled out to consider this latest development. Finally, he called Martin and asked him if he was available to talk things through. A few minutes later, he'd fed the dogs and drove to the Frontier restaurant. Martin was waiting for him. They both ordered enchiladas and coffee and headed to a booth. As they dug into dinner after some small talk, Pitcairn described his plans. "I spent a lot of time walking while I was up at Rancho Sereno . . . and crying." He paused and reached for a tortilla. "By the way, it's a good name for your place, but it sure doesn't meet with any expectations I had for what it would be like."

Martin nodded, smiled, and shrugged with sheepish understanding as Pitcairn went on.

"I don't know if I'm prepared to talk about all of it yet, but I do want to tell you what I'm planning. Maria Elena really launched over this, so I figure I ought to check it out with someone. Fortunately, Clint told you about my situation."

Pitcairn proceeded to lay out his plan. He hoped the column would run soon in *Contours*. In the meantime, he was absolutely certain he needed to talk to his aunt about his mom as well as talking to the loved ones of Davidson's Santa Fe victim. Then he planned to head down to Texas to interview more families of Davidson's victims. While the story may have seemed finished to some people, he knew it wasn't for him. He had no idea where his work, and his thinking, would lead. It was simply what he had to do.

Martin listened intently all the while, his blue eyes boring into Pitcairn's. In the end, he said little. "I'm not much for providing feedback unless it's specifically sought. But will this column do harm to others?" he asked gently through drawn lips.

"That's been on my mind," Pitcairn replied quickly. "I'm certainly not planning on it. I'll just follow where the conversation needs to go. As long as I'm respectful, I don't know how else to approach it. I just know I need to do this."

A slight smile showed on Martin's face. "And what about Maria Elena's feelings?"

"Martin, I don't know what to say about that. Her concerns and points are valid. I know what I'm doing doesn't seem to make sense. But I sure do know I've got to do this, even if I don't know why. It seems to me she's got some inner work of her own to do. The best I can do is love her while she sorts it out." He shrugged awkwardly.

A curt nod followed, though Martin's smile had grown. "Sometimes there are things we simply must do."

They chatted a while longer. Pitcairn decided he needed to talk with Martin at a later date about Rancho Sereno and the land that he owned there. He thought there was a story to be told about the care of that land. He was still surprised by the lushness of the grass, and wanted to know more.

Parting was easy. Pitcairn thanked him, to which Martin replied wryly, "I couldn't do it without you." They both chuckled. The words didn't really mean anything, but using them, as Clint had done so often, symbolized their common connection to him.

When he came home, Maria Elena was already in bed. He said hello, but she did not respond. As he crawled into bed, he could feel iciness emanating from her. Gingerly he put his hand on her shoulder, again to no response. An awkward night followed, and he slept only intermittently. While he was ill at ease, and the sadness and dread had combined into an unyielding knot in his gut, a sense of anticipation and resolve energized him.

▸ 17 ◂

A DIFFICULT WEEK FOLLOWED, THOUGH IT BEGAN WELL ENOUGH after Maria Elena wordlessly left for work. A few minutes after nine Amy Miscione called about his column. "Pitcairn, this is really great," she said. She was sure she could find a place for it in the following Friday's *Contours*.

While he had received much praise over his years in journalism, which he usually fended off uncomfortably, this time he felt himself blush. He felt exposed, without the usual distance he had from his writing, and without his customary defenses. The experiences of the last few weeks had stripped away his bluster as well as layers of his emotional control. He muttered a thank you and hung up a little too quickly.

Despite the continuing, unrelenting sense of doom that had settled in him as a result of his time at Rancho Sereno, Pitcairn plowed into research on Davidson's victims and their families. He broke away regularly to stretch, his neck and jaw muscles locked with tension. Despite efforts to shake it, an ache began just above and behind his eyes, a pain that seemed to ease only slightly in the face of an onslaught of ibuprofen. He dared not step it up to heavy-duty pain killers; narcotics were too seductive.

On Monday night, Maria Elena avoided coming home until late. She was not speaking to him at all, and the silence was brutal. He followed the high road he had been taught through A.A. and by Clint, loving her and giving her the space she needed. He improvised by leaving her notes with the bare essentials. And he was up very early each morning for walks with Lincoln and Lucy that grew in length. The nightmares spared him but not the ache in his head and the tension in his gut.

He would leave on Sunday for a week in Texas. The goal was to talk to the families of six of Davidson's victims. Pitcairn had researched the circumstances of their deaths. He had found information but not understanding. For that, he felt, there needed to be patterns. If he could see a pattern in what the families could tell him, the missing pieces in the puzzle that was Daniel Davidson might begin to be filled in.

In preparing himself to talk with them, and to cope with the stress he couldn't escape, Pitcairn went to at least two A.A. meetings a day. Though he knew how long since he'd had his last drink, he also knew sobriety could not be taken for granted. Reassurance, reinforcement, and emotional support were constant needs. And in times of upheaval, extra effort was always needed. He updated Martin when he ran into him a couple of times a week.

On Wednesday, he finally reached his aunt. Her voice was steady though frail.

"Hi, Aunt Jeanne, it's Kevin."

"Oh!" she responded with a start. "It's nice to hear your voice. You know, there's a lilt in your voice just like your mother's. Did you know that?"

He laughed. "You've only told me about a thousand times, but thank you. Again!"

True to form, she prattled along for a while. Pitcairn mumbled an occasional acknowledgment and wedged in a word here or there. Jeanne was caught up in her own little world, a world revolving around her retirement community and the extensive activities that kept its residents busy.

A short time passed before she thought to ask about him. He told her he'd been quite involved in reporting a very high profile case. "In fact," he admitted, "that's in part why I'm calling."

"Really, Kevin!" she replied with sweet enthusiasm. "Why in God's good name would you call me about your reporting?"

He cleared his throat as he thought carefully about what to say. "Well, it's an ugly situation, so I won't go into details. It involves some pretty violent behavior. And believe it or not, it has got me thinking about my mom."

A pause followed before she mustered a tentative reply. "Your mom?"

"Yeah, Jeanne, I have some rather painful memories that have come up about her. I know she was never very happy, but . . . ." He composed his thoughts quickly. "Mom seemed to have a strong response to sex, almost an aversion. But she never spoke about it. It was all kind of veiled . . . I think."

He heard a sharp intake of breath and gave his aunt some space. It was awkward, but he imagined her steeling herself. When she spoke, her voice had lost the gaiety that marked it for as long as he could remember.

With a conspiratorial tone infused with melancholy, she began. "Kevin, we never talked about these things." An audible breath followed. "As the oldest child, your mother was expected to take care of many things. That included some things that involved your grandfather that I will not speak of. Your mother never said a word, but her behavior spoke loudly. She was very protective of me. Once, she drove him from our bedroom while I was still in bed. She scratched him and drew blood. He hit her and gave her a black eye. But he didn't come into the bedroom ever again, at least not while I was in it."

Pitcairn sighed heavily. "I'm sorry, Jeanne."

"Oh, I'm fine," she said calmly, "but thank you for saying that."

"So that's it, huh?"

His aunt's steady breath filled the line again. "No, Kevin. That's not all of it. Your mother also protected me from our brothers . . . your uncles. They were just like your grandfather." He could almost hear the cracking of the facade Jeanne had used to protect herself over the years. Her next words were said with a quavering voice: "Anna paid a terrible price for standing up to them, Kevin. They hurt her in unspeakable ways."

Now it was Pitcairn who had to take a steadying breath. Feelings of anxiety flitted wildly in his chest. "Thank you, Jeanne. It's very helpful to know all this, both personally and for this work I'm doing."

"I'm happy to help, honey. Just let me know if you need to discuss it further. I suppose all things must come to light sooner or later."

"I'll do that, and I'll also send you a copy of the piece that's going to run Friday. It will probably seem a little strange to you, but maybe not."

"Do send it," she replied brightly, already regaining her balance.

"Love you, Jeanne."

"I love you too, Kevin. Don't wait so long before calling again."

"Yeah . . . sorry I'm not in touch very often . . . ."

"It's fine and I'm fine. Bye-bye."

He needed a walk to burn up his feelings, and glanced out the window. Clouds were building in the west, but he could sneak in a fast trip around the neighborhood. Calling the dogs to him, they left at a near trot.

* * *

That night, he tried to talk to Maria Elena about what he had learned. But he backed off quickly when he saw her stoic, black eyes. Her emotional unavailability hurt and added to the weight he carried. That was enough to keep him from remaining silent.

"Maria Elena," he began before stumbling. Shaking his head, he started anew. "Emmy, I have tremendous respect for you and the work you've done on your own demons. And I will keep respecting your need for space and your intuition. But you need to let me trust my instincts too."

Their eyes locked briefly in what felt like recognition. Then she turned and moved away.

He shook his head once to acknowledge the situation,

and retreated to his office, where he sat with his sadness. He slept on a couch there that night, unable to bring himself to face her.

Early Thursday morning, he took a lengthy and painful hike with Lincoln and Lucy. Tears coursed from him as he walked through the darkness. It seemed like his heart was breaking. Or maybe it was his life. Regardless, he felt the weight of his weariness.

Still, all he knew to do was push forward, to take more action. So during the day, he finalized his plans for Dallas, deciding to leave a day earlier on Saturday. He could not imagine spending any part of the weekend with Maria Elena, given her demeanor.

He called Martin and brought him current on his affairs and plans. As usual, the quiet man offered little other than supportive comments.

Then Pitcairn made the first of his difficult calls about the victims. Mateo, the father of the girl killed in Santa Fe, answered on the third ring. Pitcairn introduced himself and told him he was researching the circumstances of Marissa's death and wanted to learn as much as he could about what had happened to her. He was exceedingly careful to say nothing that might injure or offend the man. While it had been several years since the girl was brutally raped and strangled in a forlorn corner of the local community college, Pitcairn could sense the pain her father felt. In the brief silence that filled the phone line, he felt tears of sorrow creep into the corners of his eyes. *How horrible it must be to lose your child in such a way,* he thought. *Loss . . . is loss . . . is loss. This man and I are linked by it.*

"Mr. Pitcairn, I cannot speak of Marissa still. You must understand, I am sure. We still badly miss her."

"I do understand, and I'm sorry for disturbing you, Mr. Sandoval. I'm terribly sorry for the loss of your daughter."

"Thank you for asking about *mi hita*. Good afternoon."

Before the phone was in its cradle, tears rushed down Pitcairn's face. He leaned back and began to rock himself gently. *So much heartache.*

He felt Lincoln nudge his head beneath his hand, sensing his distress, which precipitated still more tears. It was all he could do to sit and feel the mass of emotions crashing through him. The anxiety and uncertainty were overwhelming. He jumped in the Jeep with the boxers and drove west into the gathering thunderstorms. The night was spent at a hotel in Gallup after leaving a voice message for Maria Elena.

► 18 ◄

FRIDAY EVENING, HE ARRIVED TO A QUIET HOUSE. HE LEFT another note. It said little, only acknowledging that he was home and heading to an A.A. meeting. He knew he would be helped by the talk there of how others had fought successfully to maintain their emotional sobriety. Pitcairn fed the dogs before rushing out the door, realizing he had eaten nothing since breakfast but still had no appetite.

He sat morosely through the uninspired recovery story of Belt Buckle Johnny, a Navajo with a huge belly beneath which hung the monstrous turquoise and silver source for his nickname. It was a long-winded account of sordid escapades, a drunk-a-log as they called it. When the meeting ended, he couldn't leave fast enough, striding along a circuitous route around downtown. It was a measure of his inner state that even A.A. offered no solace.

Turning the corner onto Gold Street a few blocks west of their home, he saw a phalanx of police cars ahead, lights flashing. Pitcairn moved more quickly, his journalistic curiosity quickly piqued, though it gave way even more quickly to concern as he realized they were parked in front of his house. Moving into a sprint, his long legs rapidly covered the distance.

Swinging through the gate, he almost barreled into a police officer reaching for his weapon. With instant recognition, he realized how it appeared and raised his hands to his shoulders. "I'm Kevin Pitcairn. Is Maria Elena okay?"

The policeman nodded curtly as his hand relaxed, then wordlessly flicked his head over his shoulder. It was then Pitcairn saw the shattered window and the crimson words sprayed across the wall. "Pinche cabron" they announced boldly.

Bewildered, he strode past another officer near the front door. "Maria Elena!" he hollered as he bolted inside. The dogs scrambled to his side as he rounded the corner to the kitchen, spying her there with reddened, swollen eyes, wiping her nose with tissue. Sitting beside her were two more officers whose eyes studied him sternly.

"Are you okay, baby? What happened?"

Fury rose in her eyes. "I told you Davidson was bad news." Her jaw muscles clinched and released rapidly several times. "Then you had to write that goddamned column. How could you believe there wouldn't be a backlash?"

He sensed that her initial anger was spent as she began to weep. He came to her side and rested his hand gently below her neck. As he softly kneaded at her tension-filled muscles, the police described the crime.

Someone had painted the ugly words first, then thrown several bricks through the window before racing away in a dark, nondescript car with lights extinguished. Apparently, there were several hate messages left on the answering machine as well, all in the same voice with a northern New Mexican Hispanic accent.

It took some time to complete the reporting with the police, during which Maria Elena wordlessly slipped away to the bedroom. Before leaving, one of the officers warned him, "Mr. Pitcairn, I'd be careful if I were you. That column of yours really stirred something up. And as an aside, I think what you wrote was pretty foolish." A firm look came to his face. "Good night."

Amazing, Pitcairn thought as he moved slowly to the bedroom. Maria Elena was already sleeping soundly, or at least feigning it, so he set about covering the window with a spare tarp. The glass could wait until morning.

He hefted one of the bricks. It was so worn there was no chance of legible fingerprints. Tossing it up and down, he retreated to his office to listen to the messages, only realizing after he arrived that the machine had been taken as evidence.

Rubbing the side of his haggard face, he walked to the living room to see if Maria Elena had picked up a copy of *Albuquerque Contours*. Sure enough, there were several. He flipped through until he found it.

Kill the Killer

A haunted look fills the boys' eyes. They are desperate to please their teachers, the older women conducting the encounter session. The boys are perpetrators. They have been sentenced to a process of education and change rather than being jailed for sexual misconduct and violence.

You can see the inner conflict the boys feel. They are agitated. In order to complete this session, they have to admit their actions were deliberate. The boys have to say they willingly did wrong. No doubt they feel like bad kids.

Science now indicates the development of the brain in boys is not complete until their mid-twenties. Fifteen-year-old boys do not have some important higher levels of reasoning.

Their actions were unacceptable. But it is very likely they too are victims of sexual or other forms of abuse. They probably bear a high degree of what psychologists call trauma. There is also strong evidence that survivors of violence tend to inflict violence upon others.

* * *

A few weeks ago, a man was slain on the runway at the Albuquerque Sunport. His name was Daniel Davidson, and he was a convicted serial killer. He raped and murdered a number of young women before he was caught.

A short time before he was killed, Davidson sent me a long letter unlike anything I've ever seen. He told me that when he came of age, his own testosterone created violent and often-irresistible impulses in his mind. Once he was caught and put on drugs to reduce his testosterone levels, the inner violence lessened dramatically. He was able to easily manage his aggressive urges.

His plea is direct. "It's easy to point a finger at me, to call me evil and condemn me to death. But if that is all that happens, it will be a terrible waste. Tragic murders such as those I committed can be avoided in the future, but only if society stops turning its back, stops condemning, and begins to acknowledge and treat the problem. Only then will something constructive come out of events that took the lives of eight women, left their families and friends bereaved, resulted in my incarceration and probable execution, and caused untold shame and anguish to my own family."

Davidson goes on to urge policy change and treatment options for young offenders. His ideas and proposals are so compelling to me that I've sought to verify his claims with mental health specialists. They say the condition he describes is plausible, and see no reason to disbelieve him. And it should come as no surprise that in addition to this mental illness, Davidson was abused as a child.

His case troubles me more than anything I have reported in my career in journalism. If what he says is accurate, then our condemnation of him is part of the cycle of violence. Worst of all, he's right. When all we do is label him evil, we fail to understand such causes and conditions, and this ignorance keeps us from finding solutions and preventing future violence.

* * *

Let me be honest. I have made a lot of mistakes in my life. Like you, I am very human. People have too often been harmed by my mistakes. Regardless, let's ask some necessary questions of ourselves. Have we injured others? If not physically, then emotionally or psychologically? Did we do so knowingly and willingly? Or have we probably done our best and failed? Could it be this is true for all of us, even those committing the most heinous crimes?

* * *

In speaking with other people about Daniel Davidson, a phrase has come up repeatedly along with the disgust and condemnation: "It's okay to kill a killer."

Over and over again, I find myself wondering about the underpinnings of our Christian culture. Is forgiving our enemies just a convenient saying?

In the weeks since Davidson's death, I have been looking for answers. In a dilapidated shack on the West Mesa, I was offered a vision of innocence and this wisdom: "It is insufficient to understand all, and thus to forgive all. If we were to truly understand, we would know there is nothing to forgive."

I'm aware how daunting this idea is. Just like you, it pushes me far beyond my understanding. But I know in my heart it is true. And for the first time, I understand the words of Jesus: "Father, forgive them, for they know not what they do."

In reading his words again, Pitcairn felt their truth. Yet he also realized the truth of what Maria Elena had said. He had completely overlooked how such thoughts would be received, and it never entered his mind that someone would take action to retaliate. His naiveté was nearly total.

Pitcairn sighed and slid lower in his seat. Absentmindedly, he scratched the dogs' necks. The night passed without sleep.

* * *

When he came back from his walk with Lincoln and Lucy, Maria Elena was awake, somberly sipping strong black coffee at the kitchen table. She flinched when he touched her and did not make eye contact.

He slid into a chair beside her. "You were right, and I'm very sorry," he said as gently as he could.

She slowly turned and looked through him with smoldering eyes. Her voice was razor sharp: "And what do you think that accomplishes?"

He studied her face, and softness bubbled up within him. "It accomplishes nothing . . . absolutely nothing."

"Goddamn you, Pitcairn," she lashed at him. "There is no way this is going to go away. Those pricks who broke the window are going to make our lives hell. And they're probably just the beginning. How could you be so stupid? And how could you be so inconsiderate of me?"

Tears slid down his face onto the table. Where once there would have been anger at what she said, now he felt only grief. He shook his head slowly. "Maria Elena," he began before wiping at his nose, "you're just going to have to find it within you to forgive me."

"Oh . . . but there's nothing to forgive, is there?" she replied with his own written words, but imbued with a nasty tone he rarely heard from her. The quote cut him to the core. They resonated with truth, even when spoken hatefully.

Pitcairn nodded, knowing there was nothing more he could say. He stood up. "I'll go take care of the window, baby. When you want to talk some more, we'll talk." He turned and moved away from her but stopped at the door.

Slowly he looked back. "I love you regardless, Maria Elena."

He cleaned up the glass and called someone to replace it. The repair took all afternoon, interspersed with calls from friends, some commenting on the column. Few seemed to understand, but all were clearly curious and engaged by the idea. Late in the afternoon, he drove to a cell phone store and bought a phone and service. He had realized how inconsiderate his inaccessibility was, especially to Maria Elena. Back home, he emailed some of his contacts telling them of his planned absence and how to reach him. Then he wrote the telephone information down for her. Last, he called Martin. An answering machine greeted him. He gave a brief account before concluding, "I'm headed to Dallas tomorrow. I'll call you from there and keep you posted. Thanks for being there."

Maria Elena was brutal with him that night, accusing him of abandoning her, placing Davidson before her. He made no attempt to explain or justify. He knew there was nothing he could do but follow his instincts. His heartache grew from knowing nothing he might say could possibly explain.

In the end, she decided to stay with Darlene while he was gone. She would not say it, but she was afraid.

So was he. He admitted as much in the long note he wrote her very early the next morning before leaving for Texas. As much as he hated to leave amid all the turmoil, he could see no other choice.

► 19 ◄

ONCE HE'D DEPARTED THE CITY, THE HIGH, OPEN PRAIRIE OF eastern New Mexico was a solace to him. He abandoned the interstate and wove across the grassy expanse on state highways, stopping at whim. First, it was to view a herd of pronghorn, and later to watch a vast patch of wildflowers waving elegantly in the breeze.

The miles sped by, giving him the time and space to put together the pieces of everything that had happened. He felt he was simultaneously fleeing an unmanageable situation and moving inexorably toward an unknown one. Still, a quiet enveloped him as the wind whipped his Jeep. He knew he must do this, no matter the reason or outcome. That certainty gave him comfort. Great clarity was uncommon to his experience.

Somewhere south of Lubbock, he stopped at a convenience store and loaded up on bottled water and bad taquitos. Dinner came around Abilene where he ate unlikely chile rellenos smothered unceremoniously in nacho cheese sauce. At his hotel near Mesquite, a suburb of Dallas, he called Maria Elena. There was no answer, so he left a simple message that he had arrived safely.

Then he called Martin, who answered on the first ring. They chatted for a while, though Martin was his usual quiet self. Yet it was a comfort, as was his only suggestion: that Pitcairn stay close to A.A.

Just before they ended the call, Pitcairn mentioned a sense of disorientation that he had become aware of as he drove. He surmised it had been with him for some time, though he could only now name it.

A soft "hmpf" came over the line as Martin chuckled. "Well, I've had an idea I should share a couple of thoughts that have been percolating through my mind the whole time we've been talking. They're not advice, and I'll pass them along if you'd like to hear them."

"Of course. Go ahead."

"Well, you know Bill W. When he reflected on his role in founding A.A., he said that never in all the years of his recovery had he understood what was going on until after the fact. And I just read an interesting psychology piece that might explain that. Researchers found what the writer described as the conscious mind being like a monkey that's perched on the shoulders of the tiger of the unconscious that's hurtling through the jungle of reality at breakneck speed. The monkey creates an unending series of stories to explain things in a desperate attempt to feel in control."

The line grew quiet, but Pitcairn could hear himself breathe. "Martin, what the hell does that mean?"

Martin responded lightheartedly and with obvious pleasure: "Let me repeat it first. I think I need to hear it again too!" He described the article once more.

"So, whatever is happening is not just beyond our control but beyond our ability to know. The best we can do is hang on, try to anticipate the tiger's moves, and when the ride is over, look back to see what it all meant, if anything."

Pitcairn's laughter was hearty and genuine. "That was advice, man, but I like it a lot. I'll write it down, and I'll keep you posted on the tiger and the jungle."

"You do that. I'll look forward to hearing about your adventures."

"Me too, brother. Me too." With that, he disconnected the call.

He flipped on the television and fell asleep.

* * *

Deep in the night, thunderstorms rumbled, adding an ominous backdrop to the recurring nightmare, now accompanied by feelings of doom. Pitcairn awoke wide-eyed in a heavy sweat, panting from exertions dreamed but not remembered.

He gulped in a breath of air, then tried with all his might to quiet the inner turmoil, but to no avail. He lurched from the bed and went to the sink to splash water on his face.

When he looked up, the mirror returned a ragged image. He studied his eyes in the softly flickering light. It seemed there was a depth to them he could not recall.

He returned to the bed and began writing in his journal. It was nothing in particular, but the act of capturing his thoughts and feelings had become increasingly comforting.

After a shower he pulled out his notes about Davidson's victims. Two of them were from nearby, which is where he would begin. Then he looked at an online guide to A.A. meetings. Seeing one at nine o'clock not far away, he went in search of breakfast.

Following the meeting, he contacted Genny Royal, whose daughter Anita had been Davidson's first victim. Pitcairn had spoken with her briefly a few days before, and she'd surprised him with a generous willingness to talk. Now she invited him to her home. When he arrived, Anita's sister, Angie, also was there. It was clearly an auspicious beginning to the interviews he hoped would bring forth valuable information.

After gracious introductions, they sat at the kitchen table as Genny served fresh coffee and homemade cinnamon rolls. Pitcairn began carefully. "I'm sure you heard that the man who killed Anita died a few weeks ago."

He watched their reaction, and was surprised to sense softness. He checked inside himself briefly before continuing spontaneously. "I'm not here to talk about Daniel Davidson. I'd like to know about Anita. Who was she? What mattered to her? What do you remember that should be said of her?"

Moistness showed in her mother's eyes, and she smiled as she remembered. "I'm very sorry her father couldn't be here to talk to you. He would so appreciate remembering her. Anita was his angel girl." She cast her eyes down. "We divorced eighteen months after her death. He moved to Idaho, and doesn't communicate much now. It broke his heart."

"Do you have a picture of her, maybe a favorite shot?"

Genny left to retrieve the treasured photo. Angie jumped in with unusual directness. "Anita was sweet. Everyone liked her. But she was really pretty ordinary. An ordinary girl living an ordinary life. And she was really happy being ordinary." Angie tried to shake strands of hair from her face, then reached up to pull them away. A soft laugh stirred in her throat as she remembered.

She looked up as her mother returned with a framed portrait. It showed an appealing but plain face with green eyes, light brown hair, thin lips, and a slightly cleft chin. Pitcairn was struck by a curious thought: *She's a very unlikely target. Why would Davidson choose her?*

He glanced up and noted similarities to both her sister and mother. "She resembles both of you, doesn't she?"

A light came to their faces. Genny spoke haltingly. "Anita was an easy child, quite unlike her mischievous sister." The women exchanged a look filled with fondness. "She loved to read, especially the classics. She always found ways to bring them into the conversation." Genny reached out to touch the face frozen in time behind the glass. "I'm not sure she ever had her thoughts in the day. She was always reflecting on those glorious fictional times. She wanted to teach literature when she finished college."

As the conversation wandered across emotional territory familiar to Anita's mother and sister, Pitcairn felt privileged to be a part of something that could only be described as sweet. It was touching, and he needed to ask only a few questions.

As noon came, they offered him a sandwich, which he gratefully accepted as they continued to reminisce. A short time later, he could feel the flow waning. It occurred to him to share a long ago memory.

"You've been very generous with your time. And I've got to tell you it all feels quite nice. She was obviously very precious to you, which makes me want to share a story if that's okay."

They nodded in agreement.

"Some years ago, I visited a friend in western Massachusetts. It was October, and he took me for a walk in the Berkshire Mountains. It was a lazy, sunny day, and the birch trees were butter gold against a light blue sky. We crossed a meadow, and in the middle of it was an old foundation with shrubs growing from it. It was a strikingly beautiful day.

"John had just ended a relationship. He was sad but knew it couldn't be otherwise. I asked him how he was feeling. He looked at me with a really gentle but sad look in his eyes and said, 'Bittersweet. Sad that it's ended but so happy I knew her.'"

Pitcairn smiled in pleasant recollection. "It's the same feeling I'm sensing you have about Anita right now. And it's indescribably beautiful."

There was a feeling in the room then, and he imagined it to be love.

Angie almost couldn't contain herself. "Kevin, I've got to tell you something else." She looked to her mom, who clearly assented with a forbearing shake of her head.

"Anita knew she was going to die. She had a really terrible nightmare several times. She said it involved the man who would kill her. But it never revealed the details." She blinked slowly a few times as if mesmerized by her own words. "I told her she was crazy. But she got me to start going to Friends Meetinghouse with her. You know, the Quakers."

Pitcairn listened with great interest.

"We just sat quietly when we went. She told me it made her feel better about her fate. I thought that was really crazy, and I told her so. But she was really persistent.

"When she was killed, I couldn't believe it. I told Mom about her nightmare. It was very weird. But the funny thing is that we both go to Quaker meeting now. And I can't explain it, but I don't have any animosity. In fact, I felt very sorry for Daniel Davidson when I read how he was killed. It wasn't right."

Pitcairn was amazed. He had just heard a genuine spirit of forgiveness. He glanced toward the mother, who raised her hands in an inexplicable gesture. "I could never explain it. I just accept it as grace. There's not a better word for it."

"Thank you for sharing that story. It's very interesting and very helpful."

Genny asked, "What will you be doing with this, Kevin?"

He smiled wryly. "Honestly, I have no idea. At this point, I'm just interviewing the victims' families. There's a story here somewhere, and I promise to let you know once I have it figured out."

After a warm goodbye, Pitcairn drove away slowly. A few blocks later, he pulled into a park. He thought about the interview but could see no discernable direction. Mostly he was amazed by the conversation, as well as the two women's extraordinary grace.

He looked through his notes for the contact information for Marilyn and Bob Johnston. Their daughter, Carrie, had been the fifth of Davidson's victims. He only hoped things would turn out as well as at his first visit.

What he was doing, Pitcairn knew, was the opposite of how he'd always reported a story before—leading conversations without a deliberate approach, allowing the exploration, and in some cases just calling out of the blue and hoping for a chance to talk after having come so far. But this wasn't like any other story he'd ever worked on. It was more of an unknown investigation, something calling to him, and though he couldn't know what would happen, he trusted in the instincts that had served him so well in the past.

► 20 ◄

Pitcairn had located Bob Johnston through the small accounting firm where he was a partner. He waited a few minutes on hold before a raspy voice with a moderate drawl announced, "Howdy."

He introduced himself again and explained his intentions once more. Tentatively, Johnston agreed to call his wife and confirm that she would be willing to talk with Pitcairn. It was only a few minutes before the man called back. They wanted him to come by their home that evening at seven.

An awkward pause followed. "Mr. Pitcairn, you won't upset my wife, will you?"

"No, sir, I would never think of doing something inappropriate. All I want is to learn more about Carrie."

"That'd be fine then. We'll see you directly."

Pleased, Pitcairn turned the ignition of the Jeep. The loud jangling of the cell phone startled him. It was the first time he'd heard the ring tone.

Fumbling the phone, he jerked it open only to have it snap shut and fall to the floor. "Shit!" he roared as he reached down to snatch it up. He thought of opening the phone and trying to search the features to find out who he'd missed. *Christ, I'm going to be just one more phone-trained monkey.*

He turned off the Jeep. The phone rang almost immediately.

"Pitcairn?" Mortensen's voice echoed thinly over the miles.

"Is that you, Sean?"

"Damn it! I got your email, but what the hell are you doing in Dallas?"

"Research about Davidson," he replied defensively. "Why?"

"Because you started a damned mess with that piece you did for *Contours*."

Pitcairn interjected quickly, "Listen, I'm freelance. You shouldn't have a problem with that."

"I know that! But there's a big protest outside their offices right now, and I need to know whatever you can tell me about what you're finding out."

"A protest . . . by who?"

"Apparently it's that nut church from Colorado Springs, Evangelical Bible Church . . ."

"Christ, Sean, the assholes who've been saying soldiers are paying the price for homosexuality in the military, and AIDS is penance for abortion?"

"That's them. About thirty of them drove down to protest the publication of your column. Apparently, you're now an abomination. Guilt by association."

A guffaw shot from Pitcairn. "An abomination? Now that's a new item for my resume. Do you want me to write something for you?"

Mortensen's reply was swift and forceful. "Hell, no! For now, we'll treat it as news. Maybe later I'll let you in on it. But I want to know what you're doing down there. Keep me up to date."

For the next ten minutes, Pitcairn brought Mortensen up to speed on what he'd found in his background work as well as his plans for Dallas. When they finished, he called Amy Miscione at *Contours*. As he waited for an answer, he heard a beep on his phone and assumed it was an incoming call, but he had no idea how to get it. A recorded message told him the *Contours* offices were closed because of unforeseen circumstances.

He dug out his cell phone guide to find out how to get messages. Soon, he chuckled at Maria Elena's breathless voice. She may not have been a reporter, but she loved a juicy story just as he did. Even her anger at him was no match for it.

"Cito . . . I know . . . I've been punishing you . . . but you won't believe what's happening here. There's a big protest over on San Pedro, a bunch of fundamentalist crazies from Colorado Springs. They're all pissed off about your piece about Davidson. The cops are there in force. Call me!" An awkward silence followed, and he could imagine her twirling a finger in her hair. "Cito . . . I love you. Call me . . . bye." An instant later, she was on the line. "Can you believe it? This is crazy!"

"Yeah, Emmy. Crazy's an understatement. But it's nice to hear your voice again."

"I know. We need to talk. But we'll have to do that in person. What do you think about this protest?"

He told her what he'd learned from Mortensen. She'd heard through the mayor's office that things had turned ugly, but she didn't know the details. She'd been told the Albuquerque riot squad had been called in to quash the protest.

Then he told her about his visit to Genny Royal. She didn't reply, which meant she still didn't approve. But she seemed to be more accepting. *Then again, I didn't give her much choice,* Pitcairn thought.

"Could you do me a favor and look up Amy Miscione in the phone book?" he asked. "I can't get anyone at *Contours* and want to try her home number."

She told him the number. "Thanks, Emmy. I'll call you tonight to compare notes."

"Okay!" came her bright reply, followed by a quick goodbye.

He puzzled over everything for a few moments before driving back to the hotel. He wanted to catch the early news. But first he tried Amy's number. She answered on the third ring.

"Amy, it's Pitcairn. Are you okay?"

"Shit, yes!" she replied enthusiastically. "Circulation's going to jump, but more important, the response proves we hit the mark on something. Nice job, man!"

"Thanks, I think." He chuckled. "I'm not sure how I feel about inciting riots with my writing. Now, what do you know?"

The group had driven down on Sunday evening after a rousing sermon at their church. Somehow a fundamentalist in Albuquerque who'd seen his column had contacted some others in Colorado, and then it had all hit the fan. The protest had begun around ten in the morning. Uncharacteristic of this group, someone threw rocks through the windows, which was when police evacuated the *Contours* staff and the riot squad was called in.

"I don't know why they decided to get violent," Amy told him. "Their reputation is for being loud and obnoxious, but who knows, huh?"

"Search me," Pitcairn answered.

"Anyway, what I hear is they did something that got the cops really ticked off. We both know there's no telling what really happened. You know the Albuquerque police. They've never been known for being tolerant with this kind of thing. I can't get an exact confirmation on some of that, but there's no doubt the cops went after them with everything. I mean tear gas, batons, the whole enchilada."

"Christ, Amy! Now they'll have reason to say they're being persecuted for their beliefs."

She roared with amusement. "No doubt. But I'm sure they got caught on camera assaulting the police, and they'll have nothing to stand on. They're screwed. But it's going to be one big clusterfuck, that's for certain."

"Well, I'm just glad you and your staff are fine."

"Couldn't be better, Pitcairn. But thanks for being concerned."

"De nada. It's the least I could do."

"So how's it going in Texas? Getting more background on Davidson?"

"Yes ma'am."

"What's your plan?"

"No idea."

"Whatever it is, will you give us a shot at it?"

"Of course, Amy. I owe you for publishing the column."

"No . . . I owe you!" she shot back in a feigned chipmunk voice. "Do you remember Chip and Dale? 'No, after you.' 'No, no, you go first.' One of my favorite childhood cartoons."

He laughed freely. "Amy, you're a delight, but I was a Heckle and Jeckle fan."

"Well, when you're back and things settle down, let me buy you coffee and we'll compare cartoon notes and whatever you're doing with Davidson."

"Deal," he replied. "I gotta go, so be good."

"If you can't be good, be good at it!" she said jokingly. "See ya, Pitcairn."

He kicked back in his chair, fingers interlaced behind his head as he considered this newest, unexpected development. The metaphor of the tiger in the jungle seemed all the more appropriate. Then he checked the time before going for a walk. He needed to move.

When he got back, the television news was reporting on "the Albuquerque riots." The video footage with its tear gas and sounds of fighting looked almost surreal to him. All the Colorado Springs contingent were either in jail or the hospital or had dispersed someplace else. The explanation was short and not very accurate. The reporter said the rioters were protesting the death of a serial rapist. *What can you expect from television?* Pitcairn thought.

He headed out for dinner, a local place the hotel clerk told him was known for its chicken fried chicken. He asked her about the difference between fried chicken and chicken fried chicken, but she just looked at him disdainfully. The waitress couldn't lend any insight either, so he just dropped it. At times, there was no fathoming the ways of Texas.

Promptly at seven, he was on the Johnstons' porch. They were gracious in welcoming him, though they clearly felt awkward. Bob had a beer belly; his wife, Marilyn, was petite.

Pitcairn quickly told them he wasn't sure how he would use any information about their daughter but that he'd like to get a sense of her if he could. Hesitantly, Marilyn pulled out family albums. Bob listened as his wife leafed through and offered a flow of consciousness account of Carrie.

She was their only child. Inwardly, Pitcairn winced when he heard this. Carrie was an athlete, a sprinter and hurdler.

As when he'd looked at a picture of Anita Royal, his attention was captured by her plain appearance, though he couldn't say why. They had been a churchgoing family, but the randomness of her death had driven them from their faith. She had been attacked while on a walk near the college she attended.

As he listened, he became more and more aware of the terrible pain the Johnstons bore so heavily. Neither could give voice to it, but its weight was palpable. And he got a sense of the true depth of the tragedy which Davidson himself had acknowledged.

After an hour or so, Marilyn Johnston simply ran out of things to say. Her husband stood up. It was more awkward than Pitcairn could easily tolerate. He offered a very simple thank you, and said he'd be in touch to tell them what he was writing and make sure it was all right with them. They barely acknowledged the offer.

Marilyn Johnston remained on the couch as her husband walked him to the door. Pitcairn was seized by an urge he could not ignore: "Bob, I could not be more sorry for the loss of your daughter. And I hope my visit has not been an intrusion."

A twisted smile came to the man's lips. "No, sir. We needed to talk about Carrie." He rubbed the palm of his hand across his cheek. "We won't ever get over her death, but I'm grateful for your interest."

Pitcairn stepped onto the porch and turned to see Johnston brushing at his eyes. It was obvious he had no words. Pitcairn nodded respectfully.

A bit of a salute followed as the door closed.

Sitting in the Jeep, he was seized by an overwhelming sense of grief. He swallowed hard and willed himself to drive away.

► 21 ◄

I T WAS ANOTHER TORTURED NIGHT. HE HAD CALLED MARIA Elena, and they talked for a very long time. The emotional drought was at an end, and both had a great thirst to connect. But telling of his experiences twisted at him deeply. Afterward, sleep was impossible. When he did doze off, formless nightmares woke him. Exhausted, he dozed again, only to be shocked back awake once more. He got up and walked, but nothing could shake the upwelling of feelings inside him. In the end, he took his journal to an all-night diner and drank coffee until the first signs of dawn.

His image in the hotel mirror stunned him. He was actually looking gaunt from loss of weight. He just wasn't hungry like he used to be. And his eyes were bloodshot. Still, he was certain he had to stay the course, even if he could not construct an explanation for continuing his search into what Davidson had done and its increasingly complex implications.

After cleaning up, he scanned the *Dallas Morning News*. On Page 5 was an account of the Albuquerque rioting that included a small photo of him beneath a great shot of tear gas wafting over armor-clad, gas-masked police. "Jesus," he muttered as he read. But at least the background story was on the mark.

A pang of uneasiness struck at him. Notoriety was not for him. But it was clear there were forces at work far beyond his understanding.

His cell phone rang a short while later, and Marie Elena's outraged voice filled the line. "Those assholes broke more

windows on the house last night. Goddamn them, Cito, I'm
so furious I could kill." She growled.

"Tell me what happened, Emmy."

"I went by to check on things. Those shits had shattered
the picture window this time. I called the cops. They said
they'd patrol more. But . . ."

"It's okay, baby," he injected. "It's just glass."

"That's not the goddamned point! Even I don't like what
you wrote, or that you wrote it, but that doesn't give any-
body the right to take these kind of cheap-assed shots at you.
Cito, they're chickenshits, and you know it!"

"You're right, absolutely right. But it's more important
that we're both out of harm's way. Who'd have guessed my
trip out here would give us both some cover."

"Cover, hell. If I was just a little more pissed off, I'd sit on
the roof all night with a gun and shoot them on sight."

"I'm glad you're not that pissed off. But I have to tell you
I love the fire in you. It's a beautiful thing."

Now she laughed. "God, Cito, what kind of a guy loves this?"

"Me," he replied emphatically.

She was briefly quiet. "You melt me, you know that?" Before he could answer, words blurted from her. "Can you
come home now?"

He considered it for an instant before replying. "I have
to see everyone I can while I'm here. If I didn't feel it so
strongly, I'd be home today."

She sighed. "I know. And your convictions are part of
why I love you so much. But it can be really frustrating."

A smile came to his weary face. "Yep . . . my finest attributes
are frustrating. That pretty well sums me up, doesn't it?"

"No. It doesn't. But I do wish you were here to take care
of the window."

"Just call Gabriel Garcia. He'll come out and give us an
insurance estimate and get it fixed quick."

"Good idea. But seriously, when will you be home?"

"I'll be there Friday. Maybe we can walk over to the Farmers' Market at Robinson Park Saturday morning and get

reacquainted. Better still, maybe Old Man Barela will be there with some of his tamales."

"Okay. I gotta go. Call me later. Bye."

Pitcairn rose wearily, noting an edginess in his gut that he'd not felt for many years, not since the turmoil of early sobriety with all its emotions and complications. He knew it was a sign of tension. It would be a good idea to find an A.A. meeting today. But first, he was driving eight-five miles south to Waco, where two more of Davidson's victims had been killed.

By late morning, he was walking a creekside path skirting the scrubby oaks where Davidson's most brutal killing had happened. Sharon Fields, at twenty-six, was also the oldest of his victims. She had apparently fought back valiantly, which must have angered him. He had beaten her savagely before raping her, and then throttled her to death. The news accounts said she was unrecognizable.

Pitcairn sat for a time on a small knoll. He didn't know exactly where the crime had occurred, but it seemed important to offer silent tribute while he was there.

He pulled his journal out of his backpack and wrote a few paragraphs. He could feel an empathy growing inside, and a kind of heartache he'd never known before. "I'm becoming more human," he wrote with surprise. He screwed up his face as he thought before writing. "It hurts." Staring at the page, he boldly underscored the words twice.

Still sitting there, he called Sharon's husband. He had been unable to make contact with him before he left.

Just before he was sent to voice mail, there was a click followed by a panting voice: "Hello, this is Robert."

He let him take a breath before he began. "Mr. Fields, my name is Kevin Pitcairn, and I'm interviewing the families of the victims of Daniel Davidson. If it's . . ."

Fields cut him off. "Pitcairn?"

"Yes, sir."

"Albuquerque?"

Now curious, he replied hesitantly. "Yes."

"Fuck you and your innocence!"

There was a click and the line went dead.

Pitcairn slumped instantly, but before the sobs he felt boiling up could take hold, rage ripped through him. There was no target; it was everywhere, made up of everything that had happened. His heart raced as he leaped to his feet and ran toward a low ridge of rock, the cell phone clinched in his hand. Nearing the layered limestone, he hurled it, watching the phone sail above its target and tear through stems of tall grass, then vanish down the slope beyond.

Pitcairn stormed over the ledge, stomping through the grass a couple of feet below as he looked for the phone. Thwarted, he bellowed his frustration while moving closer to the creek, sweeping his feet widely before him in the hope of kicking the phone in the grass.

Above the creek, he peered seven or eight feet down a steep dropoff. Three upturned faces stared at him, terrified by the raging they'd heard. The boys' eyes darted wildly, searching for escape from this madman. They knelt on another ledge of porous stone that traced the edge of the creek. They must have been exploring, and now clearly felt trapped.

Pitcairn lurched to a stop, caught by the unexpected mirror of his own unvoiced fears. He slowly drew a ragged breath, then reached toward them. "I'm sorry, boys. It's okay. I'm not going to hurt you."

The three—all about ten, Pitcairn guessed—remained still and wordless. He began to kneel to be closer to them, not wanting to abandon them, wanting the boys to understand he was no threat.

As Pitcairn stretched out a trembling hand, the one in the middle suddenly shrieked and bolted back, tumbling his friend from the rock into the pool below. Immediately Pitcairn saw that the water was over his head. He jumped to the ledge below, then into the creek, wading through chest-high water toward the floundering boy as the two others scattered screaming.

Sputtering from water he'd swallowed, the boy screeched as he fought with underwater kicks and flailing hands when Pitcairn tried to wrap his arm around him. Propelled across the creek by his struggles, the boy was soon at the opposite bank a few feet away, where he quickly scrambled up the gentler slope and raced away screaming with terror.

Pitcairn stood in the middle of the creek, water almost to his shoulders, shaking with adrenaline. He remained absolutely still, without a thought, for what seemed a long time before he returned to himself. His memory was flooded with recollections of all the times as a child and youth when he had felt that kind of terror. It was not a pleasant thought.

The water and what happened there had quenched his fury, but his conduct left him with a feeling of shame at his rage. He turned and moved toward the ledge. Pulling himself up the bank hand over hand, he suddenly saw his phone glinting in the grass a few feet away. He picked it up and marveled at how unmarred it was compared with how he felt inside. Curious, with a disconnected pragmatism, he flipped it open and noted that everything seemed in order.

He had taken a few steps toward the knoll where his belongings remained when he heard the faint sound of sirens. Immediately Pitcairn realized the bedlam that was sure to follow when three terrified boys told their tale of the crazed stranger at the creek where Sharon Fields had been killed. He picked up his things, moved slowly to a very open area, and dropped his arms to his side to wait.

Soon two sheriff's deputies came around a bend in the path, both moving carefully. They stopped, and one placed his hand on his gun. The other scrutinized Pitcairn quickly before speaking: "Move your hands away from your body."

Pitcairn complied. "I can explain what happened," he said.

"I imagine you can, but first, who are you and what are you doing here?"

Pitcairn described his encounter with the boys and was soon allowed to produce his identification. He tried to explain what had led a stranger like him to the neighborhood:

his research into the death and life of Sharon Fields. The deputies relaxed, and it wasn't long before one of them—P. Taylor, his badge said—was chuckling about the situation with the boys. The other, R. Wallace, remained somber. He pursed his lips and squinted at Pitcairn. "You're that boy who wrote the article that set off those riots, aren't you?" Matching his serious tone, Pitcairn replied, "Yes, sir, I am."

The deputy nodded curtly. "I'm pretty sure we don't need your kind 'round here, Mr. Pitcairn. You might want to be movin' along."

"Yes, sir. I can do that. But would it be possible for me to meet those boys and set things right with them? They need to talk with me so they don't have nightmares about this."

Taylor stepped forward. "That'd be fine, I think. Let's you and me walk up the way to the neighborhood, while Deputy Wallace calls in and takes care of the report." He turned to his partner. "You okay with that, Wally?"

Wallace pursed his lips again before replying. "Guess so." He turned and walked away purposefully.

Pitcairn and Taylor chatted amiably as they covered the half-mile to a housing development. As they walked, Taylor told him that Sharon Fields had lived in the neighborhood, and he didn't think they should say anything about why Pitcairn was there.

A small crowd at a cul-de-sac had gathered around the boys. The deputy gave a succinct account of what Pitcairn had told him about the incident, which produced immediate relief.

Pitcairn knelt down to be at eye level with the three boys, who came forward with some reluctance. He looked each of them in the eyes, nodding approvingly.

"Boys, I made a big mistake back there. I hope you'll accept my apology for scaring you. Men make mistakes, don't they?"

The boys murmured their agreement.

"Let's shake then." His hand swallowed each of the boys' hands in succession.

He stood and looked at the neighbors. "And I owe all of you an apology as well. I'm sorry for frightening you and your children."

One man stepped forward to shake his hand. "Name's James Henry. Call me Jake. Thanks for talking to the boys. If you'd like to come over to the house, you can dry yourself and clean up a bit."

"Thank you, Jake. That's very kind of you. Is one of these youngsters yours?"

"No, sir, mine are over at A&M. Janie's a freshman, and Luke's a senior. But I'm neighborhood association president, so I kind of feel like they're all mine. Come on now. I'll make us some coffee while you wash up."

As the crowd began to disperse. Pitcairn thanked Taylor for his assistance, and apologized. The deputy waved it off easily. "Not a problem. Just glad it wasn't nothin' serious."

They shook hands, and Pitcairn walked two blocks with Jake, then around a corner to a tidy brick home. Jake directed him toward a bathroom and gave him a pair of gym shorts and an oversized T-shirt. "Toss your clothes out here, and I'll throw them in the washer. There's towels under the sink. You hungry?"

"Jake, that's another nice offer. Thank you. But don't put yourself out."

"Naw. I'll just get the coffee goin' and throw together a sandwich. That okay?"

"Sure."

After Pitcairn had showered, Jake gave him a plastic bag for his wallet, loose change, keys, phone, and comb. Then they sat down to what might have been the strongest coffee Pitcairn ever tasted and a white bread, ham, and cheese sandwich made thick by fresh-sliced tomatoes and lettuce.

As they ate, Jake talked about his family and his work as a self-employed computer programmer. "I just happened to be around for all this excitement," he said. "Those boys'll be talking about this for a long time to come."

After Jake shifted the freshly washed clothes to the dryer, he sat down and looked directly at his guest. It was a look Pitcairn had seen before over the years running through the culture of Texas: the fair dealing look of honest pioneer stock. "Listen, that deputy did a fine job summing things up, but I'm pretty sure he didn't tell us the whole story. I don't think you were out there just piddling around on some story. You want to tell me about it."

Pitcairn looked Jake in the eye as he assessed the situation. He decided this was the kind of man for plain talk.

"That's pretty perceptive of you, Jake. As a reporter, I can tell you most people don't notice what you did. There's a lot they miss. And I'm going to trust my sense of you that I can talk honestly."

The corner of the man's lips turned up in appreciation and understanding.

"I was checking out the scene of Sharon Fields' murder. I'm talking to the families of all the victims of her killer, Daniel Davidson, after an odd encounter with him in New Mexico before he was killed. I had just called Fields' husband on my cell phone. His response was pretty ugly. It pissed me off, so I got pretty stupid. I tossed the phone, then started stomping around looking for it. The boys heard me, and had every right to be scared."

Jake's eyes wandered over him, searching.

"I know," Pitcairn said. "That's not the whole story. Apparently, Mr. Fields heard about a story I wrote for an Albuquerque weekly that caused quite a ruckus. My photo was in the Dallas newspaper along with an account of rioting yesterday at the Albuquerque paper's office. He obviously didn't care for my perspective ... or me for that matter." Pitcairn shook his head seriously. "His words made that pretty clear."

"You want some more coffee?"

"Yes, sir. Fill 'er up."

As Jake turned to grab the coffee, he spoke slowly. "That Sharon was a sweetheart. She and Robert lived over a couple blocks. When she was murdered, Robert nearly went crazy. Started walking the creek with a pair of Colt pistols his granddaddy left him. Almost shot a few folks. Made the rest of us crazier than coots. Eventually, he moved away. It wasn't like we wanted to shun him, but he didn't give us much choice. Can't be around that kind of crazy for too long without being affected."

"Can you tell me a little more about her?"

"What are you going to do with the information?"

"I don't know. If I knew I'd tell you. But believe me, it's honorable."

"I'll buy that. And because I can see you're a square-dealing fella, let's see what I can think of."

Seized by intuition, he asked, "Jake, have you read what I wrote?"

His baritone voice rattled the room. "Damn straight. The Dallas story made me curious. Found it this mornin' on the web. Wanted to know what could set those Christian crazies on a run like that. I can't say as yet what I think of it, but my daddy raised me to keep an open mind." He smiled broadly. "So I have to admit I didn't tell you everything I knew. I've been playing you. I apologize, but I'm real curious about this here deal."

"Thanks. I'm afraid I'm a little leery of how people are going to react, so I'm holding my cards pretty close."

"Can't blame you. Now before I tell you what I know about Sharon, my wife makes a fine berry cobbler. I can hear it callin'. You want some?"

It was clear to Pitcairn that Jake was a pretty good student of human behavior; not much got by him. As he described the relatively normal life of an office manager and her physician assistant husband, Pitcairn couldn't help wondering how all these seemingly ordinary women could have found themselves in the sights of a serial killer. He shared his curiosity.

"Don't know," Jake said, "but it is odd that Davidson didn't go for pretty women instead."

"Right. I've studied the profiles of serial killers, and this is not untypical. It's apparently never about appearance, or even being attracted. But somehow that's at odds with what I expected."

Jake nodded, then changed the subject. They chatted about the development and how it was expanding until the clothes were dry. Then Pitcairn thanked his host profusely.

"Do me a favor," Jake replied. "Here's my card. Send me what you write. I'd like to know what you come to."

"Deal. I never expected to be so well treated."

"I'd love to take credit, but it's what my folks taught me. Couldn't be otherwise."

► 22 ◄

THE BALANCE OF THE AFTERNOON WAS SPENT TRYING TO TRACK down the family of Kip Kelly. Pitcairn left information on how to contact him at several numbers but with no luck. He ended up walking the Baylor University campus where she had lived as a graduate student, eventually finding the corner of the parking garage where she'd been assaulted and slain.

A nearby wall had been dedicated to her memory and was filled with an eclectic collection of artistic expressions. He was deeply moved by them. The news materials Pitcairn had collected on her made clear that she was a solid though unexceptional student. Kip had been a member of the women's chorus and an efficient graduate assistant in the department of biology.

After a few minutes taking in the wall and its many messages, he slipped back to the Jeep and pulled out his file. His photo of Kip was poor, but he was sure she too was plain in appearance.

He drove to a nearby coffee shop and went in for an iced tea. He pulled out his journal, and began to write. More than anything else, he was struck by the utterly ordinary nature of the women's lives and the stark contrast of the violence visited upon them. More than ever, he related to the profound tragedy of it all. Davidson had told it right. His acts had shredded the lives of many people, and had rippled then to affect countless others.

He called Maria Elena and left a message. Then he called Martin, who answered promptly.

"Martin, how you doing?"

"Passable, Pitcairn. You?"

"Riding the tiger, brother, and watching the jungle speed by."

"You remembered."

"Too good to forget. Let me give you the details." He proceeded to describe his experiences since they'd last talked.

"That's quite a ride you're on," Martin said. "Any conclusions so far?"

"Wouldn't want to rush it."

"Of course not. But you've got me really interested."

"Welcome to the club, brother. All I know to do is keep putting one foot in front of the other until something else becomes clear."

"Did you see that movie about that Maori girl who rode the whale?"

"Yeah, sweet movie, Martin. And very inspiring."

"It reminds me of you. She just had to ride that whale. No matter what."

"No matter what. That sounds like a very compatible strategy for me."

"Keep me posted."

"You got it. And thanks, Martin. You're a great help."

Pitcairn walked to a nearby pizzeria for a couple of slices for the road, then drove north back to Dallas. His phone rang twice but the reception was too spotty to have any luck answering. When he pulled into a church near his hotel for an A.A. meeting, it was almost seven o'clock. Maria Elena had left two messages, both bubbling with talk about the rioting. He didn't want to be late for the meeting, and planned to call back later.

He slipped into a metal chair in a cool basement room just as the gavel fell to start the meeting of nearly thirty recovering alcoholics. A woman named Gloria opened the session and then started talking about a topic from the organization's literature. It was on the ninth step—about making "amends" to those one has harmed—and Pitcairn listened with great interest. The group was diverse, and as the members shared their stories, it was clear through the diversity of perspectives that there was a great deal of long-term sobriety in the room. What he heard made him think deeply about the amends he felt he could make through Davidson's victims. Too many people, he knew, think an apology is sufficient, or changing the behavior that caused the harm. Clint had helped him see that these were only markers along the way to inner healing. "Fix the insides, and the outside will follow," his sponsor had often said.

When Pitcairn's turn came to share, he noted that Gloria's topic was a timely one for him, since his visit to the area was part of his process of making amends. He acknowledged that it was challenging but said he was persevering. He briefly mentioned the reception he'd received from Robert Fields. The others in the basement loved it, easily relating to being told off in similar ways.

At the end of the meeting, a bear of a man made a beeline to him. With a voice made husky by too many cigarettes, Mikey D introduced himself. He was slightly shorter than Pitcairn and very stout, with a crushing handshake.

"Saw your mug in the mornin' paper, buddy. Did a little pokin' 'round. You and me gotta talk. You wanna grab some coffee?"

A few minutes later, they were in the same all-night diner Pitcairn had gone to early that morning. He realized it had been a very long day. "What's up, Mikey?"

He lit a cigarette and took a deep drag. A look of great pleasure came into his eyes. "Let me tell you, buddy, I like what you wrote. But I gotta tell you why."

He took a couple more deep puffs and squinted as smoke rolled into his eyes. "Me and Junior are the foundin' members of M.A."

"M.A.?" Pitcairn asked.

The big man laughed heartily. "Murderers Anonymous, of course." A twinkle showed in his eyes. "Our motto is, 'Just let them bastards live, one day at a time.' They may deserve killing, but don't do it." He broke up with more laughter, followed by a spasm of coughing. Pitcairn laughed with him, equally amused by the use of A.A.'s motto of one day at a time.

"I'm just shittin' you, buddy. But Junior and me was mercenaries. Used to git called out any time of day or night. Never knowed where we might have to go."

"Yeah?" Pitcairn asked skeptically, well aware of alcoholics' propensity to embellish their personal stories.

Mikey realized this immediately. He may have been rough, but he wasn't stupid. "I know. You figure I'm full of shit. But it's straight, buddy. And because of that, I like what you said."

"You found the column?" he asked with surprise.

The big man extended his arms with a shrug and a smug look. "I read a lot."

"So what was it you liked?

Mikey stubbed out his cigarette and promptly lit another. An exposed, almost-childlike look came to his face and eyes. "I joke about Murderers Anonymous, but I've killed." He glanced up furtively, "Not since I got off the sauce, mind you."

Pitcairn gave the nod of validation he knew the man needed.

"It was hard to find, but there was a lotta hurt and hate in me. My sponsor in the joint, Big Bobby Blue, helped me feel, deal, and heal. But I still hated my fuckin' folks for what they done to me." He sucked on the cigarette as a frown creased his face. "And what they done to my baby sisters was the worst. They're both crazy as loons from the shit they took."

Mikey leaned back for a deep breath. "So, ol' Bobby helped me bore deep down in my soul. It was black as hell. And then Bobby hooked me up with this dude who brought A.A. meetings in to us. Danny was a counselor. He spent a lotta time with me, pullin' that ugliness out."

Mikey chuckled and scratched the back of a hand. Sadness shone in his moist eyes. "Danny and Bobby showed me how to forgive my folks. What they done was wrong. But now I know it was the same shit was done to them. And as soon as I got ahold o' that forgiveness, I stopped hatin' people.

"Then I had to stop hatin' myself for what I done. That was the hardest thing you could imagine, Pitcairn. I was a nasty son-of-a-bitch. And I could never make right what I did wrong. But we got my insides cleaned up—me, Bobby, and Danny—and now I'm living a different life."

A light shone in Mikey's eyes. "Killin' and hurtin' people was the only thing I knew." He smiled with giant teeth, beaming right at Pitcairn. "You got it right in your column, buddy."

Pitcairn realized his breathing was shallow, and he had to force air into his lungs. "Jesus Christ, Mikey. I can't tell you how much I appreciate hearing that."

"Damn, don't get all warm and fuzzy on me now," the big man replied, but the smile remained on his face. "Now enough of that crap. You been out to El Malpais ... the badlands west of Albuquerque?"

"Yeah, a few times, especially climbing around the sandstone overlook."

"You been down in the really rugged badlands? Where there's nothing but broken rock and a few piss-ass shrubs?"

"No, not there."

"I walked out in the middle of that mess. Sat down and waited for God knows what. Sat long enough that I saw how purty it was. Awful ugly on the outside, but sweet as can be when you get past the ugly."

"Mikey, you've got the heart of a poet."

"Screw that, buddy! But you can buy me a sweet roll."

"Done," Pitcairn replied as he waved to a waitress.

They traded stories until nearly ten o'clock, when they declared it a perfect meeting after the meeting. As Pitcairn moved past Mikey's truck and veered toward his Jeep, Mikey grabbed him firmly by the arm. Pitcairn turned, and the big man pointed a finger in his face. "Keep telling them it ain't what they think. No matter what, don't stop."

With a serious look of agreement on his face, Pitcairn gave a curt nod as they shook hands.

He checked the cell phone he'd left on the seat. The first message was a tersely worded demand from the Kellys' attorney that he cease his attempts to contact the girl's family. He swallowed as it sank in, but words he had heard in the A.A. meeting just a few hours before flashed back to him: "We can never ease our conscience at the expense of another person's feelings. Yet how they respond is none of our business." He could do no more on that front.

The second message was from Maria Elena. She jabbered colorfully about how excited the neighborhood was over the previous day's events right up until the recording timed out and cut her off. It seemed there were many points of view, the message made clear. He made a mental note to call Mortensen the next day to get an update.

When he returned to his room, he called Maria Elena back, and they chattered away until midnight.

► 23 ◄

IT WAS NEITHER A GOOD NOR A BAD NIGHT'S SLEEP, BUT WEDNES-day morning came early. Pitcairn's body ached in more ways than he thought possible.

After breakfast, he read the newspaper while drinking coffee and planning the day. He would drive over to Fort Worth to find out what he could about Maggie Andrews. It was the murder that had led to Davidson's arrest, and was the best documented in Pitcairn's files. He read the facts again for a long time before he left the restaurant.

As he drove, following an internet map, he thought about what he knew. Maggie's story was not unlike the others. Twenty-two years old, from an old Fort Worth family, she'd been a bit of a community debutante, though it didn't seem to fit her very well. She'd completed her degree at the University of Texas, where she was involved in a number of intramural activities, none with any great distinction. A good photo taken at the auto dealership where she and her boyfriend worked made clear that she too was ordinary in appearance.

She hadn't been home from school for more than a few months when Davidson found her in the wooded area of a local park around dusk. She had just ended the relationship, and had sought solace and a place to think. A jogger heard the final acts of violence and alertly noted Davidson's license plate.

First, Pitcairn located Republic Park and walked the area, hoping for he knew not what. Then he called Maggie's last boyfriend, Aaron Hill, at the office where he worked now. Hill agreed to meet him for lunch at a restaurant a few miles away.

Pitcairn drove around aimlessly and arrived there at 11:15, shortly before he was to meet Hill. He called Mortensen as promised and updated him on his contacts and information, holding back about the more-adventurous details which might only aggravate the editor. There was nothing new to report from Albuquerque, so the call was fairly short.

Pitcairn had just slammed shut the door of the Jeep when a sports sedan pulled into a nearby parking spot. A slender young man stepped out. His headful of curly hair didn't seem to fit his wrinkled linen suit. He glanced toward Pitcairn, who swung a hand of acknowledgment in his direction. They both steered toward the entrance, pausing to shake hands.

Aaron Hill was clearly a circumspect and diligent sort of fellow, perhaps a little neurotic. His anxiety showed in a slight furtiveness. He didn't wring his hands, but it seemed that he needed to. They sat in a booth and ordered quickly since Hill had made clear he had only an hour for lunch.

"It's funny you called," he said. "Maggie's been on my mind a lot. I read that Davidson was dead." A near shudder passed through his slender frame. "I've always felt I should have been with her. If I'd been more the man she needed, she wouldn't have cut me loose. My therapist says it's not my fault. I guess I know that in my head. But that doesn't stop me from feeling it."

Pitcairn nodded with empathy. He well understood the difference between the head and the heart. "Tell me about her."

"She was funny in an understated sort of way. Maggie always had a witty perspective about everything. But she was careful with it. Her parents are really religious—Church of Christ. And they didn't approve of her sense of humor. So she was guarded. But she always made me laugh."

"What were her plans for her life?"

Hill took an almost birdlike sip of water. "She wanted to break free from her family." He smiled wistfully. "She was considering the Peace Corps, or teaching English as a second language in Japan." Pitcairn detected a gentleness growing in the young man's eyes. "The last time we talked, she said she was thinking about Portland. She thought her dad would flip. He's really conservative . . . Texas conservative. Hates liberals but can't say it because he's a Christian."

Pitcairn snorted at the remark, and Hill looked at him quizzically. "I get it, Aaron. I get it." He smiled warmly at the serious young man, who grinned briefly before being distracted by the arrival of their meals.

Soon, Hill steered the talk again toward Maggie's parents, both of them this time. "They were so phony about her death—all filled with Christian charity." He clicked his tongue with disapproval. "But it was all fake. Mrs. Andrews must have talked about God punishing the killer a hundred times. Her eyes were all wrong. She spoke kindly, but there was hate in her eyes." He nearly shuddered again.

"What about you, Aaron? How did it affect you?"

The question seemed to settle the young man, though a haunted cast showed on his face. Pitcairn imagined he was fully present now, as affectations dropped away.

"I've never stopped missing Maggie. I think about her all the time." He snorted in a self-deprecatory way. "She may be all I think about."

They were very quiet; the din of the restaurant seemed to fade. Pitcairn noticed a brief mental lapse inside himself, almost like a blink or a defocusing. It reminded him of an experience he used to have in early recovery when he was very depressed, though this was milder. He used to refer to it as his psychic reset button. When things got to be too overwhelming, his mind would just shut down for an instant.

It used to scare him. It could be really disconcerting. Now he was just curious. It was another sign of stress, but he couldn't rouse much interest in it. He remembered one of Clint's observations. When we were focused on our proper role, nothing could faze us. He resolutely turned his attention back to Hill.

"It's been hard, hasn't it?"

"Whatever," the young man shrugged.

Pitcairn felt a wave of concern and care sweep over him as he studied Hill's face. "Aaron, right now, right in this instant, are you okay about this?"

Hill blinked, and for a moment, Pitcairn saw the proverbial deer caught in the headlights.

"No," he answered firmly. "I'm not okay. I'm not sure I'll ever be okay."

It was quiet again as the two men looked at each other.

"I'm really sorry, Aaron."

Pitcairn's comment was a jolt. He could see it very clearly as Hill looked through the window and across the parking lot.

"I've got to get back to work," he said abruptly, then stood up.

Pitcairn extended his hand. "Lunch is on me. Thanks for your time."

A distracted thanks came back. Aaron couldn't seem to leave fast enough.

Pitcairn sat thinking for a long time. As he considered what he'd just seen, he remembered a hike on the West Mesa. It was mid-morning, a warm, brilliant spring day. Lucy and Lincoln were trotting along placidly. They all had more than a few miles behind them.

Unexpectedly, a rattlesnake slithered from the brush onto the path. Lincoln didn't see it even though his next few steps would take him right toward it, and neither did Pitcairn. But Lucy, the inveterate clown, moved with a burst of speed, cutting in front of Pitcairn and knocking Lincoln aside in a wild dash into the brush. It stopped them all in their tracks. He looked down as the curse he had for Lucy died on his lips. Quickly he grabbed Lincoln's collar as the snake coiled to strike.

Pitcairn tugged the dog backward out of range and then watched in amazement as Lucy careened wildly across the path just to the other side of the snake. It snapped toward her in a flash, but the change of direction made it miss widely.

Then Lucy took off into the distance barking crazily. Usually she stayed close, but this time she was gone like a shot. Pitcairn held Lincoln patiently while the snake slithered across the path into a stand of chamisa. Then they worked their way forward in search of the missing boxer.

It was a while before they found her sitting and panting with one paw held gingerly off the ground. Several nasty goathead thorns were embedded deeply in the pads.

Timing is everything, Pitcairn mused.

With that, a sudden urge to call Maria Elena swept over him. She answered almost immediately.

"I miss you," he said plainly.

Her voice was almost musical. "Is it me, or some part of me you miss?"

Her question shook him from his lethargy. "I miss all of your parts, Emmy, and the sum of all your parts too!"

"That's sweet, Cito!"

He felt another momentary mental lapse, followed by his voice. "As a matter of fact, I think I'm leaving right now. You convinced me."

"When will you be home, Cito?"

"I'm going to go check out right now. I'll get to Burkburnett tonight and find a motel. That's the little town on the Red River where one of Davidson's victims lived. Then I'll swing up to Lawton, Oklahoma, for one last visit. If things go right, I might just come in early Friday morning."

"Oooh . . . you know how much I like it in the morning, Cito!"

"You are incorrigible!"

"Only certain parts of me. The others are positively prudish."

"Which ones?"

"Which ones what?"

"Are prudish?"

"Both pinkies. Everything else is incorrigible."

He felt himself smile as he told her how much he loved her, then disconnected.

▶ 24 ◀

His cell phone rang before he left Fort Worth. "Do you believe in serendipity, Pitcairn?" asked a voice he immediately recognized as Kate Delmonico's.

"As a matter of fact, I was musing about timing only a short while ago, which probably means you are right on time. Right?" he asked pithily.

"You won't believe what I found," she replied with a tone that could not conceal her satisfaction.

"Kate, nothing would surprise me at this point. So . . . what?"

Her reply sounded self-satisfied. "A set of lectures on C.D. by a British neuropsychologist called 'The Neurological and Biological Bases for Behavior.' And this guy is all over the questions Davidson raised. I mean all over it. You are going to love what he has to say."

"No shit!" Pitcairn replied with matching enthusiasm.

"Yes, sir," she said. "Neurons and synapses and hormones and genetics that all lead to some conclusions that are pretty compelling." Pitcairn lapsed into a moment of reflection at how the timing had worked out.

"Pitcairn?" she asked as he realized his distraction.

"Sorry, Kate, too many adventures of late. All my neurons and synapses are overworked."

She laughed. "Good! This will put you into overdrive. It's really great stuff."

He thought carefully. He had a long drive back, and the C.D.s would fill the time. "You think you could FedEx them for hold and pick up in Lawton, Oklahoma?"

"Sure," she answered promptly. "Happy to do it." A click followed.

The drive to Burkburnett, Texas, was uneventful. When he checked into the Red River Lodge after grabbing dinner, he was dog tired and ready to sleep. But when he opened the door to his room and flipped on the light, he was stopped in his tracks. For an instant, he was back in Evansville, Indiana, on that long ago night that haunted him so deeply. His heart pounded, and he could suddenly hear blood rushing in his ears.

An urge to flee rose up in him; his hand clenched his bag tighter. Then he heard a still, quiet voice whisper: "It's okay, and you're okay." He blinked deliberately several times in rapid succession as if to help understand what was happening. Then he stepped into the room.

Standing and waiting, he scanned the room. The wallpaper was reminiscent, at best, with similar patterns to Evansville's but wholly different in color—beige with blue rather than burgundy. As he took it all in, a bead of sweat trickled down his cheek. He realized the entry hall was similar. Other than that, it was all an illusion.

After a few calming breaths, Pitcairn walked in and dropped his bag on the floor. Then he draped himself across the bed as it sagged slightly under his weight. He closed his eyes and was asleep almost immediately.

He awoke six hours later. The sleep, though uninterrupted, had hardly been restful, and he still felt exhausted. He lay in bed briefly cataloguing all the signs of stress he was showing. The fear of a breakdown crept into his thoughts. But the resolve that had been fueling him still held firm.

Pitcairn lurched to his feet and moved unsteadily to the bathroom. Then he dressed and headed toward the river, soon picking up a game trail that followed the bank eastward. The rhythm of his stride slowly cleared his mind and restored some semblance of grace to his movements. He marveled at the power of walking to restore him . . . like a tonic.

The moon hung giant and low on the western horizon as he cut from the trail across a network of rivulets and broken sand. The Red River was like the Rio Grande, an arid country waterway with large expanses of sand leading to a surprisingly small main channel. As Pitcairn neared the water, cooler air washed over him. He relaxed and settled onto a tree trunk long fallen and washed smooth by the action of sand and water. He needed to think about the information he was getting. He remained curious about the women Davidson had chosen. They were all from the same age group and relatively plain in appearance. Though they came from a diversity of backgrounds, they all seemed so very ordinary.

Scratching his head, he kicked at the sand beneath his feet. Suddenly he was possessed with a desire to dig. He sprawled out like a kid on the beach and began to play in the sand, shaping mounds, valleys, and holes by moonlight as his mind freewheeled.

The violence had been so utterly random, visited upon the women unexpectedly. Nothing was clear except that all the killings were crimes of opportunity, certainly not spontaneous but hardly premeditated either except in the sense that Davidson had to have a rough outline in his head to make them happen.

Pitcairn had read so much about violence, especially violence against women and the psyche of serial killers. And beyond the deaths themselves, their impact on families, friends, and communities was much more than he'd imagined. In some ways, the people around the victims were affected almost as profoundly. And there was so much rippling of the violence, if not in a physical way, then as inner damage that could take as great a toll and be passed on many times in many ways.

He lowered himself to gain a better angle for a long tunnel he was excavating beneath the little cityscape he'd made. As he reached past his elbow into the cool damp sand, a thought hit him with extraordinary force.

Everyone is so innocent. Then life comes along and brutalizes that innocence. For some, the injury heals, but for most, it seems to be perpetuated time after time.

Pitcairn sat back with his arms wrapped around his knees and began to rock gently. He remembered Kate Delmonico telling him once that any motion or movement that alternately stimulated the right and left sides of the brain was fundamentally soothing. It was why we rocked babies, though it might be as much for the caregiver as the baby. It was likely why the autistic and many of the mentally ill were prone to it. It probably explained why walking could comfort. And it had led to the development of treatments for those suffering from post-traumatic stress disorder.

Mostly, Pitcairn was aware of how much he felt for all those affected—both directly as victims of the violence and by the ripple effect that so clearly pushed forth from each event. Very few people seemed able to see it playing out in their lives. Even fewer could transcend it. The "tragedy" Davidson had talked about now seemed such a vast understatement. Violence causes injury and trauma, which far too often trigger further violence or severe disruption of other lives, all in a seemingly unending spiral.

The water tumbling over sand and rock suddenly sounded louder. Pitcairn realized why as he stopped rocking and only sat and listened. For the first time in as long as he could remember, his insides were as quiet as the outside.

The night sky was lightening, and a slight movement downstream caught his attention. He turned his head slowly and watched four white-tailed deer creep gracefully from the woods to a trickle that coursed around a sand bar. He remained motionless as they drank. One turned to study him, an unusual shape in well-known terrain. Pitcairn almost stopped breathing as he watched the doe watching him. After what seemed an eternity, the four deer moved slowly away into brush farther down river. He collected a deep breath but refused to move as he savored the experience.

Finally he stretched and rose from the river sand. He shook a foot that was tingling from the blood flow it had lost. Feeling came back, and he pivoted in the sand. As he did, Pitcairn thought of Christy Mayfield, the reason he had come to Burkburnett, the local girl fate had sucked into Daniel Davidson's vortex of violence.

He had learned about the other women like her this week, and had seen the wreckage left in the lives of those who had loved them. Now he wanted to look further—and maybe deeper too. He would try to get a sense of the community as a victim as well.

Walking briskly, he took a circuitous route back to the motel. Traffic on the riverside highway punctuated the quiet now with its increasing rumble and roar. Soon Pitcairn was standing under a hot shower, feeling surprisingly well.

He assumed that in a small town like Burkburnett, everyone would have known Christy. His inquiries began with Beth, the waitress at breakfast. Speaking in a friendly but earnest tone, he explained why he was there and—as best he could—the intent behind his mission. As he did, she opened up slowly but steadily.

The murder had shocked the small community. Twenty-year-old Christy was the daughter of a small ranching family that lived west of town. She was not notable except as a member of the community, where she worked as a bank teller. When she'd been found in bushes near a riverfront park, people had been devastated. Fear took over the lives they had always known—and taken for granted. Though Davidson was finally caught two years later, the sadness, the feeling of upheaval had not left.

Soon, the waitress, wanting to help Pitcairn understand, was taking him to meet others in the diner. He saw immediately what a favorite she was, and could sense that her introduction was giving him credibility with the group. There was the grocer, John Ralph Johnson, and Kitty Coburn, a real estate broker. Jeff Gardner owned a small trucking firm, and his brother, Rich, farmed while his wife, Donna, taught at the local high school. One young woman, Connie Blake, was a bank employee who had heard about Christy even though she began working at the branch after her death.

Each part of the story they told was imbued with an account of the life of Christy Mayfield, and the backdrop of ugliness that had descended afterward into the community and the lives of its residents. Children who'd ranged freely now were kept home. Women who had always felt safe in their insulated small community had come to live with fear. Some men felt angry and impotent. The fabric of the town had been terribly torn by the violent act.

As each person talked, Pitcairn could feel the fragility that seemed to have come as part of humans' realizing the risk inherent in living. But balancing that was a marked resiliency which manifested differently in each individual in feelings like humor, commitment, and resolve. More than anything else, Pitcairn was aware, despite the guardedness hovering over the conversation, of the privilege extended to him through their candor. He felt very grateful.

The Gardner brothers were the last left in the conversation when he asked if they thought he would be welcomed by the girl's parents, Floyd and Lou Mayfield. Both brothers looked down toward their boots for a long few seconds. "Mr. Pitcairn," Jeff began hesitantly, "there's a whole lotta hurt there for a quiet family to manage." Rich nodded sympathetically as his brother continued. "It'd be thoughtful to just drive on down the road."

Again Pitcairn felt the ache and damage. He nodded quickly. "Rest assured, I wouldn't want to bring any harm to anyone." They both looked at him with what he took as appreciation.

Pitcairn thanked them both. As he left, he pressed a ten into the hand of Beth, the waitress, and smiled as he thanked her as well.

"My pleasure," she replied pleasantly. "Thanks for asking. Drive carefully, hon."

A few minutes later, after filling up with gas, he was driving over the Red River into Oklahoma. By early afternoon, Pitcairn had arrived in Lawton. He called the number he had for Randy Curtis, the widower of Veronica Curtis. His notes showed that Randy was a retailer and had remarried to a woman named Barbara. Unlike the other victims, Veronica had had children: Randy Jr., Gay Lynn, and Cindy Leigh. Pitcairn expected a difficult conversation.

Randy Curtis answered the phone brusquely. He and Pitcairn had traded voicemail messages in the previous week, so the call was not a surprise. Still, Curtis was apparently a man of few words, listening silently as Pitcairn explained his desire to know what Veronica was like, and his interest in the effects of what Davidson had done. Curtis gave him directions to his auto parts store, where they could meet.

It took some time to drive across town, including a stop at the FedEx terminal for the C.D. Kate had sent. When he got to the store, a tall, sad-eyed man brought him quickly into his office. Pitcairn noted a number of photos of children but none of a woman who could be Veronica or Barbara. He sat in a straight-backed chair that Curtis gestured toward.

"How can I help you?" the man asked.

"As I told you on the phone, I'm just trying to learn what I can about the victims of Daniel Davidson. I'm not sure yet what I'll write, but there's no way I want to hurt you or the memory of your wife."

In a tone that seemed almost disembodied to Pitcairn, Curtis described his former wife. They were high school sweethearts, and had married as soon as they graduated. All Veronica ever wanted was to be a mother, and in four years, they had three children. She had always been happy, and the children only added to her joy. Their life had been unmarred by hardship.

As Pitcairn listened, he knew what psychologists would call the lack of affect he was seeing: disassociation. He was looking at a man whose inner wounds had caused him to shut down some part of his emotions. He may never have been able to grieve his terrible loss. Indeed, Curtis mentioned immediately that he had remarried within a year, perhaps for reasons in addition to his children's need for a mother, Pitcairn hypothesized to himself.

They stood and moved to the photos of the kids. With practiced eyes, Pitcairn studied the images. It was clear to him that the children had changed. Once, there was a gaiety, but not after their mother had died. Randy Jr.'s reserve was obvious, while the eyes of the girls were guarded. These, he knew, were the marks of trauma, scarring the children in ways that might not easily be known for years to come.

For a man short on words and with obvious emotional impairment, Curtis had continued the meeting longer than Pitcairn expected.

Once it was over, he grabbed road food from a burger joint and called Maria Elena from the parking lot. She didn't answer, so he left a message that he was just getting on the road. If things went well, he'd be at the house around five or six on Friday morning.

► 25 ◄

PITCAIRN DROVE WEST THROUGH SCATTERED THUNDERSTORMS and then into an incredibly beautiful sunset that lit up the clouds with a heavenly glow. As night took hold, lightning flashed in the distance in many directions. The air, already cooled by rain, became increasingly comfortable as he gained elevation from Oklahoma into Texas. The high plains of eastern New Mexico would be chilly.

He filled the time listening to the first few hours of material by Dr. Stephen Pfalzer, a second-generation immigrant Brit renowned for his neurological studies. The background was rich with genetics, anatomy, biology, and evolution that the professor said laid the foundation for key points that would follow. Pitcairn's innate desire to learn was captivated by the steady but engaging flow of information.

Around eleven, he pulled onto an exit ramp in Amarillo for fuel and food. The roadway was wet, and there had been a collision that made for quite a logjam. A number of cars were negotiating the crash scene carefully. The police had not yet arrived.

As Pitcairn waited, a pickup pulled behind him and flashed its lights. With the glare, and the disorientation of the traffic, it was confusing. He continued to wait for an opportunity to move forward. The truck behind him honked a few times.

His annoyance increased. When the driver flashed his brights again, Pitcairn put the Jeep in neutral, set the parking brake, stepped out to face the truck, and gestured with open arms. He couldn't tell for sure with the lights, but it looked like three men in a Ford King Cab.

The driver honked again. Pitcairn shook his head, shrugged, dropped his arms with a sense of finality, and climbed into the Jeep. He glanced in his side mirror and saw that the driver had opened his door and was stepping down. He seemed to wobble a bit as he swung his second foot to the ground. Pitcairn instantly knew that the guy had been drinking.

The man reached into the truck to get his hat and pulled it down firmly on his head, then hitched up his pants. Pitcairn had been in enough rough places during his drinking days that he could see the signs of a fight before it began. He steeled himself, an old response he knew well. His fists were clenched, one on the steering wheel and the other on the gear shift.

Pitcairn sized the man up in the mirror. The fellow was smaller than he was, though wiry and undoubtedly tough. Pitcairn rolled down his window and placed a hand on the door latch so he could roll the cowboy with the door if need be.

"What's up?" he asked as the man positioned himself just far enough away to avoid the door.

The man spat on the pavement, then squinted at him through reddened eyes. "What's your problem, buddy?"

"My problem?"

"Yeah, that New Mexican attitude shit."

"Man, you flashed me and honked. I didn't start this. Seems to me you're the one with the attitude."

The man reached up and ran his hand across his chin. Pitcairn could sense the move coming and got ready to jerk the door open. But in a surprising instant, the still voice he'd heard but not acknowledged in the hotel room whispered to him again: "Violence begets only violence. Go now."

With unlikely obedience and certainty, he popped the clutch and whipped swiftly to the left as the man swung his fist, banging it off the doorframe. Cutting onto the shoulder and then with tires on grass, Pitcairn accelerated forward as cars began to honk at him. Just as he got to the end of the ramp, the first police car arrived on the scene. "Timing," he muttered to himself as the cruiser blocked his way. The officer came out of the car like a bull and stormed toward him, his face a mask of fury.

"What the hell's the matter with you?" the policeman screamed as he moved toward him.

Pitcairn raised his hands and announced through the still-open window, "I can explain everything. Just give me a minute." Pitcairn saw the officer glance behind the Jeep to see the Ford truck careening across the grass in the opposite direction toward the service road. Seeing it in his rear view mirror, Pitcairn spoke firmly: "Those drunks were trying to start a fight with me."

The policeman's eyes darted back and forth. "Don't move!" he barked, then ran to his car to make a quick radio call. A few seconds later another cruiser raced down the service road in pursuit of the truck, lights flashing and siren howling.

The officer returned and stood closely, peering into the Jeep. "You been drinkin'?"

"No, sir, not in many years."

"Recovering?" the officer asked.

"Yes."

A quick nod followed. "Me too . . . fifteen years. Swing the Jeep around the wreck. You're good to go."

"Thank you!" Pitcairn responded, appreciation surging inside him.

After navigating carefully with the officer's help, he drove into a gas station and convenience store. As fuel flowed into his tank, he stretched his hands over his head and yawned. Arms extended, he realized they were quaking faintly. His system was flooded with adrenaline. Regardless, he was very curious about that small voice he'd heard. It was a new experience.

After visiting the restroom and splashing water on his face, he grabbed a Mountain Dew and some chips. He paid for his purchase and threaded his way back onto the highway.

In less than an hour, he had to pull off the road to nap. Weariness and carbohydrates had defeated the caffeine. At a lonely exit, he parked and dropped his seat. It took longer to fall asleep than he expected. Thoughts flew in his mind, though they too were slowly overcome by the weariness.

A monstrous thunderclap startled him awake about an hour later. Pitcairn shook his head a few times to clear the fog, then watched the splashes of light across the sky before he climbed out to take a leak.

It was very dark and deeply quiet except for the sound of the wind preceding the storm. Then he heard the approaching hiss of pea-sized hail that began pelting him along with the rain as he zipped up his pants.

Leaping into the Jeep, invigorated by the nap and the cold rain, he roared away into the night. As he drove, Pfalzer's lectures combined with his accumulated weariness to produce a focused reverie, a strange flow of consciousness and thought as he hurtled homeward.

Pfalzer taught that there is nothing remotely resembling normal where human behavior is concerned. The fringes of behavior are inevitable as part of the continuum. What marked these outliers was their unpredictability, both in their forms of behavior and, more important, the extremes they could represent. We should not be surprised by aberrant behavior; it was built into the design of life.

Emmy slipped into his thoughts. Damaged but indomitable. A rock of reliability in the shifting sands of the psychology of abuse, she had been driven, like Pitcairn, to excel in education and professionally, overcompensating for long ago childhood wounds. Those injuries had kept her from relationship commitment until he came into her life. Sometimes, the trauma made her flighty, other times loyal. And she could fight if need be, like a pit bull if she had to. It was not hard to imagine how close some of her adaptation might come to multiple personalities, alternate realities carved from a core to avoid shattering the self. Maria Elena's was a story of healing and rehealing.

Who knows what pressures had caused Daniel Davidson to fracture into the violent streak that marked the fringes of human behavior?

Pitcairn suddenly focused back on Pfalzer. Genetics and neurochemical functioning were only part of the tale. Environmental factors interacted in so many ways as well. Deep in the brain, the amygdala ran strangely parallel tracks of sexual arousal and excited aggression. Throw in the frontal cortex's capacity to control disinhibition, and the tendency for violence to desensitize along with a chemical cocktail of hormones, and anything could be possible. Every situation was a unique mix of nature and nurture, most tending toward stability, a few flying toward extremes.

Pfalzer summed it up: "There but for the grace of God go I."

Pitcairn's thoughts returned to the conscious monkey on the shoulders of the unconscious tiger racing through the jungle of reality, the monkey mind of the self telling stories of what we believe we are doing and why. In fact, the difference between self-will run amok and self-will run lucky was greatly dependent on happenstance. And not one of us could easily imagine we were not fully in control of ourselves and our actions.

Testosterone won't cause violence, Pfalzer emphasized, but it can ratchet up a preexisting tendency due to other circumstances. Somewhere within each of us lurks a soul-self separate and apart from our behavior.

"In the end," Pfalzer concluded, "we find ourselves facing only one road . . . that of kinship and compassion."

▶ 26 ◀

JUST AFTER SEVEN O'CLOCK, BONE TIRED WITH A HEAD FULL of swirling thoughts, Pitcairn drove down Gold Street to their home. He could see immediately that Maria Elena had dealt with Gabriel, and the repair had been done quickly. Everything looked perfect.

With the first creak of the door, Lucy came barreling down the hallway with a few soft barks of recognition. Lincoln moved down the hall with stately demeanor a minute later followed by Maria Elena, who bore a huge smile and a spatula in her hand.

"Cito!" she squealed as she kneed the dogs aside and pressed herself to him. "I got home early from Darlene's just in case . . . but I have to go to work . . . ." Her voice trailed away. Then she kissed him deeply before pulling away. "You look awful, Cito!" she said as she took a good look at him. "God, I'm impossible aren't I?" she asked with a mischievous smile.

"Absolutely," he replied with ease. "And the only thing better than you are your burritos. So I'm a happy man!"

"Panza llena corazón contenta!" she replied. "Fill up a belly, and the heart follows." Then she darted away.

After things settled down and he'd napped a few hours to recharge, Pitcairn grabbed some leftover burritos and went out with the dogs. First thing, he decided, they all could use a good walk. So he headed for the foothills of the Sandia Mountains, to Embudito Canyon, where they trekked up the stream even though it was heavily overgrown and almost impenetrable but for the game trails. Within minutes, the sounds of the city had vanished, and they climbed steadily toward the line of ponderosa that began around seven thousand feet.

Once past the area where most hikers stopped, he and the dogs found a comfortable slab of granite with a trickle of water flowing across it. They settled in, the dogs to rest and he to contemplate.

He sat for more than an hour as the sun climbed. The quiet refreshed him and made up for the lack of sleep. Lucy became restless as he was finishing off the burritos, so they retraced their route back to the trailhead and a quick drive home. On the way, he made up his mind. It was time to do something he had long considered but could never be sure was right. Today he was certain.

With monsoonal clouds towering in the west, he stood under a portal poised to knock on the door of Tomas and Raquel Maldonado. He had never met them, since Maria Elena no longer had any contact with her parents.

He paused and lowered his hand, listening for an inner certainty as he scanned the old neighborhood to the west of Plaza Vieja, Old Town's center. It was interesting that they lived so close though he'd never met them. His sense of clarity was confirmed as he stood quietly, so he turned and rapped sharply on the door.

He heard footsteps approaching. The door opened to reveal a petite woman who so obviously resembled Maria Elena it stopped him for an instant. He recovered his balance just as her mother asked tentatively, "Yes?"

"Hello, Mrs. Maldonado. We haven't met, but it's overdue. I'm Kevin Pitcairn, and I've been seeing your daughter for a long time."

A look of fear crossed the older woman's eyes. "Is Maria okay?"

"Yes ma'am. She's fine. I'm sorry to worry you. May I come in and speak with you."

She glanced nervously over her shoulder.

"Is your husband home? I'd like to talk with him as well."

She blinked with obvious discomfort. "Are you sure?"

"Yes ma'am. There's no question."

Hesitating for a moment, perhaps taken aback, she stepped aside and gestured with a short sweep of her hand. "Please come in."

The interior of the home was dark with dated furniture that spoke to their frugal nature, though a pleasant odor of spices and cedar leant a sense of comfort. Still, the home was so obviously formal that the scent was at odds with the feel of it.

She showed him to a large sofa and then quickly left to find her husband, who soon appeared and extended his hand as Pitcairn rose to meet him. "Mr. Pitcairn, my wife has gone for iced tea. Please sit," he said pleasantly as he gestured. Then he moved to a side chair and settled stiffly and awkwardly.

"What brings you to our home? Raquel said Maria is fine, so I'm not sure why you are here."

Pitcairn nodded readily. "Yes, sir, I can imagine you would be surprised. I've been doing some very interesting research in Texas about families, and it led me to want to learn more about your daughter. Her childhood, and anything else you can remember."

An odd look crossed the man's face. He was suspicious. "And why would you ask this?"

Pitcairn chuckled. "Mr. Maldonado, I love your daughter very much, so I don't think there's anything strange about my request. I simply realized that I didn't know that much about Maria Elena. So here I am."

"You call her Maria Elena?"

"Sure, it's the only name I know her by."

The older man nodded, then glanced up as his wife entered with a tray of tea and biscochitos. "Raquel, Mr. Pitcairn would like to learn more about Maria."

A look passed between them that Pitcairn could not interpret, but he was quick to speak. "Please call me Kevin."

They both looked at him oddly, perhaps off balance from his implied intimacy. "Kevin then," Tomas said somewhat awkwardly. "Where should we begin?"

"Well, as I've interviewed other families, photo albums seem to help a lot."

With that, Raquel moved to pull them from beneath the coffee table. He noticed her hands shaking as she opened the album. But the photos quickly drew them into the story of their lives. Pitcairn mostly listened as he studied the photos. Pictures of the entire family revealed little bits of information. The awkward posing of girls on men's laps, with the occasionally obvious inappropriate touch.

He noted with sadness photos of Maria Elena, with the loss of light in her eyes becoming clear to him around the age of six, followed by a steely-eyed anger in her teen-age years. A shot at about nineteen almost broke his heart with the hopelessness he saw in her face. Then he remembered the light she carried within her now, and tears welled up. She had worked so hard in therapy, and had healed so very much.

Her mother noticed and asked, "What is it, Kevin?"

He glanced up at them both. "Nothing . . . I was just thinking how sweet she is."

A look of suspicion came to her father's face. "Mr. Pitcairn, enough of this. Why are you here?"

The atmosphere was pregnant with tension. Raquel clasped her hands so hard he could see little strips of white appear around her nails. Her father seemed ready to pounce like a cat. Anger flashed in his eyes.

Pitcairn thought carefully. The principle of do no harm to others buzzed loudly. A place of quiet reserve held sway within him. He recalled a phrase that an older woman, long sober, had said once at an A.A. meeting: "The next right thing is the thing that wants to be said or done." And he knew what wanted to be said.

"Mr. and Mrs. Maldonado, I intended nothing but to hear more of the story of Maria Elena's life. I'm sorry this has been uncomfortable for you, so I'll go."

A look of relief came to her mother's face, but her father eyes revealed the inner storm that raged inside him.

"But before I leave," Pitcairn added, "I need to say that your daughter was profoundly injured as a child. I think you know why." He smiled with compassion, though her father looked about to explode. "I'm here to bear witness to that pain. And to a remarkable woman who has incredible strength. I could do no less for the woman I love."

He rose as Maria Elena's father pointed to the door. "Get out of my home," he snarled.

Pitcairn nodded as Raquel scurried toward the door. "Mr. Maldonado, I apologize for intruding and for your discomfort. But that does not change what you did."

Briefly, he thought the old man was about to charge at him. But Pitcairn looked back so calmly and intently that it gave him pause. The quiet voice spoke at that moment: "He's innocent too."

With that, Pitcairn smiled kindly. "Thank you for seeing me, Tomas, and for welcoming me into your home." Her father was clearly stung by the compassion in his voice, and looked ready to bolt. Pitcairn turned and walked with a measured pace to the door where her mother awaited. "Thank you for sharing the photos with me, Raquel."

She shrank from him with a troubled nod of her head.

The door closed behind him as Pitcairn stepped toward the street. It was dark outside from the clouds, but the light of day remained vastly different from the interior darkness of their home.

► 27 ◄

THAT NIGHT, OVER A LOVELY DINNER AT CASA DE LOS GENTES in the North Valley, Pitcairn told Maria Elena about his experiences since he'd left for Texas, culminating in the visit to her parents. At first, he thought she was going to fly into a rage. But as she listened, her eyes softened and she slowly relaxed into the cushioned seat. When he finished a full account, she gazed at him for a long time before she spoke.

"I don't know what to say," she began. "In my wildest dreams, I couldn't have imagined you talking to my parents."

He raised his eyebrows sheepishly to validate her surprise, but said nothing.

"What did you think of my dad?"

"Hmm . . . he's tough and very defended. Probably not going to be redeemed in this lifetime."

She looked inquisitive, so he continued.

"I guess, to be consistent with this perspective on violence I've been dabbling in, he must have had a rough time somewhere. Not that that excuses what he did to you, Maria Elena, but I sure do wonder what happened to him. I mean, he seemed to have only a couple of modes when we were together, suspicious and bristling. So I have to figure something bad happened to him. If it's true that violence begets violence, that must be the case."

She squinted, and he could see she was thinking. "Well, I'm not planning on cutting Tomas Maldonado any slack anytime soon, but I remember Tio Tony making a joke that I never thought much of until now."

Her hair swayed as she shook her head with the memory. "Uncle Tony, my dad's oldest brother, told me they used to joke that Abuela Victoria beat them so often she stripped every tree in the yard of anything she could swing."

"Really!" Pitcairn replied.

"Yep. Then Tio said he always admired my dad because he would never utter a sound. That really pissed off my grandmother, who would beat him even more. Never a tear shed, not a single word of protest, not even resistance. He just took it."

"Christ, Emmy!"

"Sure, it sounds bad, but when does the buck stop, Cito? I can appreciate that my dad had a crappy childhood, but that doesn't excuse him molesting me. That bastard is not innocent, no matter what you say."

He smiled at her, loving her all the more for her directness. "I think the problem is in how we understand innocence, Emmy. It doesn't mean he didn't do what he did, and it certainly doesn't make it okay. It's like I'm beginning to see that there's always a story that puts people in a different light. That's exactly what happened with Davidson, and now I'm having the same experience with your dad."

A sweet but very curious expression came to her face. He smiled at her. "Okay, so here's the really strange thing. I've been having this quiet voice speak to me . . . ."

"Cito, you're exhausted, you're stressed, you're not sleeping well, and you've not been eating right. Don't you think voices in the head are more than just strange?"

He shrugged. "Hell, I don't know what to think anymore. All my bearings have been swept away. But I sure don't feel crazy. So just hear me out. Okay?"

Her eyes twinkled as she replied, "Okay. Knock yourself out."

"All right. So it's only happened a few times. It's a very still voice, and it seems to be pointing out things I need to see about innocence and violence. I didn't tell you that it told me to haul ass just before that cowboy in Amarillo swung at

me. If I had taken him on, it would just trigger more violence. At a minimum, those other dudes in the truck would
have wanted a piece of me. Beyond that, who knows?
"Then it happened with your dad. Just when I thought
he was going to jump up and say or do something crazy, the
voice said, 'He's innocent too.' And damned if it didn't completely change how I felt about him. Everything I said there-
after was as kind as it could be. Don't get me wrong, I
named what needed to be named. But I felt entirely different. And it sure looked to me like a hammer falling on him.
Your dad went from wanting to fight to wanting to run.
Emmy, it was unreal. Oh, and I just realized something else.
I walked out of there without a shred of judgment. In fact,
I may be feeling empathy, especially now that I know he was
physically abused as a kid."

Maria Elena studied him with an open and pensive look,
unable to express her thoughts. Just then, their waiter came
with the dessert menu and proceeded to describe the selections one by one. They ordered a crème brulée to share,
and coffee.

She spoke very softly. "I have never loved you more than
I do right now, Cito. Whatever it is that you're going
through, it's changing you in ways I'm not sure I have
words for. But I like it . . . a lot. And I am so honored that
you would confront my parents like you did. That tells me
more than anything how you feel about me."

Pitcairn was overwhelmed with feeling at that moment.
He leaned back and took a breath.

"Shit, Cito, you looked Tomas Maldonado in the eye and
told him the truth. And right in front of my mom. That
makes you like Sir Galahad or something."

Now he laughed. "If Clint were here, he'd make it very
clear that I am not a knight in shining armor."

"Screw Clint. You're my knight in shining armor!"

The waiter picked that moment to slide dessert into the
space that had narrowed between them. He smiled as he
poured the coffee. "Sweet," he said with a wink.

After dinner, they strolled wordlessly in the bosque, hand in hand as lightning flashed in monsoonal clouds gathering in the southwest. Later, after shooing the boxers away, they made love to the sound of thunder and lashing rain. For the first time, Maria Elena was actually shy in bed. They fell asleep with heads cradled together on the pillow.

A huge thunderclap woke them at two o'clock. She immediately rolled over and began snoring lightly. Despite a great sense of weariness that clung to him, Pitcairn lay in bed unable to sleep. Nothing in particular claimed his thoughts, but there was far too much stirring inside him to allow sleep. Soon he arose and sat to write in his journal.

The rain stopped, and he took the dogs for a long walk through the neighborhood. The city was washed clean by the heavy rains. He thought he caught a hint of autumn in the air. It was the first day of September, and if the usual weather pattern held, the monsoons would break with the final day of the state fair on September 16. With that change would come the breaking of the heat. Every year he relished the yielding of the oppressive weather.

Just before seven, he woke Maria Elena, ignoring her groan. "We agreed we'd walk to the farmers' market. Up and at 'em, Sunshine!" She didn't move or respond. "Okay, this calls for the dog patrol." He whistled, and the boxers piled onto the bed. Lucy began to lick her ear.

Maria Elena squealed her reluctance, then rose upright. "You are just plain mean."

"Come on, we'll get Barela's tamales for later. If we're lucky, Flying Star will be there with their fiesta sandwiches and kickass coffee."

After she'd assembled herself, they wandered with Lincoln and Lucy down Gold Street toward Robinson Park on the western fringe of downtown. She reluctantly admitted it was a glorious morning, and the walk was a great idea.

Cutting across Park Avenue, they steered toward the Hotel Blue. Coming around the corner, it was immediately apparent that something was happening at the west end of the park. People, though still sparse because of the early hour, were staring across the park, a few pointing. Two more paces and they could almost see past the trees that lined the park. Pitcairn dropped into a crouch to get a better look. "Jesus Christ! Look at that, Emmy. There are upside-down crucifixes with people standing on them."

A hush came over them, as it had to the others who were there. They crossed the street and moved toward what now could be seen to be three crosses, each with a person standing on a small platform positioned at the crosspiece. Several police cars were on the street just beyond the crosses, but it was apparent the officers had no cause to act, or perhaps no idea how to act.

Nearing, they saw that the two men and a woman on the crosses were each garbed in a simple, rough-spun garment. Their hands were cupped together at the waist, and their eyes cast down. They were quiet and composed, silence seeming to ripple around them. People approached but were respectfully quiet. There was no mistaking the power in the image of the upside down cross, a clear statement of Christianity in distress. Beside the crosses, a sign read: "Judge not—the real message of Jesus."

A simple wooden sign hung beneath each crucifix as well. Pitcairn read them: "Forgive seventy times seven"; "Neither do I condemn thee"; "Father, forgive them for they know not what they do."

Pitcairn knew it had to be a response to the previous week's evangelical Christian rioting. And it was incredibly powerful.

Maria Elena leaned over to whisper to him. "It's got to be that liberal Catholic group from the South Valley, the Center for Enlightened Spirituality. You know . . . the Catholic heretics?"

He nodded as he too spoke softly. "That makes sense. But man, what a statement!" He walked over to a woman next to the crosses who was silently holding pamphlets, took one, and glanced at it.

Several statements on the back seized his attention: "The loudest voices are not the truest"; "When angry voices lie, our actions must speak louder"; "The truth shall set you free."

Even when the news vans pulled up a few minutes later, the hush held. With unusual respect, not one of the reporters attempted to speak to those on the crosses. Instead, they trickled around and interviewed those who were watching.

Soon, a young woman journalist approached them, apparently recognizing Pitcairn. He shared their best thinking, that it was a response to the evangelical demonstration, and might be a South Valley group.

"Do you think your column is responsible for this?" she asked.

"Sure, but who could have predicted such an outcome?"

As the woman prodded him for facts, he could not keep his eyes from the three calm figures on the crosses. Finally, she asked, "What do you think of this display?"

Pitcairn thought briefly, then spoke with a somberness that permeated his being: "They are right on the mark ... and it stills my heart."

He retreated across the park with Maria Elena to sit on a bench and marvel. "Don't you think you're seeing something pivotal, Cito? Like Rosa Parks on that bus, or one of Gandhi's nonviolent demonstrations? Can you feel the shift?"

"Yeah," he replied. "And whoever thought of turning those crucifixes upside down is either a genius or very dangerous. Nothing is more powerful than co-opting a symbol. And no symbol is more powerful than the cross."

Indeed, they looked around to see a park full of very, very quiet people. It was simultaneously inspiring and disturbing.

At eight-thirty, by obvious prearrangement, three pickup trucks drove onto the grass. The trio stepped off the crosses and helped load them into the truck beds. Then they climbed into the cabs and left. News trucks followed, and it would be only a matter of time before their identity was known.

Pitcairn found it curious that they had consciously avoided greater exposure for their views. He and Maria

Elena walked home wordlessly. Breakfast, tamales, and the farmers' market had been forgotten.

▶ 28 ◀

THE EFFECT OF WHAT WAS BEING CALLED THE "CRUCIFIX Protest" was like a tsunami. News broadcasts from coast to coast were filled with coverage that included this most potent of images. Reactions were as varied as one could imagine. Some religious groups were extremely offended. Those who spoke for them were overly strident in their criticism. Others voiced their views with great humility and introspection. By Sunday, copycat crucifixions had occurred in Tulsa, Jacksonville, and a couple of towns near San Francisco.

In some cases, the response to them was volatile as people who felt offended by the protests tried to disrupt them; altercations and fights forced the police to step in. A psychic nerve had been struck.

Though the trucks with the crosses had been followed to the Center for Enlightened Spirituality, the group locked the world out. No one was available to speak to the media, and it appeared that no one would be. The individuals involved, though identified by family and friends, did not emerge. Despite the journalists surrounding them, that front was quiet.

Pitcairn stayed put at home, ignoring the reporters appearing at his front gate. He found himself in the unlikely position of being the only source with an overall perspective on what was happening—and the fact that ultimately it led back to Daniel Davidson. By Sunday evening, he had received a dozen calls asking for interviews, including one from Jennifer Frank, the highly successful national television personality. While Pitcairn thought of her as no better than a carnival barker, he agreed to travel to Minneapolis for a live interview a week from Monday. Another interview was arranged with a local TV shock jock and philanthropist, Lenny Morris, who broadcast from his ranch in eastern New Mexico during the summer. Pitcairn would drive there Tuesday morning. The speed of the response was amazing. It seemed as if he had been on the phone all weekend. When contacts weren't calling for interviews, friends were checking in on him. Even his Aunt Jeanne had seen a broadcast that included clips from an interview with him. Amid the flurry of activity, he had spoken several times to Martin, just to keep his emotional bearings.

The hubbub only added to his inner disquiet. He awoke shortly after midnight on Monday morning and was able to sneak away for a long walk on the West Mesa with Lucy and Lincoln. As they covered the perimeter trail that traced the edge of the escarpment to the south, he was very aware of pervasive weariness.

He sat for a long time on a slab of basalt from which he could see far up the valley. Lights twinkled, exacerbated by his bleary-eyed vision and the strange mental defocusing that was now regularly interrupting his thoughts. Like a mental blink, for a moment, he would vanish into nothingness.

He felt an edge of fear, a signal of the concern that dogged him. Would he be able to see this through? Was his strategy of persistence one that could work? Everything had become far more convoluted than he could have imagined. Never before had he been so clear that his best efforts might not be enough.

He whispered quietly in the dark, "God, if you're there, I need some help here." Nothing changed, and no voice spoke. But he felt renewed resolve.

With an effort, he rose and moved back to the trail. The boxers followed. The three looped back on a spur and were soon home, well before dawn.

Pitcairn spent the day researching and organizing articles he was writing about the Bisti Badlands and a controversial district judge, though his efforts kept being interrupted by more calls. The following morning, he left at three o'clock for the two-and-a-half-hour drive to the ranch north of Santa Rosa that Morris broadcast from.

It was a beautiful drive, with the morning air cooling as autumn approached. When the Jeep bumped over the cattle guard at the entrance to the Park Springs Ranch, he was interested to see beneath the sign three connected crosses and the words "Tres Cruces." Perhaps it was coincidence, but he made a mental note to inquire about it.

Six miles along a muddy road from the entrance, he drove over a rise and saw the ranch house backlit by a huge stone barn with light streaming through windows and cracks. Morris had refit the old structure for his studios, and stories abounded about state-of-the-art lighting and sound systems. Wrapping around the structures to the south was what appeared to be a fairly large pond.

Heading for the barn as he'd been instructed, he was met at the door by a striking woman who introduced herself as the broadcaster's wife, Deana. Rumor had it she was the marketing genius behind his success.

She spoke with confidence as she led him inside. Morris was on a very large, glass-enclosed broadcast stage surrounded by cameras. To catch the East Coast markets, the show had already begun. Pitcairn was slotted for seven o'clock local time, more than an hour away.

Deana escorted him to an area cordoned off in a corner of the barn where she briefed him while a staff member worked with his appearance. The information took only a few minutes, so Pitcairn asked about the three linked crosses.

She offered a short history of the ranch, which had once been part of a Spanish land grant. It had been settled as a small ranching community because of the excellent springs which kept the pond so lush. Eventually, the land had been purchased by a cattle baron and the ranch house built from the initial structures. At that time, the ranch had been renamed Park Springs, but the Tres Cruces brand had continued.

"Given that I'm here to discuss the Crucifix Protest, the crosses on the entrance sign seemed serendipitous."

She smiled and said, "Probably so." Then she left him to tend to a problem her assistant had come with.

During a later break, Pitcairn was escorted onto the stage and introduced to Morris, who offered a firm handshake and leaned forward to gently lay a hand on his shoulder. When the show resumed, they talked through the events that had resulted in the Crucifix Protest. Morris asked him for a summary of his *Contours* piece, carefully studying his guest as he described it.

Then Pitcairn briefly described the Center for Enlightened Spirituality, and added his most recent thoughts about innocence.

"Okay, Kevin. Let's get real. A serial murderer is *innocent*? Who's going to buy that?"

Pitcairn laughed. "Yeah, it seems likes a stretch to me too at times. But with everything we're learning about genetics and psychology, increasingly it sure looks like things are at work within us that we don't really have any control over."

"But the whole foundation of human civilization is based on the presumption that we have choice. Are you saying that assumption is wrong?"

He had to think for a moment. "Lenny, I guess I really don't know. Maybe we have the potential to choose, but until the potential is realized, there is no choice. Look at everything we've learned about addictions. Once you're hooked, there's no choice. And most people who end up with problems start drinking or smoking or doing drugs before the age of fifteen. Evidence is now coming forth that the ability to make good decisions doesn't develop in the brain structure until the late teens, if not later. That's why the cigarette manufacturers target kids. They know they don't have good reasoning skills. Did you know that something like 57 percent of kids who get hooked on smoking will die as smokers? There's no choice there."

Pitcairn knew that Morris brought abused children to his ranch every summer for camps with professionals intended to help them heal. The look in the broadcaster's eyes told him he had struck a chord.

"How'd you learn all this, Kevin?"

"Not by choice," he said. "I've been researching all kinds of things since the day I received Daniel Davidson's letter. It's been enlightening to say the least."

"So, no free choice?"

"Only the potential, I think. I mean, who knows. But how about the kids you bring to the ranch? I hear some are severely abused. After all that, can they choose to trust you? Or even this experience at the ranch?"

Morris peered at him before answering. "Not fair, Kevin. You're talking about my kids. And I'm quite partial to them." Then he smiled at him. "But you're right. The worst cases result in kids who have a terrible time trusting no matter what we do."

"You don't judge them for that, do you?"

"Hell, no! We're really patient. It's the only solution."

"I agree. That's the point. Those kids aren't choosing to not trust. It has to be reawakened in them. And for some, it doesn't work. And for the majority that never get any assistance, they become adults who can't trust, a large number of whom become abusers themselves."

"But some don't become abusers. What about them? Do they have choice?"

"I don't know, but Ralph Fitzhugh, who headed a big study at Yale, says that some of us have resilience and some of us don't. Some can be taught to be resilient, and some can't. So if you're born with resilience or the capacity for it, and can overcome the abuse, then you're lucky. If you can't, you'll need help. If you don't get that help, there may be no choice."

"So what are you proposing as a solution?"

"That's way beyond me. I'm just telling the stories and trying not to judge anyone. The only thing that seems clear to me is that violence begets violence, in every imaginable form. So our only choice is to find ways to stop the violence anywhere we can, and I think that starts inside each of us."

"Was the Crucifix Protest violent?"

"I'd say not. But some people have clearly felt judged by it, and they're responding with some rather strong language, and in some cases physical force. Those who espouse peace can find it pretty hard to stay true to their values."

"Well, I seem to recall that the leader of the Center for Enlightened Spirituality talks a lot about cleaning up the insides before doing anything on the outside. Is that the point?"

"I think he says, 'Until we get right on the inside, our actions will always miss the mark.' By the way, that's the original definition of what I believe is the Greek word 'sin.' It's an archery term, and it means to miss the mark."

Pitcairn shrugged. "At any rate, I don't know if that's the point or not. But it does seem to make sense that each time we judge or condemn others, we are adding to the violence, and that will only produce still more."

"Hence your point about Jesus in your article—which ironically seems to have been the cause of the riots and now the protest. It's strange that citing Jesus Christ has caused some Christians to erupt in reaction."

"Indeed it is, Lenny."

The broadcaster turned to face the frontal camera. "We've been talking to Kevin Pitcairn about the Crucifix Protest. We'll be right back."

They froze for a few seconds for the cutaway. Then Morris extended his hand. "Stick around, Kevin. After I'm done at nine, we'll have some breakfast. It's a special thing my wife and I do ourselves after the show. Take a walk around until then."

Pleased by the invitation, Pitcairn nodded in agreement.

He headed for the pond, which seemed extraordinarily tranquil and oddly out of place in the high plains. He found a very comfortable chaise next to the water, settled into it, and promptly fell asleep.

A dream came to him as he slept. It was the same hotel room where he had murdered a man so many years ago. But the room was empty. Not even Pitcairn was in the scene.

It was eerily devoid of meaning, and strange enough to cause him to shiver in his sleep.

A hand touched him awake, and he sat bolt upright. "It's okay, big guy," said Morris with an empathetic nod.

Pitcairn looked up at him, his face showing how startled he was.

"For a minute there," Morris said, "I was afraid you were going to take a swing at me, which I completely understand. Deana learned a long time ago to go easy with me for the very same reason. I almost clocked her one night when she woke me up."

Pitcairn stood up quickly, landed on the sloping bank and almost toppled into the pond. Morris grabbed his elbow and steadied him. "That must have been some deep nap you were having."

"It was, Lenny. I've been running on empty for a while now. That was just a bit of what I need to catch up."

"You can tell us all about it over breakfast. Deana is in the kitchen. I hope you're hungry. She loves to feed guests."

They walked to the far end of the ranch house and stepped up onto a sun porch. Beyond it was the kitchen. The air was heavy with the scent of bacon as they pointed him toward coffee on the sideboard. Soon Pitcairn was seated with a very large ranch-style breakfast in front of him.

It was an easy conversation. Mostly, they spoke of the kids that Lenny and Deana hosted there, mainly from abusive homes in the city. They came out for two weeks each summer in three cohorts: late June, early July, and late July. The three talked at length about the camp Lenny and Deana had on the Pecos River which accommodated fifteen at a time, plus a number of horses, counselors, and therapists. The kids hiked, fished, cared for the horses, and helped with cooking and chores. They offered to show Pitcairn the site, but he declined with a wave of his hand.

After they had eaten, Morris asked him about his plans.

"Honestly, I don't know. There were some things about Davidson's death that weren't right, but I'm not sure that's my course. What I really want to do is give voice to the effect on those all around the victims themselves, and I need to do a little investigation of those. I really want to find some way to give the victims voice."

"Just Davidson's victims?" Deana asked.

"Haven't thought about anything more than that. Why?" She considered her thoughts as she sipped coffee. "It seems like there's a lot of energy in this right now. I'd guess the time was right to do something."

Pitcairn grunted in agreement. "I don't suppose you have any ideas—do you—that might help me disseminate what I'd like to get out there?"

They thought for a few minutes before they both acknowledged they had no clear suggestions to offer him.

"Well," he replied, "my mentor always said that the way will be made clear. I don't know that I've ever believed that as much as I do now. Davidson's letter seems to have launched something I'm caught up in regardless of my wishes."

Deana laughed knowingly. "Well, it's said the times make the leader, so maybe it's your time."

A surprised look flashed onto Pitcairn's face. "I'm certainly no leader, but thanks for the thought."

"You sure sounded like a leader in the interview," Lenny inserted quickly before adding, "Maybe you just don't know it yet."

Puzzled, all he could do was lift his hands in a defenseless gesture. "I surrender," he offered quietly. "All I know is I've got to see this thing through. And there is no question I'm blessed and cursed with persistence. So if that's where it leads, then I'm in for the ride."

With that, the conversation swung to the ranch and its operation. They chatted a few minutes more before Pitcairn said he had to leave.

Lenny and Deana suggested a circuitous but scenic route back to Albuquerque which mostly followed ranch, county, and state roads meandering around the Ortiz Mountains before looping into the funky little tourist town of Madrid. He wrote down the directions and was soon on his way.

► 29 ◄

THE DRIVE RANGED OVER COUNTRYSIDE HE'D NEVER TRAVELED, and offered a pleasant diversion. He stopped for an ice cream soda at The General Store, a well-known institution in Madrid, where he also found a unique silver necklace for Maria Elena. It was a braided knot that folded in on itself with the deceptiveness of an Escher graphic. She would love it.

Then Pitcairn opted to follow a secluded canyon road that skirted the crest of the Sandia Mountains before dropping down through Placitas. The small town was founded by hippies, but the glorious views had turned it into a much-desired bedroom community. Mid-afternoon thunderheads looming over the mountain crest blocked the sun but filtered the light beautifully. It should be a spectacular drive.

An hour later, after driving almost to the crest, he diverted the Jeep down the dirt road snaking through a canyon that folded in on itself as it drained the northern slopes of the range. It was greener than Pitcairn could imagine, and flush with wildflowers resulting from a very wet year.

Puttering along beneath the canopy of trees that filled the canyon floor, he felt a sudden sense of urgency quicken in his chest. Given all the odd things he'd been experiencing, he noted it but continued his easy pace.

A mile or so later, he pulled into a small turnoff to look at the stream. As he opened the door, he experienced an intuitive thought that he should not stop.

With one foot hovering above the ground, he stopped to think it through. He remembered his experience with the voice in Amarillo, and against all reason, decided to heed his instincts.

He put the Jeep in gear, revved the engine, and zipped onto the road. It was still dirt, but he knew it would soon become pavement, so he endured the bone jarring rattle of the washboard surface. As he crossed onto asphalt, he could smell the ozone that preceded the storm. He accelerated and raced around curves, now fearful of what might be occurring farther up the slopes. A canyon was a bad place to be in the event of a flashflood, which he now suspected.

Long minutes passed before he exited the narrowest sections, but he raced on until the road opened into the broad, high desert. There, the stream trickled into a wide arroyo where it soon vanished into the sand.

Pitcairn pulled to the side of the road, which now ran substantially above the drainage. He released the steering wheel from a white-knuckled grip just as he heard the roar. Hopping from the Jeep as the first spatters of rain began to fall, he turned to watch a mad rush of whitewater careen into the arroyo, carrying with it trees and other debris.

While he had seen a number of flashfloods, this one was awe inspiring as it crashed into the wider but still deep arroyo, then spilled over the banks. He cast his eyes up to the mountains where a dark curtain of rain encased the entire crest. He imagined it had easily engulfed the canyon where he'd stopped.

Curiosity filled him. The first time the voice spoke to him, he had been oblivious even though he knew he had heard it. Then, when it spoke just before the cowboy swung his fist at him, Pitcairn was still inclined to lean toward some kind of telegraphing of the violence. Frankly, he'd discounted the experience. Now, a knowingness had emerged that was impossible to ignore. He couldn't fathom what to make of it, but he felt a need to consider it further.

He drove home, where he found Maria Elena preparing green chile stew. After giving Lincoln and Lucy the required attention, he swept her off her feet and up into his arms.

"My! Aren't we frisky!" she squealed.

"Nope, just very happy to see my one and only."

"Your one and only what?" she asked as her eyes sparkled. He scowled at her. "You need to ask?"

She scrunched up her face to match his. "No, of course not! You need to say it."

"It," he said solemnly.

She pinched his cheek. "Kevincito, you are such a pain."

"Yeah, but I'm your pain, and you love it."

"Okay, you can put me down now. Tell me about the interview. Darlene said you were great, but I want to hear it from you."

He released her, and they settled at the table as the stew simmered. "Before I talk about the interview, let me tell you what just happened. It's the damnedest thing," he said as he launched into an account of the canyon.

She listened with rapt attention. When he finished, she just shook her head. "I told you before that I like how you're changing. So whatever it is, and I have no idea what to say about it, I like it." She paused, then added, "I'm just glad you got out of that canyon." She pressed her lips firmly together and nodded to signal closure on the subject. "Now tell me about the interview!'

Pitcairn gestured helplessly. "You have got to be the most direct woman I have ever known. How you can move so quickly past an episode like that is beyond me, but you're consistent." He touched the back of her hand lightly with his fingers, then proceeded to describe his discussion with Morris.

As he wrapped it up, she moved to get bowls of stew. She tossed a glance over her shoulder and asked, "So what do you think of that experience?

"Honestly, Emmy, I haven't the foggiest. And I'm even more baffled by their suggestion that I'm some kind of a leader."

She placed the bowls down and returned for tortillas. When she came back to the table, she cocked her head to study him. "You are a mystery, Kevin Pitcairn. But I sure do love you." She beamed at him. "Eat!"

He chortled in response. "Like I said . . . direct."

As they ate, she told him about her day, then suggested an after-dinner walk in the bosque. The dogs jumped at the word "walk," and they were soon strolling beneath cottonwood boughs.

The next two days were filled with more work on the Bisti project and looking into the judge's background, an effort interspersed with many phone calls. He scheduled dinner for Friday night with Martin, who offered to take him to an invitation-only meeting of recovering alcoholics. Pitcairn knew it would be a session that didn't quite fit in the usual A.A. structure, with its subjects sometimes going beyond the larger group's more-limited focus. They couldn't call it an A.A. meeting since it wasn't open to all alcoholics. They called themselves Group X, and Pitcairn had heard less-than-flattering talk about how far they stretched the boundaries of their conversation. Martin told him it would be an enlightening experience, and he simply embraced the opportunity as yet one more open door.

Just before he wrapped up his work on Thursday afternoon, Father Anthony de Franco, the leader of the Center for Enlightened Spirituality, called. Members had remained secluded at the retreat center to avoid the reporters who continued to seek them out, though the news cycle was still filled with ripples related to their protest.

The priest invited him to visit their compound the following morning to discuss the protests. Pitcairn leaped at the offer, and agreed to arrive at eight o'clock for breakfast.

► 30 ◄

FATHER DE FRANCO WAS A PORTLY FELLOW WITH A RUDDY complexion and sandy hair. He exuded an air of gentleness beneath which Pitcairn could sense a deep well of conviction. It was reminiscent of the Dalai Lama's demeanor, and authority was the only word that seemed to fit, though the priest laughed even more than the Tibetan. De Franco conversed easily over breakfast, ranging freely from his own background to the history of the center. With a personable approach, he drew out a great deal of information about Pitcairn. Before they turned to the business that had brought them together, de Franco uncovered much of Pitcairn's background, including his alcoholism, Davidson's letter, and the quest that had ensued.

The priest prepared two large mugs of tea made from herbs grown in the center's gardens, then led him to a small, secluded patio beneath a huge cottonwood. Chickens scratched in the soil across the yard, milk goats bleated softly from beyond a hedge, and several rabbits skirted the edge of the building as they nibbled at grasses.

After the two men had settled into comfortable wicker seats, de Franco began. "Kevin, let me tell you about the underpinnings of our practice here. Some know us as a mystical community, which in part is a throwback to ancient practices of the church throughout New Mexico, which I suppose is as good a term as any for describing us. But we do not practice what some would consider extreme actions associated with monasteries or penitence." He chuckled. "Some would think of us as a rather unusual retreat center."

After a shrug and a moment of refocusing, he continued. "We believe that Jesus made it very, very clear to anyone who is open to his teachings, despite those around us who pervert them for their own reasons: We know not what we do—thus, there is no guilt to be absolved, even though forgiveness of ourselves and others is practiced as often during the day as we can remember. We think of forgiveness as atonement, or at-one-ment, and each of us has a daily practice that asks us to remember our spiritual perfection as often during the day as we can. Then of course, we have several community practices scheduled during the day when we are to remember our collective perfection."

He paused to sip his tea. "By some standards, we are heretics within the Catholic Church. The church would insist on our inherent sin, a notion we reject." He chuckled. "Frankly, it is a curiosity that we have not been sanctioned by the church for our beliefs. Our members generally believe our efforts to abstain from judgment create more access to grace, which then makes the crooked way straight for us. As a result, trouble does not come to our doorstep.

"Our decision to protest in the park was well considered. We have known for several years that a time was at hand for that expression. Each of the phrases you saw on the crosses is central to our practice and beliefs. Forgive seventy times seven. Neither do I condemn thee. Father, forgive them for they know not what they do."

He studied Pitcairn for an instant as an almost-whimsical look came to his face. Sipping tea again, he continued. "Your article was exactly what we needed. We knew as soon as Sister Christina brought it to our council. The choice of words and your own admitted failings made it clear. Then when the church members from Colorado acted so abhorrently, it was assured."

He laughed again. "It has certainly had an effect, I would say. We don't care for some of the actions it has triggered, but awakenings can be very uncomfortable. And we feel there is substantial change afoot."

With a look of gaiety in his eyes, he asked, "What do you think of that, Kevin?"

"Honestly, Father, I had guessed it almost on the mark, which I find amazing. I don't think of myself as intuitive, but I guess I am." He clucked his tongue. "I'm interested in your belief in perfection, though. That seems to stand out from all you said."

"Ah, of course. That's very perceptive of you. The original meaning of perfection did not suggest without flaw. It translated from the Greek roughly as 'well suited for a particular purpose.' So the scripture, 'Be ye perfect as thy father in heaven is perfect,' calls us to be spiritually purified and awakened enough to serve the Lord well. Many of our efforts are to wash away the inner obstructions sufficiently to allow the Spirit of the Lord to pour forth . . . to be available for his use of us, which is to be well suited for his purposes. That's why we had long considered our actions. We had much inner work to do individually and collectively to make ourselves available for the message. I would guess we did our work well enough given the impact the action has had." He nodded humbly, then added, "Notwithstanding the judgment some still felt."

Pitcairn cleared his throat. "Why have you asked me here today, Father?"

"Oh, partly out of curiosity. I wanted to meet a man who could write with such clarity. You must have done a great deal to make yourself available."

"Ha!" Pitcairn exclaimed. "If there is a divine to offer guidance, it had to be true in this case. I can't claim the ideas in that piece."

De Franco smiled warmly. "You see, God does not need you to believe in him to use you. He only requires sufficient openness in you in order to act through you."

The words stopped Pitcairn in his mental tracks for what felt like a very long time. "I need not believe?"

"Of course not. At least not in all the rules and dogma. There was that fine moment in the gospels when all a man had to do to receive a miracle was to act with enough faith to touch the hem of the Master's robe. That's all you've done, Kevin." A feeling descended over him. It was the same feeling he had felt with the Dalai Lama.

The priest looked at him with obvious kindness. "You just received the miracle of atonement. I can see it in your eyes and feel it oozing from you. It's unmistakable."

Pitcairn stared at him, then the story rushed forth. He told de Franco of his experience on that long ago day when he was struck sober after an interaction with the Dalai Lama. Then he described in great detail the murder he had committed. All the while, the priest offered only kind expressions. When the pouring forth was complete, Pitcairn slumped in his seat, drained by the outpouring.

After an extended silence, he looked at de Franco. "Aren't you supposed to give me some kind of release now?" he asked with an uncomfortable wince.

The priest roared with laughter. "You need nothing from me. You could never fall from grace except in your own thoughts. That's the teaching of the prodigal son ... which is your story, Kevin. Welcome home."

Pitcairn just blinked a few times. "So do I walk on water now?"

"Probably unnecessary, though it might be fun. Nonetheless, I think you are ready for something else. Do you have the rest of the day free?"

"Sure, I'll just have to make a couple of calls to make a few arrangements. What did you have in mind?"

"First, let me be clear. What we've spoken of thus far you should feel free to use in any way you wish. But what we are to do next must be completely confidential. If you can't promise that, we cannot proceed."

Pitcairn thought about it and then, with absolute trust, agreed.

"That's good, Kevin. If you would be willing to drive, I would like to take you to the Ponderosa Sanctuary. You probably know of their facility in the Zuni Mountains, but most do not know the heart of their work. They are known to themselves as the Community of the Blessed, and I think you will like it. Shall we go?"

"I'm in, Father. Let me make those calls. It will only be a few minutes. Oh, and I need to be back by about five. Is that okay?"

"Certainly."

A short time later, they were on their way west. Over the next ninety minutes, there was a comfortable quiet between the two men, with occasional comments about the beautiful terrain as they climbed through high desert into ancient red rock country. A few miles beyond, they turned onto a dirt road that ascended steeply until it came to an open expanse beneath soaring canyon walls. The views were spectacular. And in that serene realm was the two-story, hacienda-style adobe retreat, whitewashed, gleaming in the sun, and trimmed with a beautifully muted tone of the color known as Taos blue.

Before they entered, de Franco insisted they take in the views. A pearlescent blue sky hung over the canyon, though the highest tops of gathering monsoon clouds could be seen to the west just above the canyon rim. Ponderosa pines filled the terrain where it was not too steep, and a breeze trickled across from the south carrying with it the calls of ravens.

As they entered through the gate, the central courtyard was a spectacular garden filled with native flowers and many vegetable plantings. The porches offered comforting shade that contrasted starkly with the whitewashed walls. Several men could be seen working in various spots.

De Franco greeted those they neared, who in turn welcomed him pleasantly. The visitors stepped through the central door into a vaulted common area with exquisite murals and wood carvings. Pitcairn remarked on the beauty of the room as they swung through a doorway to the left.

De Franco acknowledged his remark with a softened voice, "Yes, the priests care very much about beauty here. You'll see it everywhere."

Indeed as they turned into an office, Pitcairn immediately noted a massive oil painting of St. Francis of Assisi surrounded by birds and ground squirrels. Beneath that re-markable work sat an old, wiry man with very small specta-cles perched on his nose.

"Father Paul, this is Kevin Pitcairn, the journalist I told you about." Turning, he added, "Kevin, let me introduce our host, Father Paul Cavanaugh."

The thin man's face split into an engaging and generous smile. "Kevin, I'm so pleased to meet you. Anthony has told me some very good things about your work."

Surprised, Pitcairn glanced at de Franco, who bowed ever so slightly. "Well, thank you, Father, but I'm not even sure why Father Anthony wanted to bring me today. And I certainly am curious about what he told you. I feel completely out of my depth with those who are so deeply involved in religion."

The older priest turned to de Marco. "Anthony, I'm sure you told Kevin about the need for absolute privacy. But have you mentioned our work here?"

"Not a word. It's not my story to tell."

"Well then," replied Father Paul, "we make very fine lemonade that is positively heavenly when sipped in the shade. Let's make ourselves comfortable, and I'll tell you of our mission here."

After asking one of the priests to bring drinks, they strolled down the broad patio to the very end where they could see out over the canyon. The two men settled com-fortably into handmade, oversized wooden chairs. Small talk held their attention until their lemonades arrived in very tall tumblers without ice. They all pronounced the lemon-ade perfect, as Father Paul explained that it was sweetened only with local honey, and that in moderation.

"So," began the old priest, "Anthony believes what we do here will aid your understanding of your own work. Again, this must be held in the strictest privacy."

Pitcairn nodded quickly, his interest substantially piqued by the emphasis on secrecy. "I'm a journalist, Father, and I'm very good at protecting a confidence."

"No doubt," he replied. "And I might add that you would not be here if you could not be trusted. Father Anthony would never allow that." He smiled at his peer with obvious approval, then began.

"While there is the occasional rumor, we are cloistered here because of the men who come to us. We are not the only such retreat, though we are probably the most notable for this type of work. Most of the priests who are here have broken their vows in the most inappropriate ways." He was quiet for a short time, and his voice took on a very somber tone. "Our ministry here includes those who are guilty of sexual offenses, and even a few who have committed terrible criminal offenses."

He looked at Pitcairn, who nodded with genuine appreciation for the reason he had been invited. "I see," were all the words he could muster, though they were more than sufficient.

Father Paul continued. "I'd enjoy telling you we rehabilitate them, but that is seldom the outcome, though sometimes there can be a true atonement. The sanctuary is a safe haven for those who may never again find a place in the world. We are the Community of the Blessed not because of our deeds but in spite of them."

Pitcairn interjected quickly, "That's a notion I have quite an interest in. I'm a recovering alcoholic, as I've told Father Anthony, and so much of that is made possible by making peace with our terrible shortcomings. Many members of A.A. feel like it's that common bond that makes our recovery possible."

"Precisely, Kevin. So too are we bound in this fellowship. And like your A.A. community, we achieve that through the candid admission of our failings. There are no secrets among us, including the deepest of insights into the root causes of our failures."

The old man sipped from his lemonade, then pointed across the canyon to a rift in the rocky wall. "Our failings and their causes are as much a part of us as that fissure. The two are one, and cannot be separated. Our humanness runs very deeply, as a few of our residents prefer to describe it. It is in the acceptance of those failings that we finally find release. We cease trying to be good and simply offer the entire package of ourselves up for God's use."

Pitcairn nodded and then waited for the priest to continue.

"We have found that almost without exception, we can trace the wrongs done by each of our residents to wrongs directed at them sometime in the past. Some of those may be quite subtle, yet there they are. And they can be quite persistent over time. So we long ago stopped trying for rehabilitation, trusting that if something needs to be made right, God will most certainly do so. Every now and again, there are healings of the most profound sort, though we rarely speak of them."

A quiet rose up to surround the three men. It was as if they were all listening.

Pitcairn broke the silence. "Of late, I find myself saying that violence begets violence. That is what you have seen, isn't it—or the aftereffects of that violence?"

Both Father de Franco and Father Cavanaugh turned to study him, each with an obvious respect that confirmed his question.

He laughed. "And I bet you realized that in attempting to remedy their failings, we can sometimes inflict subtle forms of violence on them ourselves, which must necessarily perpetuate still more of the same." He glanced at them. "Yes?"

Obviously pleased, Cavanaugh replied simply, "Yes."

"So the only things to be done are acceptance and prayers for assistance."

Now the priests looked surprised. Father Cavanaugh asked, "How have you come to have such clarity, Kevin?"

He shook his head slowly from side to side. "Well, I had a very good teacher, another drunk named Clint. But he passed away not long ago. To be honest, since then, it's been just showing up. I seem to be being taught in a way I don't think I understand." He laughed loudly. "To be even more honest, it's often against my will, but apparently, I can't escape it."

Their respect was palpable. The quiet rose up and silenced them again.

Finally, de Franco spoke. "Father Paul, Kevin should tell you about his experiences related to Daniel Davidson, the serial killer." He turned to Pitcairn, "Kevin, would you mind describing them?"

He shrugged then proceeded to describe the entire story up until that moment. The priests offered rapt attention as he spoke.

When he finished, Father Cavanaugh smiled at him. "When Father Anthony said you were coming, Kevin, I thought that you should speak with Brother Samuel. His story will be very useful to you."

Pitcairn accepted the offer immediately.

► 31 ◄

AFTER WALKING AROUND THE PERIMETER OF THE RETREAT under clouds beginning to boil tens of thousands of feet above the canyon, they found Brother Samuel reading beneath a shady wooden ramada. It stood beside a cemetery with about forty simple crosses scattered among well-tended native grasses and plantings.

Introductions were brief. "Brother Samuel, this is Mr. Pitcairn who I mentioned to you earlier," Father Cavanaugh said. Then the two priests left to allow Brother Samuel to speak with Pitcairn free of their presence.

Lightning flashed farther up the canyon, then thunder echoed off the rocks. The sun slipped behind huge thunderheads.

Brother Samuel swept an arm up toward the storm and smiled with pleasure. He turned with a grin. "As a boy in Oklahoma, I loved the power of storms. My mother used to drag me to our storm cellar when tornadoes were around. All I wanted was to watch the clouds and rain, and feel the wind tearing over me. It's glorious." A hint of a drawl colored his words, though his eloquent tone seemed to Pitcairn to come from a very good education.

He placed his book on a weathered wooden table and gestured for Pitcairn to sit down. The two men faced the coming storm. Brother Samuel looked to be in his mid-fifties with dark hair tinged with gray that he combed straight back. Hazel eyes contrasted softly with his ruddy complexion.

"Father Paul told me earlier you were coming, and that

I should speak freely with you about anything you would like to know."

Pitcairn gestured humbly. "Everyone seems to know a lot more about things than I do. But let me tell you about my work of late, and we'll see where we go."

After a little background information, a gentle look came to Brother Samuel. He nodded with empathy.

"Yes, I see. Let me tell you how I come to be here." He stared off as lightning flashed a few miles away, then turned to speak as a few large raindrops spattered around the ramada. "I fled my boyhood home in Tulsa to attend Gonzaga University, and later I studied for several years at Oxford and Cambridge. I wanted to go very far away, and to study sociology, which seemed like the greatest thing I could imagine. I was raised as a Methodist along with my three sisters but was enthralled when I was a teen-ager by reading about the priesthood and the majesty of the Catholic Church. In retrospect, it seemed safe."

A touch of sadness came to his eyes. The storm broke around them at that moment, and a clap of thunder rocked the two men. A look of great pleasure came to Brother Samuel's face. "The sky weeps." He locked his gaze onto Pitcairn's.

"My family was not a bad one, though both my parents came from severe poverty. My mother was very unhappy most all of her life, and my father was distant. As years passed, I pieced together an understanding of their backgrounds, though they spoke little enough about it. My father's family used to joke about never wearing shorts. Apparently, his mother, my grandmother, used to punish them with anything she could swing. Today, it would be called child abuse. They were routinely beaten, so much so that my father and his siblings always wore long pants because of the scarring on their legs."

Pitcairn could feel Samuel's grief as he continued. "Mother came from a matriarchal clan that hated men. Rightfully so, it seems, given all the philandering they apparently practiced."

The rain was now roaring down around them and cascading across the terrain into the network of arroyos that fed the Zuni River. "How Mom and Dad managed to be as kind as they were is extraordinary. But they were still damaged. I can't recall a single kiss, hug, or caress as a child. They were not capable of it. Tenderness had been driven out of them.

"Along I came, a little boy that neither seemed able to nurture ... through no fault of their own. So when I discovered a local Catholic church at the age of nine, it became my sanctuary. The local priest was very kind and gentle, and unafraid of touch, though I now know it was not the kindness it seemed.

"For seven years, the priest molested me." A mix of feelings showed in the smile that crept to Brother Samuel's lips. "I craved the attention he lavished on me. Even though I knew what we were doing was wrong, I could not resist. And somewhere during that time, my sense of my own identity, and certainly my sexuality, became very, very confused."

Pitcairn could sense a slight embarrassment in Brother Samuel, so he nodded gently to assure him. The rain eased.

"I joined the brotherhood after college. It just seemed to fit as well as allowing me time to continue to study my first love, sociology." He looked up, his eyebrows raised. "And when the chance came to be around young boys, I resisted. I knew what stirred within me—though I was unable to sustain my resistance." He turned again to look at Pitcairn with an utter, stark frankness. "Mr. Pitcairn, I became a molester."

It was very awkward, but before Pitcairn could register the thought, he heard his own voice. "It's okay, Samuel. You're speaking to a murderer."

The words registered deeply in Brother Samuel, who roared with laughter. "Perfect!" he exclaimed, "Absolutely perfect!" Appreciation flooded his face as he shook his head in amazement.

"I'm here at the Community of the Blessed because I cannot be trusted in the world. None of the spiritual and psychological counseling has yet dispelled the twisting of my psyche and my sexuality." Ruefully, he continued, "My prayers have not yet been answered, though not for lack of effort or willingness. If necessary, I will stay here until my death and then join my fellows in this cemetery. Most of them were not able to return to society."

The two men lapsed into a lengthy silence. Eventually, Pitcairn asked: "How do you feel about this sanctuary?"

Brother Samuel looked as if he would cry. "Thank God for this place. Everyone knows my entire life story. They do not judge me."

He spoke wistfully. "Better still, the community allows me to live in the full and certain knowledge that I will not harm another boy. That is likewise a priceless gift."

Pitcairn was filled with awe. It was a terrible tale with an unconventional and bittersweet ending. "How do you spend your time?"

"Ah," came the pleasured response. "I am a scholar, an author of more than twenty books on sociological matters. Obscure though they may be, the work greatly pleases me.

"Mr. Pitcairn, does writing please you?"

"Without a doubt!"

"Then I'm sure you understand. As long as I am immersed in sociology, I am a very happy man. And for those who have similar interests, I am able to make a contribution through my books. Nothing can be more important than feeling useful, especially when one must face the darkness within oneself."

Pitcairn cocked his head with interest. "That's a truth about A.A. as well. Usefulness is priceless."

The rain had become light but looked as if it would be steady for some time. Mountain canyons, Pitcairn remembered, often trapped the monsoonal systems until the night cooled.

"Oh," Brother Samuel continued, "I forgot to mention. Of all the things in the world I did not expect to do and enjoy, I am our lead goatsman. We make a very fine cheese that is a staple as well as a source of income for the sanctuary. And I seem to have become a favorite of the goats."

He shrugged his shoulders. "It was not the flock I expected."

They both chuckled as Brother Samuel rose. "Will you join us for supper? We eat our main meal at two o'clock, which is now at hand."

"Thank you, I'd be delighted."

► 32 ◄

THE DRIVE HOME FROM THE SANCTUARY WAS UNEVENTFUL though slowed by heavy runoff on the mountain roads. He and Father de Franco chatted all the while. As the priest got out of the Jeep at the center, he asked Pitcairn about his plans. He pondered the question. "I don't know, Father. My girlfriend and I fly out to Minneapolis on Sunday for a live television interview with Jennifer Frank on Monday. I don't think I can see beyond that. But this has been a really valuable day for me. Can I call you when things become clearer? I'd really appreciate your guidance."

"Most assuredly. Consider me available, whatever you may need."

"Thank you, Father. I can't tell you how much that means to me."

"De nada. One more thing, Kevin. Do not doubt that God uses our flaws in his service."

Silence filled the Jeep. It was potent, the measure of a truth spoken. "Thanks for that too, Father."

"Sure enough. Keep up the good work. Bye for now."

Soon Pitcairn was home, much to the delight of Lincoln and Lucy, who assailed him at the door with their typical exuberance. Maria Elena was right behind them with a quick kiss as she slipped out the door to meet two friends for dinner. He promised to tell her about everything the following morning over breakfast.

After a short walk with the dogs through neighborhood streets damp from the same storm he'd encountered at the sanctuary, he met Martin at the Flying Star in the North Valley for dinner. Except for details of his time at the Community of the Blessed, he talked about everything that had taken place since they'd last spoken.

Occasionally, Martin remarked at the amazing experiences Pitcairn had been accumulating. At one point, he said pointedly, "Well, if you ever needed proof there are forces at work beyond our knowledge or control, this would certainly satisfy the need. I have no idea how this will all turn out, but count me as curious."

"Me too!" Pitcairn replied. "Me too."

"I presume you have no idea what's next."

Pitcairn whistled before speaking. "Martin, I'm not sure it matters what I think is next. Using your monkey metaphor, it seems to me the best I can do is hope to lean the right way at the right time."

"Yes, that would appear to be true. Do you have any questions about Group X tonight?"

"Is What's Left of Dave running it?" he asked, using the A.A. nickname the gathering's host had taken for himself. It was a macabre acknowledgment of Dave's amputated leg and withered arm, the results of a drunken motorcycle accident.

"Yes, just north of here."

"What will we talk about?" Pitcairn asked.

Martin chortled. "Not to worry, Dave will pick a topic, and we'll kick it around. We'll talk the subject back and forth until we're done with it."

"Let's go then."

Ten minutes later, they walked onto a back patio where five men had gathered. Pitcairn knew them from other A.A. settings, and settled into a chair. Suddenly aware of how incredibly tired he was, he rapped his breastbone sharply with his knuckles. Clint had insisted it stimulated an energetic response from the hypothalamus. Pitcairn had never verified the truth of the idea, but it did seem to have an energizing effect.

The group didn't bother with any formal opening. What's Left of Dave soon offered the topic: "I've been thinking about prayer and meditation. I'm not sure there's anything we need to pray for. God's will is God's will. You think God's going to be swayed by me asking? The highest power in the universe surely is above me and my requests for anything."

Two men shifted in their seats, seemingly ill at ease with what Dave had said. One of them, named Roger, leaped at the question: "Of course we're supposed to pray for things, Dave. God wants us to ask for what we need. That's the deal."

Pitcairn listened uncomfortably as the conversation ranged over varying perspectives on prayer. The consensus seemed to gravitate toward prayer for others, though Dave remained adamant that even that was presumptuous.

Martin had been mostly quiet as well, when an intense fellow named Michael asked him what he thought. Martin smiled as he lifted his eyes to think for a moment, a behavior Pitcairn noted was very similar to what Clint would do, saying he could not go on without listening for guidance.

"Honestly, I'd like to hear Pitcairn before I comment," he said, turning toward him with a mischievous look.

Pitcairn was immediately aware of his discomfort. He nodded an acknowledgement. "Look, guys, I remain unconvinced about the existence of God. But I gotta say I listen to an awful lot of this kind of debate in the meeting rooms of A.A., and I like to think I've been blessed with pretty good reasoning. So it seems to me that the God you all like to talk about is a human construction. If God exists in the ways you describe, he's going to have to be a lot larger than human concerns."

He checked the faces around him, which showed interest. "I think part of what Dave is saying is on the mark. But surely a force like that would be ever-present and responsive. Probably through many of the things we know . . . like gravity . . . or for that matter, the human ego. From a logical point of view, you can't have the omniscient God you like to talk about and then exclude anything from it."

His comments had silenced the group. Martin added enthusiastically, "What he said!'

Pitcairn squirmed with discomfort. "But remember, I don't believe in God."

What's Left of Dave grinned almost lewdly. "Fuck me if you don't believe, Pitcairn."

Everyone laughed, and that just stirred the conversation further. Twenty minutes later, after a wide range of viewpoints had been said and heard, Dave went into the kitchen and came back a few minutes later with a tray filled with bowls, spoons, and containers of Ben & Jerry's—Phish Food, Chocolate Therapy, and Cherry Garcia. Sugar demonstrated its status as a true "higher power" as everyone helped themselves.

Long after the group had adjourned, Pitcairn and Martin leaned against Martin's car gazing toward the sky and chatting. Lightning flickered to the east beyond the Sandia Mountains. A few breaks in the cloud cover revealed an indigo sky.

"Are you prepared for the interview?" Martin asked.

"I don't know, man. She can be really tough sometimes. I'll spend the entire flight writing everything I can think of just to get as clear as I can. I don't know what else to do."

"I suspect you're already aware of an option you have, but I would never want to hold back a thought that's been with me for some time."

Pitcairn nodded.

"Maybe you should stop calling it innocence. People misunderstand what you mean. And speaking personally, I'm just not sure your thesis is right. It leaves no room for personal choice or freedom of action. Who knows what's true, but it's very hard to accept. I like to think people make choices. And all the evidence in people's reactions suggests it's an offensive idea."

"You're right, Martin. It's the craziest thing in the world to tell people. You have no idea how much I've been thinking about it. I don't know where it's come from. But it's the only thing that seems to have come from beyond me. Besides that, what the hell else could I call it. I keep arriving at part of A.A.'s bedrock . . . to thine own self be true."

The shine of Martin's smile showed in the dark. "There you have it then. And I know you don't need my half-baked preaching."

"Nah, thanks for being true to yourself."

"Pitcairn, you've become a heretic."

"No shit," he replied.

"In that case, enjoy the ride."

► 33 ◄

AFTER A NIGHT OF MENTAL DISCOMFORT AND DISRUPTED SLEEP, Pitcairn and Maria Elena sat waiting at the airport Sunday morning for their flight to Minneapolis. The front pages of all the papers and the endlessly droning CNN broadcasts were filled with stories and photos of crucifix protests. In a few days, they had multiplied in number, size, and intensity, including several overseas and one that had precipitated a violent response in Mexico City. Religious commentators were referring to the symbol now as the "crucifix in distress," and one pundit spoke of the "need to redeem the great redemption."

Not surprisingly, the underlying message had been lost in the reporting. The Albuquerque group's role in initiating what had become a full-fledged movement was noted only minimally.

The press had forgotten the message of the original crucifix protesters and become caught up instead in what they had unleashed. Led by rabble-rousing TV commentators, the media had succumbed to sensationalism and accepted the rage of those who were angered by the protests—seeing the upside down crosses as anti-church whereas Pitcairn knew they reflected the church's deepest message.

He read several related news stories and commentaries, then listened to the television as a Catholic bishop from Boston offered a thoughtful suggestion that the upwelling of feeling the protests had led to might be something the church should pay attention to—that perhaps it was missing the mark on the subject of judgment and non-judgment. It was incumbent on every Christian leader, he said, to examine these matters carefully.

"Emmy, this could prove to be pretty promising," he said. She rolled her eyes in exasperation. "You are so naive. First and foremost, the church must be right. All they can believe is that they are persecuted or misunderstood. The church has no desire to change, and never will."

"You are beyond tough," he said as he squeezed her hand. Light flared in her eyes as she smiled magnanimously. "Just be grateful I'm on your side."

"Believe me, I'm grateful," he said playfully, then reached up and pinched her cheek.

"You know, Cito, your nighttime disturbances are becoming mine. I'm not having nightmares, but you know I haven't slept well for the past couple of weeks, and last night felt almost feverish. Is your obsession contagious?"

Concern raced through him. "I'm sorry. I know I'm up and down a lot; fitful is kind of an understatement."

"Oh, it's not that. I can blow that off anytime. But it's like the energy of this thing has taken up space inside me too. In fact, as I think about it, things really began to shift for me when you confronted my parents."

"How so?"

She settled into her seat to think about it. Then she turned to him and pressed her face close enough to whisper. "No one has spoken up for me like that, Cito. Not on something as important as the way he molested me. You're the first to not only truly believe but act on it enough to stand up for me."

As she caressed his cheek lightly with her fingertips, he found the intimacy almost unbearable.

"Whatever has changed inside you has changed me too. And I give you the belief you gave to me. Your fight has become my fight, though I can't possibly share the experiences you describe."

He could not even blink, so intense was the connection he felt. They stayed locked in a near trance for an interminable time before the voice uttered a single word, "*Preciosa* . . ." then trailed away into an ethereal vacuum.

Maria Elena's eyes widened in surprise, though the energy that bound them to each other was not disturbed. He saw tears welling above her lower eyelids as she bit her lip and the experience crept away.

"Cito, no one but my Auntie Susan called me '*Preciosa*.' "

Now shock came to him. "Maria Elena, you heard the voice?" She countered with a puzzled look.

"What the hell just happened, Emmy? And who is Auntie Susan?"

Her staccato laugh rang out. "Cito, this is not my gig. If you don't know what happened, I certainly don't." She shrugged helplessly. "Auntie Susan was a neighbor who always made me feel safe when I was a girl."

"You heard the voice . . . '*Preciosa*'?"

"Yes."

"I thought it was just in my head."

"Apparently not."

"But it wasn't out loud was it?"

"No, it was in my head too."

"Jesus . . . ."

They lapsed into silence before she turned to him again. "So now I've shared one of your experiences."

"Yeah, what do you make of that?"

"Your fight is my fight, Cito."

"Okay then. We're schizophrenic together."

She whacked him in the arm. "No, you buffoon! I don't know what just happened, but you shouldn't belittle it!"

He could only gesture helplessly as they heard the boarding call, then walked toward the gate with Pitcairn muttering to himself.

After they'd both settled comfortably into the first-class seats the TV show provided, Maria Elena promptly pulled a blanket over herself and slipped into slumber. Pitcairn pulled out his journal and began to write, not about innocence and violence but on this most recent experience.

By the time they landed in Minneapolis, Maria Elena felt refreshed, but Pitcairn's writing had left him greatly agitated. She asked about things they could do in the city, which neither had ever visited before, as he only fretted. "Come on now," she implored. "Where's that pragmatism you're so fond of? Either everything's going to be fine or we're screwed, no matter what we believe in." She tilted her head impishly, which caused him to drop his concerns.

"Okay. Let's just take a long walk and see the city. Maybe walk over to the Mississippi River?"

"Ooh, that would be fun! Then let's let serendipity find our dinner for us!"

They walked into the terminal with that simple plan. After a limo sent by the show dropped them at their hotel, the afternoon was spent wandering. They strolled across a bridge to St. Paul and the University of Minnesota campus, and spent a delightful hour in an art museum.

When time for dinner came, they discovered a small Polish restaurant and indulged in fare that was utterly foreign to them. The Sinatra music and overstuffed vinyl seats reminded Pitcairn very much of Villa di Capo where so much of the adventure seemed to have begun for him emotionally. Only six weeks had passed since that night and his ruminations on Davidson's letter.

He turned to Maria Elena and observed, "A lot has changed in a very short time, Emmy."

She fawned over him. "Isn't it wonderful? '*Beautimas*,' Auntie Susan used to say. She loved to invent Spanish-sounding words. I haven't thought of her in such a long time. And I can't get over '*Preciosa*.' It's all too weird." She smiled at him again. "*Beautimas!*"

A long sigh slipped from him. "I'm glad you think so. Mostly, I'm just worn out. And I have no idea what to expect tomorrow on that show."

"It will be fine, Cito. Don't you remember Clint saying, 'Fine is the only possibility?' "

"Yeah, but it never seems to look fine, does it?"

"Of course not, silly! The point is not how it looks, or even how it feels. It's how it eventually adds up."

"When did you become so wise?"

"I've always been wise. You've only recently become smart enough to notice it." Her eyes twinkled mischievously. "Welcome to sagedom!"

"Sagedom?"

"Sí, mi amor. Wisdom becomes you."

"Why do you suppose you and everyone else seem to be now accusing me of traits I can't see in myself?"

She rose up in her seat primly. "Because you are called."

"Called? That is a very troubling notion for an agnostic."

"But Father de Franco said that all you had to do was cooperate, didn't he?"

"Those are not exactly his words."

"No, but Cito, that's exactly what is happening. You're on a path you are willing to follow, and it's amazing to watch."

He just stared at her.

"I wonder how it ends," she said coyly. "In bed?"

Pitcairn laughed. "Some things don't change."

"I've never been done in Minneapolis."

"Well, for goodness sake, we wouldn't want to miss adding that to your résumé, would we?"

► 34 ◄

PRODDED BY YET ANOTHER VARIATION OF THE NIGHTMARE, Pitcairn began the day of his television interview with terror. As Maria Elena slept, he walked through downtown Minneapolis in predawn darkness. His anxiety was so great he had to resort to counting his steps.

Somewhere inside him, a great disturbance was rising. He knew it from the nightmare—a succession of eyes conveying the full range of all the troubling emotions he had experienced: pain, fear, doubt, disillusionment. And amid them all arose a great foreboding for the interview with Jennifer Frank. He wondered if the prospect of an audience was the cause of his disturbance.

A long, very hot shower soothed him somewhat. By the end, as he stood before a mirror too steamed to offer a good look at himself, he resolved that he would yet see these matters through. It came with the kind of stomach-settling, grounded feeling he had come to recognize. For better or worse, the tiger was in charge.

By early afternoon, they had arrived at the studio, which included a good-sized auditorium. The technician prepping him said there would be about four hundred in the audience, and told him to relax.

"That's easy for you to say," Pitcairn replied.

The man shrugged with disinterest.

When he was called to the stage by a pretty young assistant, Pitcairn swallowed hard. As he stepped toward the lights, he saw Maria Elena perched in a front row seat slightly to stage right. She saw him and waved. The assistant held him by the elbow as they awaited his introduction.

Jennifer Frank was strikingly attired in a white suit that made him feel awkward in his own dark off-the-rack suit. He was not accustomed to this dress up world. Her eyes flashed in the bright lights, and her teeth gleamed. Turning to the audience, she began: "Everyone has been watching the Crucifix Protests with great interest, and the violence they sometimes spawn is alarming. The assault on values central to our society has many people up in arms. Today I'm quite pleased to welcome, Kevin Pitcairn, a journalist with the *Albuquerque Chronicle* who has played a central role in this wave of social conflict."

Applause rose in the audience as the assistant pressed him forward onto the stage. He moved briskly toward Frank. She rose and shook his hand firmly, then gestured for him to sit on the couch beside her.

"Welcome, Kevin."

"Thanks, Jennifer. I'm very pleased to be here, and to see your city."

"Great. Now give us the background on what led to the Crucifix Protest."

He described Daniel Davidson and his letter, then the article he had written. He could feel the tension in the audience. It caused him to recall Clint's prediction that few would offer any slack to a serial killer.

Then he quoted from the article: "It is insufficient to understand all, and thus to forgive all. If we were to truly understand, we would know there is nothing to forgive."

Pitcairn could see muscles flexing in Frank's jaw, almost as if she were chewing on the quote.

"Then there was a riot at the office of the weekly paper that published the piece. Members of a well-known right-wing church, Evangelical Bible Church from Colorado Springs, drove to Albuquerque and protested quite violently. I was in Texas at the time, interviewing the families of Davidson's victims. But shortly after I returned, the Center for Enlightened Spirituality, a liberal Catholic group, staged the Crucifix Protest. The rest you all know quite well from the news coverage and the spreading of the protests."

A hard look shone in her eyes as she asked, "And you have described Davidson, and others, as innocent?"

"Yes, ma'am," he said with an easy smile, though he sensed her growing impatience. In the dimly lit audience, he could feel the agitation.

"Innocent? I can see not condemning people. But innocent!"

Empathy surged in his heart as Pitcairn replied. "Believe me, I understand your consternation. Everyone feels the same way, Jennifer. And I've had to think about it a lot. Look at it this way. Think of someone you believe is wrong or guilty, and think of something really bad that they did, which is all the better for illustration purposes. Can you possibly imagine not judging or condemning them for their acts? Even if you don't demonstrate it overtly, doesn't it permeate your attitude and creep into your thoughts, words, and gestures?"

He paused while she looked at him stonily.

"See, that's the point. That's a subtle form of violence. And violence begets more violence, and its consequences. I got a note from a schoolteacher. She said she'd been thinking about what I wrote. Her fifth graders always know when she's judging them if they're right or wrong, and they invariably act it out. You have to conclude that forgiveness is finding a way to see no wrong . . . to see innocence."

"Kevin," she began sternly, "that's rubbish. Hitler was not innocent. Nixon was not innocent. Daniel Davidson was not innocent."

"I know exactly how it seems to you, and probably to the whole audience." He gestured around the auditorium, and as he did, Pitcairn could feel not just resistance to the idea but also the violent thoughts behind it. As if on cue, he could hear murmurs of disagreement. "It's just human vanity to think we would do differently. Put any one of us in their shoes, products of their experiences, and we'd be very likely to act similarly."

He took a steadying breath. "It's that great line: There but for the grace of God go I. Or if you prefer, Maya Angelou said it beautifully: 'You did then what you knew how to do, and when you knew better you did better.'"

A collective, audible murmur filled the space, and Frank raised a hand to silence the audience, even as she was poised to attack him.

"You are an agnostic as I understand it."

"Yes, I am, though in recent days, I've adopted the idea that more than anything else, I'm a free thinker. I don't know what powers there may be in the universe, so I don't know about a God. That makes me agnostic. But in a discussion with Father Anthony de Franco, the leader of the Center for Enlightened Spirituality, he assures me I'm on solid ground."

A look of disgust came to her face as she nearly spit her next comment: "They are heretics!"

"Absolutely, Jennifer. And so was the Jesus so many proclaim to follow."

A chorus of boos rose now, and Frank looked slightly apoplectic.

Pitcairn felt deep within him the profound reminder: "They're all innocent." The voice had marked him indelibly. He could feel the truth of what it said as much as he could feel his hands and feet. Tennyson's words about God popped into his head: "Closer than breathing, nearer than hands and feet." The thoughts grounded him deeply, and he smiled with a patience and empathy that formerly would have been far beyond him.

"Jennifer, despite all the appearances, somehow we're all doing the best that's available to us. And that's the basis for our innocence."

There was fire in her eyes, but he returned her gaze with neutrality. She spoke with cool animosity: "You moral relativists are the downfall of all we hold dear."

A cheer cascaded from the audience. "And it disgusts me," she sneered.

Pitcairn held his hands to the sides to show his openness. "Believe me, I know about this subject. I once murdered a man, many years ago." A hush fell in response to his words. "I'll never forget that, and I can never make it right. I've lived with nightmares because of it for so long they've become my norm. But somehow, we have to be able to live with what we've done. Innocence allows that ... for me and for you."

"Mr. Pitcairn, that is the most harebrained idea I believe I've ever heard."

A cheer rose again, but it was quickly pierced by an anguished screech. The crowd turned as Maria Elena stormed up the steps to the stage. A shocked clamor came over the hall. Pitcairn could see the fury in her eyes, but he made no effort to move.

"You sanctimonious bitch!" she screamed at Frank, who cringed as she retreated into the cushions.

The audience roared. Pitcairn imagined the long ago bloodlust of the Coliseum in Rome as his lover quickly closed the distance.

Two security guards raced across the stage. The first to arrive, a wiry young man, clearly underestimated Maria Elena. She nailed him with a swift and lucky kick to the crotch that left him writhing as he collapsed to the stage.

The second guard, a beefy fellow, quickly waved to someone offstage for support before slipping in between Maria Elena and Jennifer Frank. She tried to get around him, but two more guards took hold of her.

As they put their hands under her armpits and lifted her in the air, she kicked and snarled like a wildcat. Then suddenly, realizing the hopelessness of struggle, she slumped in surrender.

The audience was in pandemonium, drowning out Maria Elena's passionate words to the host: "How dare you condemn a man bearing a message of love and forgiveness."

Frank recoiled and sank back farther, straining to catch her breath as the point struck home.

Pitcairn's eyes and face softened as he watched the guards carry Maria Elena off the stage. Then he turned to Jennifer Frank, who was slowly reorienting herself.

"Well," she began, "that was certainly unexpected." She offered a weak smile. "And I see we cut to a commercial during all that. Where should we resume?"

He touched her arm gently. "I've said all I can say. And I believe my girlfriend summed it up pretty well." He stood up slowly.

"You can't just walk off the show."

"I most certainly can. Maria Elena needs me now."

Surprise filled Frank's face.

"By the way, Jennifer. She's innocent—and so are you." He smiled as he turned and left the stage.

A staff member directed him to a briefing room where Maria Elena had been taken. She looked up sheepishly as he walked in, but there was still a righteous fire in her eyes.

"Sorry, Cito," she offered with a feigned look of regret.

"Maria Elena, you were magnificent," he replied. "And your parting words were much more profound than your graceless exit."

She bounced toward him. "Do you think so?"

"Abso-damn-lutely, to quote Clint." He wrapped her in his arms.

"Jesus, I was so scared. And that poor guard ... he dropped like a bag of sand." She giggled with obvious uneasiness.

"I am so glad you are on my side, Emmy."

She leaned back to look up at him. "Me too!" Then she burst into nervous giggle again. "I need a cigarette, Cito. I haven't smoked in years, but now's the right time. Can we go?"

"Yep, the guards said to get you the hell out of here."

"Now?"

"Let's split."

► 35 ◄

"UNBELIEVABLE!" MARTIN SHOOK HIS HEAD AS HE HEARD the culmination of Pitcairn's blow-by-blow account of his day on the Jennifer Frank show. "I didn't see it, but a couple of the A.A. guys told me. The truth is even more outrageous than they could paint it." He eyed Pitcairn. "So how are you after all that?"

"Good," he replied glibly.

"Good is good."

"And they say good comes to good, Martin."

"Have you become an optimist now?"

"Who knows? It probably doesn't matter, given the tiger and the jungle. But it sure beats the alternative."

"What do you mean?"

"Martin," Pitcairn said before taking a swallow of coffee, "it seems to me that if we have no business judging anyone, we probably ought to stop judging the events of the day too. Somehow, it must all be good."

"You know, it's ironic that everywhere you write or speak about innocence and violence begetting violence, peace does not exactly break out around you."

"Isn't that the truth?" Pitcairn agreed with a puzzled look. "Clint told me this would really push people to the limit."

"There was a fellow who wrote that Gandhi and Martin Luther King couldn't have been successful with their nonviolence practices if others weren't paralleling them using violence the whole way."

"Hmm, I don't know about that. I think there's just something so threatening about these ideas it nails people right between the eyes. The result is a defensive, and sometimes violent, reaction. Maybe that's why both of those guys were toast. Jesus too."

They were quiet a short time before Martin asked about Maria Elena.

Pitcairn laughed hard. "She is so into her new rock star status. Her friends are loving it. I mean, how many people can say they got physically evicted before a national television audience?"

"How much of it aired?"

"They were able to bleep the bitch part, and then they cut away. I can only imagine those production guys never moved so quick in their lives. It must have been a riot in the engineering booth."

Martin laughed. "So what do you plan to do now?"

"Who knows, Martin?" He scratched his head. "First, let me tell you how much I appreciate the support you've given me."

"No problem," he shrugged in response. "Just pass it on."

"Can do." Pitcairn paused. "As a matter of fact, I got a call from Lenny Morris—actually it was his wife, Deana, that called. She was so turned on by what Lenny and I talked about that she contacted a friend at the *North Country Reader*. You know, that left-leaning rag?

"They're in Minneapolis too, which is a strange parallel. I told them about what I did in Texas, and they want me to write a series on the families of victims of violence. So it looks like I've got a wide open opportunity to tell the stories about how violence keeps playing itself out."

He suddenly felt incredibly grateful. It filled his chest, and tears came to his eyes. "Damn, what a gig. Those stories need to be told. I'm so clear on that. And what a living amend that could be."

"You mean for the man you killed?"

"Sure, but it's more than that. There's a need to keep framing this thing in a way people can see. So it's kind of an amend for a lot of bad situations. Some good could come out of that."

Martin looked at him very seriously. "Pitcairn, do not become a crusader. It's bad for you, and might even get you drunk. If all you do is make your own peace, that should be enough. Anything else is gravy."

"Good point. I'll keep it in mind. For now, I just know I've got a bunch of stories to tell. And it seems like they just keep coming at me."

The two men sipped their coffee. "I'm going to take Maria Elena to see my Aunt Jeanne," Pitcairn said. "It's been too long since I've seen her, and she may not live much longer. And I've got to talk to the folks over at *Contours*. I promised them first crack at some of the things I might write. We'll have to figure out how to do that along with the *North Country Reader*."

He suddenly started. "Damn, Martin, I've got more forgiveness work to do with Mom and Dad. And there is no way that looking into Davidson's death can bring any good. I know in my gut any further reporting on his murder will only injure the loved ones of his victims. And whether I like it or not, that's going to feel like more violence to them even if it's not how they would describe it."

Martin nodded sympathetically. "Sounds pretty clear." He paused before he asked somberly. "What about your murder confession—on national television no less. I'm surprised she didn't follow up on it right away, but even still, the cat's out of the bag."

Pitcairn felt the statement weighing heavily and cast his eyes downward. "Yeah. She had to make her point for her audience. That's the only thing I can imagine would keep her from asking about it."

He sighed as his thoughts returned to his confession on the air. "I don't know, Martin. There's nothing to be done now. I suppose I'll take what comes, if it comes."

"One day at a time then."

"One day at a time," Pitcairn repeated. "Maybe I'll talk that through with Father de Franco. I'd like to continue meeting with him if he's willing. I don't know why, but I'm going to trust my intuition on that too. He strikes me as quite a man."

"So Pitcairn," Martin asked slyly, "did you ever dream you'd be using a Catholic priest as a spiritual adviser?"

"Ha!" he burst out loudly. "Heretic Catholic priest. Let's be clear."

Martin laughed. "Onward into heresy."

"Already been there, and I like the feel."

* * *

The rain fell steadily from a leaden sky as Father de Franco poured them tea on the porch at the center. It was the last weekend of the state fair, which usually foretold the final fit of the monsoons. Summer's hold was already loosened, and there was a tinge of autumn in the air. Pitcairn could feel a lessening of the tension and torpor of summer.

"The protests are having some effect, Father."

"Please, call me Tony."

"You got it, but that brilliant counter-move won't save you from commenting on the ripple effect of the protests, Tony."

The priest chuckled. "Fine. We would never have guessed the protest would have gained such traction. Fortunately, the violent responses are diminishing. Better still, many church leaders are becoming quite introspective. And I've heard that a community church in Madison, Wisconsin, has asked its leaders to reconsider their position on homosexuality. We could never have predicted that."

"Who'd a thunk it?"

"We're pleased. The timing of our protest was indeed right. The church and some of its practices really are in distress."

"Did your folks catch any grief from on high?"

"I can't comment on that, Kevin."

After the silence that followed, Pitcairn went on. "Tony, there are a few things I'd like to talk about. But first, I'd like to be able to visit with you regularly. I like you, and all you represent. The guy I'm using as an A.A. sponsor nailed it when he said I'd be using you as an adviser. He thought it was pretty ironic. I do too. But I can learn and grow a lot with your guidance."

"I'm honored by the request. Believe me, it's a mutual feeling, and I'd be pleased to talk regularly."

"It means a lot to me. Especially because I've been hearing more of the voice, the quiet one, and I really don't know what to make of it. While I was traveling to Minneapolis, which is another story to tell, the voice spoke to me and my girlfriend at the same time."

"Really! That's remarkable. And what did it say to you?"

"It whispered the word '*Preciosa*,' which was a childhood name a trusted neighbor gave to Maria Elena. The woman must have loved her a great deal."

"Have you thought of a reason the word was spoken to you both?"

"No idea, Father. No idea whatsoever. It could have been speaking to us mutually. Or it could be some kind of a joining together. I just don't know."

The priest touched his hand and spoke gently. "Then stay in not knowingness. Leave it be. Let it remain mysterious. There is a philosopher, Ken Wilber, who says that we make a tragic mistake when we try to take the divine and its expression, and render it into a human perspective. He calls it flatland. And we kill the mystery and the wonder, to say nothing of turning the inexpressible and infinite into a material expression. Simply relish the voice as long as it lasts."

"I feel obliged to remind you I don't believe in God." Pitcairn looked at him with chagrin as he apologized softly, "Sorry."

"Kevin, please don't ever feel you need to mention it again. And certainly don't apologize. You've been honest with me, and I have assured you I believe God lives and expresses through you whether you believe it or not. Regardless, the manifestations of the Holy Spirit are pronounced through you, which you cannot deny even if you don't name them as I do."

Pitcairn's face showed his surprise. "That's crazy, you know? You religious dudes are supposed to chastise us non-believers."

De Franco raised his eyebrows. "And you have evidence of how that turns out, don't you?"

"You betcha! I get that."

"Kevin, a few summer ago, there was a marvelous story told about a couple of drunken men. They were with their families for a summer vacation on Lake Erie when, inexplicably, they rode two wave runners out into the lake. Who knows what they were thinking ..."

Pitcairn interjected. "Yes, I heard about that. They were drunk, Tony. They weren't thinking."

"Well, yes, there is that, isn't there?" He chuckled. "At any rate, they ran out of gas and spent a very frightening and sobering night in the water. With hypothermia approaching, the sun rose on the horizon the following morning.

"Unbelievably enough, a Coast Guard cutter sighted them despite being to the west of the men and having to see their heads bobbing amid waves flooded with sunlight. The officer who spotted them called it a miracle."

The priest sipped his tea and sighed with a shake of his head. "News reporters talked to the men, one of whom said, 'God sure was with us when they found us.' As soon as he said it, one of the priests who'd been comforting the families blurted out a comment loud enough to be picked up by the microphone. He said, 'Rest assured, God was with you even as you rode foolishly out into the lake.' "

He laughed at the story. "You see, Kevin. Grace is not conditional on anything. It's ever present. All we need do is open ourselves to it." The priest turned to smile at him. "And you, my friend, have had an unusual glimpse of the grace in which you are immersed."

"That is a completely foreign idea to me," Pitcairn instantly replied.

"Not just to you. Most everyone is caught up in the delusion that grace resides only in the good. Isn't that the whole point of this principle of innocence to which you now adhere?"

"I hadn't thought of it that way, Tony." He tugged at his ear distractedly. "Then is there some kind of obligation . . ." he caught himself with a cluck of his tongue. "Of course not, but isn't there some kind of responsibility that comes with that?"

The priest raised his hand with the sign of a blessing. "No, though you do get to choose whether to embrace the grace, which I would say you are already demonstrating."

Pitcairn thought for a while. "Tony, that's what happened when the Dalai Lama looked at me, isn't it? I mean, for a moment, I must have been bathed in what you call grace, and it was life altering." He paused before whacking himself on the head. "Christ . . . that was the same feeling I had when Maria Elena and I were locked in that near trance and the voice spoke to us. I know it by the feeling of it. Does that sound right?"

De Franco patted him easily on the shoulder. "Who knows? But I would say you are on track."

"Man, if Clint were here, he would be more amused than I could stand."

"Why is that?"

"He insisted over and over again I was a testament to God's work and just couldn't see it."

"What do you think?"

Pitcairn took some time to ponder. "Father, I'm going to keep being completely honest with you because it seems to be a really good thing. And for the life of me, I cannot get my head around the God idea."

The priest poured more tea, then scrutinized Pitcairn's face. "Then I would stay in not knowingness on that as well. Whether your thoughts cooperate or not, you are living a remarkable life.

"So, what next, Kevin?"

"I've got an offer from a magazine to write about victims and the cycle of violence. I'm going to accept. It's kind of a living amend, if you know what I mean."

"A fine plan, I think."

"I'm glad you think so. There are a lot of stories that need to be told. And I can't get past the thought that some part of my path is with the guys up at the sanctuary. Do you think I could spend more time there?"

"To what end?"

"As usual, no idea. But I know their confidentiality can't be compromised. So it must be more about what I need to learn rather than what I might do with any of it."

"Kevin, that sounds like an act of service."

"Ha! You jump to the same kind of conclusions that Clint did. But I'm very suspicious of labels that sound good when I'm a living contradiction in so many ways."

"Kevin."

"Yes, sir."

"God only needs you to be available. I will talk to Father Paul."

"This is all very amazing, Tony."

The priest nodded with a smile. "Let me pass along yet one more story." He raised his eyebrows as if for permission.

"Fire away."

"Just a few days ago, I heard a report on National Public Radio. A neurological researcher had a most remarkable result from an experiment with a man who had a brain injury that destroyed the part of the cerebral cortex that processed vision. He was completely blind.

"I can't recall why they decided to do the experiment, but they lined a corridor with obstacles like trash cans and floor fans. Then they had the blind man walk down that hallway."

A look of mischief showed in de Franco's eyes as he leaned toward Pitcairn. "Without any guidance, the man avoided the obstacles. And when he was done, the researchers asked, 'How did you do that?' "

"Do what?" the man answered.

"How did you avoid the things we put in your way?"

"I didn't," the blind man replied firmly.

Pitcairn was deeply entranced and leaning forward as well.

"Kevin, here is the piece of the tale you will undoubtedly be able to use." A wry grin came to the priest's face. "His eyes can see, but his mind doesn't know." Pitcairn blinked several times as he pondered the implications. "Jesus," he muttered before laughing in disbelief. "Tony, that's more proof there really are things at work within us we can't begin to understand. Hell . . ." he shrugged sheepishly in acknowledgment of the word. "To not even know . . . ." His voice trailed away.

"Yes, Kevin." De Franco nodded in affirmation. "It's just like your principle of innocence. In some way, Daniel Davidson knew what he did was wrong, but he was as powerless to act on it as the blind man was to realize his eyes could see.

▶ 36 ◀

FALL HARVEST WAS AT HAND. AT MARIA ELENA'S REQUEST, THEY drove north of the city to Wagner's Farm for their annual supply of green chile. The smell of chiles roasting hung heavily in the late morning light, crows called raucously from nearby cottonwoods, and somewhere in the distance, a mule brayed.

While she shopped inside the farm store, Pitcairn lounged across bales of hay drinking mulled cider. He watched families wandering around and children playing.

Across the yard, he spied a slender man staring at him. It was one of those occasions when Pitcairn could predict the man's approach even if he couldn't know why. Indeed, the man sauntered toward him, a study in conflictedness.

As he neared, he asked, "Aren't you Kevin Pitcairn?"

"Yes, sir."

He extended his hand, "Pleased to meet you. I'm Davis Jefferson. I'm a real fan of your writing."

"Thank you," Pitcairn replied graciously. "Am I to assume your name is linked to the South?"

The man nodded his head. "My mom and dad were dyed-in-the-wool southerners . . . South Carolinians, in fact. Dad was a practical joker and just couldn't resist the name." He snorted. "I've caught more than my fair share of shit from his gag."

An awkward pause followed before Jefferson spoke again. "I saw you on Jennifer Frank's show."

"That was quite an adventure," Pitcairn said simply, though with an obvious sense of humor.

"Yeah."

"What'd you think?"

"She blew it."

With his interest piqued, Pitcairn leaned forward. "How so?"

The man looked around the yard with some discomfort. "I can't believe I'm telling you this, but I have to talk to someone. Look, can I tell you the truth?"

Pitcairn nodded.

"Not long ago, my son was picked up by the police for hurting a dog. He's only fifteen, but I'm certain he's a good kid. It's just . . ." He looked around the yard again with obvious unease.

"It's just that he's acting out. I've not been a very good father."

Pitcairn could feel the ache inside the man and gestured for him to sit.

Lowering himself somewhat gingerly to a bale of hay, Jefferson sighed. "It's such a shitty story, Kevin. My wife is not very well . . . you know . . . psychologically." He looked down between his boots for an instant, and when he looked up, his eyes were slightly reddened. "She's really hard on Donny. Really hard. I don't know what happened to her, but she's so distant to him it's painful for me to watch."

"I know about that," Pitcairn offered.

The man looked at him. "Yeah?"

Across the yard, Maria Elena appeared on the porch of the store. Pitcairn waved at her, and she seemed to intuit the situation. She nodded with a smile and wandered back into the store.

Jefferson continued. "My wife, Constance, is not physically abusive, but my God, how she punishes Donny. It's in the way she looks at him more than anything else, because she doesn't even talk to him much anymore." The man clenched his fists and wrung them lightly. "She was really good with him up until the past couple years. But now when she acts like that, he gets pissed off, really pissed off."

Pitcairn felt an urge to speak but waited.

"I try to be the middle man, but sooner or later, I blow up." His voice shook. "Donny gets the worst of that too." The silence that followed was not awkward. If anything, it was sympathetic. Pitcairn cleared his throat.

As if on cue, Jefferson stood up and extended his hand. "Anyway, I just wanted to let you know I like your work." "Thank you." He smiled broadly. "And thanks for talking about your situation at home. I appreciate hearing it."

An embarrassed shrug was the only response as the man turned and moved purposefully across the yard. He walked up to the rotating chile roaster where a slender boy stood, and draped his arm across the boy's shoulders.

Pitcairn watched as they chatted, then saw a woman come from the store. Jefferson moved to position himself between the boy and the woman. Soon they all walked away.

Sitting quietly in the sun, no particular thoughts in mind, Pitcairn felt a pervading sense of compassion, or at least that was the best word he had for it.

A short time later, Maria Elena approached with several bags. "Who was that?" she asked as he rose and put his arm around her waist.

"Just a guy who wanted to chat about my writing."

She scrutinized his face. "And . . ." she said knowingly.

He gazed at her. "You are so dangerous, Emmy." He paused for an instant. "And it's another story that needs to be told."

They moved as one toward the chile roaster.

* * *

That night, with Lucy and Lincoln settled in the shade for an after-dinner nap, Pitcairn sat in the yard with a pen and a pad of paper. At times, he found it the best way to write, to feel the material in a way the computer just couldn't allow. With a steady flow of thoughts, he began:

There has been much in the media lately about the Crucifix Protests spawned from a demon-

stration at the office of *Albuquerque Contours.*
That near-riot was the result of a column I wrote
titled "Kill the Killer," about the murder of
Daniel Davidson. Everyone seems to have an
opinion on the protests and that column. Most
of those opinions are strongly held.

It's time to stop the rhetoric, even my own.
The fact is that while we argue, more important
matters are being overlooked. I refer to the
many who are the victims of violence, whether
brutality was visited upon them or their loved
ones. Some of these are people who will never
overcome their injuries. Some of them will injure others.

Violence creates a terrible pattern that devas-
tates the fabric of our humanity, to say nothing
of our lives and communities.

After much consideration, I realize that what
has most deeply affected me in following up on
what Davidson did are the stories I have been
told. Let me tell you one of the true-life accounts
of those who are still living with the effects.

Her father thought of her as his angel girl.

Anita Royal was brutally raped and murdered
for no reason other than randomness. She was
not particularly distinguished. She was simply in
the wrong place at the wrong time. And Anita
forfeited her life. We can't imagine the terror
she must have felt.

Since then, her father has divorced her
mother, abandoned the family, and retreated
into seclusion. Loss of his angel girl has hurt
him so deeply he is unable to maintain the most
important relationships in his life.

Anita's mother and sister have been able to
make remarkable progress toward forgiveness.
They have made peace, but the ache of their loss

is still apparent in what they say and how they
see the world.

The dogs were suddenly startled as the back door burst
open and Maria Elena emerged. Her face was unreadable.
"Emmy, what's wrong?"
She stepped from the porch and moved toward him.
"Momma just called. She and Daddy want to talk."
"No shit! That's a surprise, huh?"
She sat next to him but couldn't speak. He moved closer,
hip-to-hip, and placed his arms around her. It was clear
there was nothing to be said.
A moment later, she began to tremble. Tears were not far
behind, and soon she was sobbing and quaking in his arms.
He began to rock her with the same gentle movements he
had learned so well from his own deep grief.
When her emotions were spent, she turned to him and
smiled shyly, then kissed him on the cheek. Her lower lip
quivered as she spoke. "Thank you." She managed another
strained smile. "I need a very hot bath."
Pitcairn nodded and kissed her forehead. She rose and
went into the house.
For the longest time, he sat very still, gazing at the sky
now darkening with the onset of evening. "*Preciosa*," he
whispered to himself.
He picked up his pad, though he knew he would write
no more this day. Beneath where he had stopped, he jotted
a few thoughts to return to.

► 37 ◄

MARIA ELENA GIGGLED AS LUCY LICKED HER FACE, A PAW ON EACH *shoulder as the boxer stood easily at her height. The more she laughed, the more Lucy slathered her with her tongue.*

They stood in a pool of yellowish light cast downward through the dark. Behind them lay the old eroding corner of a three- or four-foot-high adobe wall at the southern reaches of Plaza Vieja, the Old Town Plaza.

A high-pitched whine rose behind her as a low rider careened around the corner. A look of innocent surprise froze on Maria Elena's face as the front fender clipped her at the hip. Lifted into the air, she tumbled like a rag doll over the wall. At the same time, Lucy yelped as the car's grill slammed her, crushing the boxer as she rolled under the car. It came to an abrupt halt. Drunken voices rose as the gun-metal smell of metabolized alcohol filled the air.

Suddenly all light vanished. Through an impenetrable darkness, a deeply resonant voice spoke to Pitcairn, "Innocence . . . ," then trailed away softly.

The adobe wall reemerged from the darkness. Like a spreading vine, lurid wallpaper from the seedy hotel reconstructed itself in slow motion. He stood before the hotel wall, right hand clenched at the end of his extended arms. He peered down to see the ugly little man on the floor desperately squirming as he sought to suck air into starved lungs. Strangled curses and gobbets of spit flung from his lips as he lashed out with arms and legs. Muscles contorted as demons raged inside him. From a measured distance above, disembodied, Pitcairn watched himself turn and walk away from the writhing man, gasping but still alive.

Impenetrable darkness fell yet again, then to be replaced by eyes of every kind hovering over him like stars in the sky. Slowly, the eyes merged into a single pair placed in a kind face that reminded him of his Aunt Jeanne, though it was not her. Just beyond the face, two more eyes emerged, wise and gentle eyes mirroring a look reminiscent of Clint. He was held at the woman's bosom, and he felt her caresses. For what seemed a very long time, he felt loved.

* * *

The strange dream awakened Pitcairn early on October 1, the anniversary of his sobriety. As the images reformed themselves with almost visual clarity in his mind, it was too much to bear. He touched Maria Elena to reassure himself she was alive, then choked away sobs as he eased himself from the bed without waking her. Stumbling to the portal outside with Lincoln and Lucy moving nearly soundlessly behind him, he collapsed across a lounge chair and wept.

The heartache of the deaths he had dreamed of Maria Elena and Lucy was real, as was the helpless rage he felt. But they could not hold him in the presence of the deep love he had also felt being caressed at the woman's breasts.

The altered reality with the ugly man confused him. Facts long held to be true now swam in a sea of doubt. But what was clear to Pitcairn was a palpable sense of release.

He was suddenly aware of Lincoln and Lucy's steady presence. He held them close as gratitude surged within. And with it came a question out of nothingness: "Are you willing to forgive even this?"

Even what . . . he asked.

No answer came, only the memory of a news account of a boy and his girlfriend. Pitcairn had read the story a few days earlier. The young man had tried to protect his girlfriend from four gang members. The thugs had taken turns raping the young woman while holding him pinned to the ground, knife held to his throat. A quiet, suburban park had become another setting in the cycle of violence. They had released the devastated woman but took the young man with them into the desert. They tortured him there, then burned his body in the remains of an old abandoned car rusting beside an arroyo.

Somehow, Pitcairn knew he was to build a memorial where the boy had died with a cross he'd recently found poking around a local metal yard. He had bought it thinking it would be for Father Tony. But now, a different purpose had been shown.

A few hours later, he stood in the early morning light beside a cairn of rock, placing wildflowers around the cross. He recalled something the priest had said only a few days before: "Every action matters. Beneath it is meaning that matters even more."

The idea spurred him to keep gathering flowers, each a bit of healing for the young man who had died there and the woman who was brutalized. As small as the action seemed, to put each tiny flower there did its little part to help calm the ripples of violence. And floating above them were victim and perpetrator alike.

Soon Lucy stuck her snout into his leg. He caressed her ears, then rubbed them vigorously, leading her to launch into a playfulness that was contagious. He picked up a stick and threw it down the arroyo, where it barely came to rest before the boxer snapped it up and raced back. Lincoln watched placidly as the routine was repeated over and over. Eventually, he lay down and lowered his head to his paws.

As if cued by Lincoln's disinterest, Lucy leaped forward and collapsed into a panting heap beside him. Pitcairn followed their lead and settled to the ground. He closed his eyes to an inner solitude. Mentally replaying the past few months, he pulled Clint's final letter from his pocket.

Dear Pitcairn,

Never did get used to calling you by your last name. It sure looks strange in writing. Anyway, time you open this, it will be your birthday. And

you need to know how proud I am of you. I
admire the hell out of the inner work you've
done. I'd claim some credit if I could get away
with it. But God knows the truth, so I won't try
to bullshit him or you.

I've had a sense I won't be around much
longer. And I had an even stronger one that
you're going to go through hell and back. I
wonder what an old friend could tell you when I
have no idea how it will turn out.

Remember that every day really is a day in
paradise. Treat it as such. You'll know you finally
see paradise when you feel it in your heart. The
whole damn design is laid out for your growth
and development. You can trust life completely.

When you get to that point, you'll understand
the greatest promise in the Big Book. "Relax
and take it easy." Until you can do that, you've
not seen the truth.

Guess I can't know if the work you've done
will let this make sense. But it will. Sooner or
later. In the meantime, don't ever forget you
can't do it alone, but you have to do it yourself.

Love,
Clint

Pitcairn allowed himself to feel. Something was finally becoming right inside him. It felt very good.

He stretched and realized suddenly that in all his efforts
building the memorial, he had failed to remember Daniel
Davidson, the man who had started him on this path. Raising himself wearily, he strolled in a wide arc and found a
few late season red and yellow gallardias. They were his favorite expression of beauty on the mesa, strangely delicate
in color amid the usual sea of brown but remarkably tough.
Returning to the cairn, he placed them securely at the base
of the cross.

Pitcairn took a deep breath and thought first of Clint, then Maria Elena. Tears crept from the corner of his eye and slid down his cheek. Closing his eyes, he offered up thoughts directed toward Davidson, the man who had changed his life though they never met. Then he slowly thought of each and every person who had had a hand in his good fortune. A long list of names and faces slid through his mind.

Moving easily toward the dogs, he sprawled on the sand with his head between Lincoln's outstretched paws. Above him was a striking New Mexican sky. He felt morning breezes playing over his skin accompanied by the gentle sound of grass rustling.

* * *

Along an arroyo near the burned shell of a car, a tall man reclines, bookended by two dogs. Beside him stands a cairn of volcanic rock. A sturdy metal cross extends up from it. Wildflowers are arrayed around the altar, trembling delicately.

An evanescent light hangs over the West Mesa in full autumn bloom. Countless yellow snakeweed blossoms shimmer like gold in the early morning, accented by scattered stands of purple aster. For millions of years, this season has transformed desert and rock into a garden, changing even the most formidable terrain into a vision of Eden.

The Light and the Shadow: Two Tales of Innocence

THE STORY IN THIS BOOK AND THE ONE IN *MY NAME IS WONDER* are like bookends in one of the most important learnings of my life. Much of my time now is spent working with people who need to forgive and to heal. From that work has come an understanding of inherent innocence, which is a subject I will be exploring more fully in coming books. Regardless, if *A Killer's Grace* represents the darkness of the path to innocence, *My Name Is Wonder* is the lightness of that same path. One is yin and the other is yang, two sides of a truth and reality that cannot be separated. As a good friend says, "Damn it, you can't just take the good stuff and call it Grace!" I cannot disagree. And I am certain that innocence is our destination—or, if you prefer, it is with us all the while, awaiting our awakening to it.

To purchase *My Name Is Wonder,* visit your local independent bookstore or any online bookseller.

—Ronald Chapman

Acknowledgments

ʃOME YEARS AGO, I CORRESPONDED WITH A SERIAL KILLER. The letter that began this novel was written by that man. I've changed a few minor parts, and he is completely anonymous at his own request. He did not think it right for any acknowledgment to come his way, nor did he wish for any further ripples to harm the families of his victims. I must admit that the request impressed me. The rest of the story is fiction, and bears no resemblance to his tale.

I corresponded with this man for a short while, and he has now been put to death for his crimes. Yet I was profoundly affected by the implications of his letter. There is nothing more to be said. The stories, his and *A Killer's Grace*, stand or fall on their own merits. Any errors in the telling are mine.

I owe a debt of gratitude to Julie Mars, who offered outstanding initial guidance as the plot took shape. My daughter, Natalie Gallagher, did the backbreaking work of initial editing that shaped the manuscript. Lynn Miller provided exceptional insights that allowed the final story to emerge. Karen Villanueva believed in the power and necessity of the story. Jim Van Waggoner provided yet one more critical and essential review. Mari Selby urged me to proceed. And Sam Dement deserves a great deal of credit for providing twenty years of uncanny mentorship, without which none of these ideas could have taken shape. The fine touches by Marty and Scott Gerber at Terra Nova Books make the story shine.

For the members of Alcoholics Anonymous, there can be no adequate thanks. They were very patient with me in explaining the nature of their program. They were sometimes empathetic to the plot, and sometimes aghast. Such is the nature of their community. I consider myself privileged to know them.

One last thought warrants mention. Reconciliation with ourselves and others may be the most difficult of all things we must do. Yet we must do it . . . by ourselves but never alone.

About the Author

RONALD CHAPMAN HAS FOLLOWED MANY PATHS OF SPIRITUAL and religious study over the past thirty years. As a workshop leader and motivational speaker, he has shown countless people how Seeing True,™ his signature practice, can produce extraordinary changes in their lives.

Chapman is one of only sixty-eight International Accredited Speakers recognized by Toastmasters International. He is the author of the novel *My Name is Wonder* and the inspirational books *Seeing True: Ninety Contemplations in Ninety Days* and *What a Wonderful World: Seeing Through New Eyes*. In 2015 and 2016, Ozark Mountain Publishing released audio sets that complement his writings. *Breathing, Releasing and Breaking Through: Practice for Seeing True* explores the use of breathwork and meditation to promote inner healing. *Seeing True: The Way of Spirit* presents a psycho-spiritual philosophy and practices for transforming what and how we see.

You can learn more about his transformational philosophy at www.SeeingTrue.com, and about its application to twelve-step recovery at www.ProgressiveRecovery.org. For more information about Chapman's entire portfolio, visit: www.RonaldChapman.com.

Made in the USA
San Bernardino, CA
17 July 2016